Paul Theroux was born 1941, and published his wrote his next three nov *Play* and *Jungle Lovers*, after a five subsequently taught at the University of Singapore, and during his three years there produced a collection of short stories, *Sinning with Annie*, and his highly praised novel, *Saint Jack*. His other publications include *The Black House* (1974), *The Great Railway Bazaar* (1975), *The Family Arsenal* (1976), *The Consul's File* (1977) to which this book is a sequel, *Picture Palace* (1978; winner of the Whitbread Literary Award), *A Christmas Card* (1978), a short story illustrated by John Lawrence, *The Old Patagonian Express* (1979), *London Snow* (1980), *World's End and Other Stories* (1980), *The Mosquito Coast*, which was the *Yorkshire Post* Novel of the Year for 1981 and the joint winner of the James Tait Black Memorial Prize, *The Kingdom by the Sea* (1983) and *Doctor Slaughter* (1984).

Paul Theroux lives in London with his wife and two children.

Paul Theroux

★

THE LONDON
EMBASSY

PENGUIN BOOKS

Penguin Books Ltd, Harmondsworth, Middlesex, England
Viking Penguin Inc., 40 West 23rd Street, New York, New York 10010, U.S.A.
Penguin Books Australia Ltd, Ringwood, Victoria, Australia
Penguin Books Canada Ltd, 2801 John Street, Markham, Ontario, Canada L3R 1B4
Penguin Books (N.Z.) Ltd, 182–190 Wairau Road, Auckland 10, New Zealand

First published in Great Britain by Hamish Hamilton Ltd 1982
Published in Penguin Books 1983
Reprinted 1983, 1985

Printed and bound in Great Britain by
Cox & Wyman Ltd, Reading
Filmset in Monophoto Times by
Northumberland Press Ltd, Gateshead

For Christopher Sinclair-Stevenson

CONTENTS

★ 1 ★

VOLUNTEER SPEAKER

★

It annoyed me when people asked, because I had to tell them I had just been in Southeast Asia. That was a deceptively grand name for the small dusty town where I was American consul. But who has heard of Ayer Hitam? Officially, it was a Hardship Post – the designation meant extra money, a Hardship Allowance I could not spend. There was no hardship, but there was boredom, and nothing to buy to relieve me of that. With a free month before I was due in Washington to await reassignment, I decided to finance a private trip to Europe – another grand name. One town on my route was Saarbrücken, where the river formed the French–German border. It looked like magic the day I arrived; at dinner it seemed like a version of the town I had left in Malaysia.

My choice of Saarbrücken was not accidental. The Flints, Charlie and Lois, had been posted here after their stint in Kuala Lumpur. They had been urging me to visit them: the single man and the childless couple are natural allies, in an uncomplicated way. Charlie had accepted this minor post because he had refused to spend the usual two deskbound years in Washington. He had not lived in Washington for fifteen years. It was his boast – no good telling him that Washington had changed – and it meant that he had to keep on the move. A little patience and politicking would have earned him promotion. 'Next stop Abu Dhabi,' he used to say. That was before Abu Dhabi became important. At dinner, he said, 'Next stop Rwanda. I don't even know the capital.'

'Kigali,' I said. 'It's a hole.'

'I keep forgetting you're an old Africa hand.'

Lois said, 'One of these days, the State Department's going to send us to a really squalid place. Then Charlie will have to admit it's worse than Washington.'

'I didn't squawk in Medan,' said Flint. 'I didn't squawk in K L. I actually liked Bangalore. They once threatened me with Calcutta. The idiots in Washington don't even know that Calcutta morale is the highest in the foreign service. The housing's fantastic and you can get a cook for ten bucks. That's my kind of place. Only squirts want Paris. And the guys on the third floor – they like Paris, too.'

'Who are the guys on the third floor?'

'The spooks,' said Flint. 'That's what they call them here.'

Lois winked at me. 'He's been squawking here.'

'I didn't think anyone complained in Europe,' I said.

'This isn't Europe,' said Flint. 'It's not even Germany. Half the people here pretend they're French.'

'I like these border towns,' I said. 'The ambiguity, the rigmarole at the customs post, the rumours about smugglers – it's a nice word, smugglers. I associate borders with mystery and danger.'

'The only danger here is that the ambassador will cable me that he wants to go fishing. Then I have to waste a week fixing up his permits and finding his driver a place to stay. And all the other security – anti-kidnap measures so he can catch minnows. Jesus, I hate this job.'

Flint had turned grouchy. To change the subject, I said, 'Lois, this is a wonderful meal.'

'You're sweet to say so,' Lois said. 'I'm taking cooking lessons. Would you believe it?'

'It's a kind of local sausage,' said Flint, spearing a tube of encased meat with his fork. 'Everything's a kind of local sausage. You'd get arrested for eating this in Malaysia. The wine's drinkable, though. All wine-growing countries are right-wing – ever think of that?'

'Charlie still hasn't forgiven me for not learning to cook,' Lois said. She stared at her husband, a rather severe glaze on her eyes that fixed him in silence; but she went on with what seemed calculated lightheartedness, 'I can't help the fact that he made me spend my early married life in countries where cooks cost ten dollars a month.'

'Consequently, Lois is a superb tennis player,' said Flint.

A certain atmosphere was produced by this remark, but it was a passing cloud, a blade of half-dark, no more. It hovered and was gone. Lois rose abruptly and said, 'I hope you left room for dessert.'

Charlie did not speak until Lois was in the kitchen. I see I have written 'Charlie' rather than 'Flint'; but he had changed, his tone grew confidential. He said, 'I'm very worried about Lois. Ever since we got here she's been behaving funnily. People have mentioned it to me – they're not used to her type. I mean, she cries a lot. She might be heading for a nervous breakdown. You try doing a job with a sick person on your hands. It's a whole nother story. I'm glad you're here – you're good for her.'

It was unexpected and it came in a rush, the cataract of American candour. I murmured something about Lois looking perfectly all right to me.

'It's an act – she's a head case,' he said. 'I don't know what to do about her. But you'd be doing me a big favour if you made allowances. Be good to her. I'd consider it a favour –'

Lois entered the room on those last words. She was carrying a dark heap of chocolate cake. She said, 'You don't have to do something just because Charlie asks you to.'

'We were talking about the Volunteer Speakers Programme,' said Flint, with unfaltering coolness and even a hint of boredom; it was a masterful piece of acting. 'As I was saying, I'm supposed to be lining up speakers, but we haven't had one for months. The last time I was in Bonn, the ambassador put a layer of shit in my ear – what am I doing? I told him – bringing culture to the Germans. The town's a thousand years old. There were Romans here! He didn't think that was very funny. It would help if you gave a talk for me at the Centre.'

Lois reached across the table and squeezed my hand. There was more reassurance than caution in the gesture. She said, 'Pay no attention to him. He could have all the volunteer speakers he wants. He just doesn't ask them.'

'Herr Friedrich on Roman spitoons, Gräfin von Spitball on the local aristocracy. That's what Europe's big on – memories. It hasn't got a future, but what a past! There's something decadent about nostalgia – I mean, really diseased.'

'Charlie doesn't like Germans,' said Lois. 'No one likes them. For fifteen years, all I've heard is how inefficient people are in tropical countries. Guess what the big complaint is here? Germans are efficient. They do things on time, they keep their word – this is supposed to be sinister.'

Flint said, 'They're machines.'

'He used to call Malays "superslugs",' said Lois.

'And Germans think we're diseased,' said Flint. 'They talk about German culture. What's German culture? These days it's American culture – the same books, the same music, the same movies, even the same clothes. They've bought us wholesale, and they have the nerve to sneer.' His harangue left him gasping. With a kind of mournful sincerity he said, 'I'd consider it a favour if you did a lecture. We have a slot tomorrow – there's a sewing circle that meets on Thursdays.'

He was asking me to connive at his deception, and he knew I could not decently refuse him such a simple request. I said, 'Doesn't one need a topic?'

'The white man's burden. War stories. Life in the East. Like the time the locals besieged your consulate and burned the flag.'

'All the locals did was smile and drink my whisky.'

'Improvise,' he said, twirling his wine glass. 'Ideally, I'd like something on "America's Role in a Changing World" – like, What good is foreign aid? What are the responsibilities of the super-powers? The oil crisis with reference to Islam and the Arab states, Are we at a crossroads? Look, all they want is to hear you speak English. We had to discontinue the language programme after the last budget cuts. They'll be glad to see a new face. They're pretty sick of mine.'

Lois squeezed my hand again. 'Welcome to Europe.'

The next morning, trying sleepily to imagine what I would say in my lecture – and I hated Flint for making me go through with this charade – I was startled by a knock at the door. I sat up in bed. It was Lois.

'I forgot to warn you about breakfast,' she said, entering the room. Her tone was cheerfully apologetic, but her movements were bold. At first I thought she was in her pyjamas. I put on my glasses and saw she was in a short pleated skirt and a white jersey. The white clothes and their cut gave her a girlish look, and at the same time contradicted it, exaggerating her briskness. Tennis had obviously kept her in shape. She was in her early forties – younger than Charlie – but was trim and hard-fleshed. She had borne no children – it was childbirth that left the marks of age on a woman's body. She had a flat stomach, a server's stride, and as she approached the bed I noticed the play of muscles in her thighs.

She was an odd apparition, but a woman in a tennis outfit looks too athletic in a businesslike way to be seductive.

She was still talking about breakfast, not looking at me, but pacing the floor at the foot of the bed. Charlie didn't normally have more than a coffee, she said. There was grapefruit in the fridge and cereal on the sideboard. The coffee was made. Did I want eggs?

'I'll have a coffee with Charlie,' I said.

'He's gone. He left the house an hour ago.'

'Don't worry about me. I can look after myself.'

Lois's tennis shoes squeaked as she paced the polished floor. Then she stopped and faced me. 'I'm worried about Charlie,' she said. 'I suppose you thought he was joking last night about the ambassador. It's serious – he hasn't accomplished anything here. Everyone knows it. And he doesn't care.'

Almost precisely the words he had used about her: I wondered whether they were playing a game with me.

'I'm his volunteer speaker,' I said. 'That's quite a feather in his cap.'

'You don't think so, but it is. He's in real trouble. He told the ambassador he was thinking of taking early retirement.'

'Might not be a bad idea,' I said.

'He said, "I can always sell second-hand cars. I've been selling second-hand junk my whole foreign service career." That's what he told the ambassador! I was flabbergasted. Then he told me it was a joke. It was at a staff meeting – all the PAOs were there. But no one laughed. I don't blame them – it's not funny.'

I wanted to get out of bed. I saw that this would not be simple while she was in the room. I could not think straight, sitting up, with the blankets across my lap, my hair in my eyes.

Lois said, 'Can I get in?'

I have always felt that if a person wants something very badly, and if it is not unreasonable, he should have it, no matter what. I usually feel like supplying it myself. Once, I gave my hunting knife to a Malay. He admired it; he wanted it; he had some use for it. Generosity is easy to justify. I always lose what I don't need.

I considered Lois's question and then said, 'Yes – sure,' convinced that Charlie had not misled me: something was wrong with her.

She got in quickly, without embarrassment. She said, 'He's mentally screwed up, he really is.'

'Poor Charlie.'

We lay under the covers, side by side, like two Boy Scouts in a big sleeping bag, sheltering from the elements in clumsy comradeship. Lois had not taken off her tennis shoes: I could feel the canvas and rubber against my shins. Her shoes seemed proof that Charlie had not exaggerated her mental state.

'He thinks it's funny. It's me who's suffering. People pity mental cases – it's their families they should pity.'

'That's pitching it a bit strongly, isn't it?' I tried to shift my hand from the crisp pleats of her skirt. 'Charlie may be under a little strain, but he hardly qualifies as a mental case.'

'A month ago we're at a party. It was endless – one of these German affairs. They really love their food, and their idea of fun is to get stinking drunk and sing loud. There's no social stigma attached to drunkenness here. So everyone was laughing stupidly and the men were behaving like jackasses. One of them took my shawl and put it over his head and did a Wagner bit. And there was this Italian – just a hanger-on, he wasn't a diplomat. He suggested they all go to a restaurant. It's two in the morning, everyone's eaten, and he wants to go to a restaurant! There was a sort of general move to the door – they're all yelling and laughing. I said to Charlie, "Count me out – I'm tired."

' "You never want to do anything," he said.

'I told him he could go if he wanted to. He gave me the car keys and I went home alone. I was asleep when he came back. There was a big commotion at the front door – it was about five. I go to the door and who do I see? Charlie. And the Italian. They're holding hands.'

I almost laughed. But Lois was on the verge of tears. I felt her body stiffen.

'It was awful. The Italian had this guilty, sneaky look on his face, as if he'd been caught in the act. I saw that he wanted to drop the whole thing. He wouldn't look at me. Charlie was grey – absolutely grey. He wasn't even drunk – he looked sick, crazy, and he kept holding this Italian by the hand. He told me to go back to bed.

' "I'm not going back to bed until he leaves," I said.

'"This is my friend," he said. His friend! They're holding hands! He dragged the Italian into the house and I really wanted to hit both of them. Charlie said, "We're staying."

'"Not him," I said. "He's not staying in my house."

'"You never let me have any friends," said Charlie, and he starts staggering around with this other guy. I thought I was dreaming, it was so ridiculous.

'"I don't care what you do," I said, "but you're not taking this creep into my house." Then I got hysterical, I started screaming, I hardly knew what I was saying.

'Charlie said, "All right, then, let's go." And off they went, hand in hand, out the door. I don't know where they went. I didn't see Charlie until that night. He looked terrible – I don't even think he'd been to work. He hasn't mentioned it since. And you deny he's a mental case.'

Listening to her story, it struck me that I hardly knew Charlie Flint. He was as frenzied as anyone in the embassy, and he had a theory that the embassy wives were going to start an insurrection, but our relationship was mainly professional. I knew nothing of his personal life beyond the fact that he drank too much; that fact applied to everyone I met in the foreign service. I regarded his determination to stay out of Washington as a worthy aim. He wasn't ambitious. And he had prepared me for his wife's oddness.

I replied to her in platitudes: Don't jump to conclusions, things will settle down, and so forth. What else could I offer? I did not know her well, and I was in bed with her. I said, as an afterthought, 'You're not suggesting he's gay, are you?'

'Do you think I'd care about that?' she said. 'You've been in the bush for two years, so you don't know. But being bisexual is a big thing in Europe these days. Everyone's gay. The men think it's fashionable, almost masculine – proof that you don't have any hang-ups. They're always hugging each other, holding hands – God only knows what else they do, though I have a pretty good idea. I'm telling you, Europe makes Southeast Asia look civilized. I get propositioned about once a week – by women!'

'Are you tempted?'

'No,' Lois said, 'I tried it.'

'With a woman?'

She nodded; her whole body moved, and she wore a curious

15

half-smile. 'A German chick. About nineteen. Very pretty. It didn't work out.' She made a face. 'Charlie wanted me to. That's why I didn't take it seriously. I thought it would encourage him in his craziness. Now, when I think about it, I just laugh.' She shifted sideways on the bed, propped herself up on one arm and said, 'How come you're so normal?'

'Everything is human.'

'You're making excuses for Charlie.'

'Charlie has a conscience.'

'Don't you?'

'I don't know. But I know that the lack of it can make some people look fairly serene, even harmless and normal. Charlie hasn't hurt anyone.'

'He's hurt me!' Lois cried, and I felt her shoe. 'I'm sorry,' she said. 'I didn't mean to kick you. But what good is it saying, "Everything's human and everything's normal"? We were in Indonesia, India, Malaysia – yes, things were normal in those places. But Europe's different. And I'm telling you, I can't handle it.'

I felt sure she was mistaken, but I didn't want to contradict her, since she appeared to take everything as a personal attack. She saw Charlie's drunken hand-holding as an affront to her, but this casual mention of *A German chick* – wasn't that equally odd? She didn't appear to think so. I understood why she was lying to me, though it was not in character for her to belittle Charlie. Adultery is a great occasion for lying; the wife in another man's bed usually talks about her husband.

I said, 'I'm glad I came to Europe. I had no idea it was so lively. It makes Ayer Hitam seem rather tame.'

'Where are you going after this?'

'Up the Rhine. I'm leaving tonight, after my talk. I'll be in Düsseldorf for a few days.'

'Are you staying with Murray Goldsack?'

'Charlie gave me his name. But I'll probably stay in a hotel.'

'Charlie gave you his name,' Lois said bitterly. 'He would. We were up there three weeks ago. Another disaster.'

I didn't want to hear it, but she had already begun.

'The Goldsacks have been there about a year. She writes poetry, he's big on painting – he'll show you the gallery he opened. It's full of pretentious crap – stupid, simple, neurotic blurs. Doesn't anyone paint people anymore? The Goldsacks don't have any children. In fact, when they got married they signed a contract saying they wouldn't have any kids and deciding who'd get what when they split up. They assumed they'd split up eventually – Murray will give you all the statistics. They're very modern laid-back people with a house full of crap art and heads full of crap opinions. Over dinner they told us how they keep their marriage alive.

'Get this. They play games. Like "White Night". Sue puts on a white dress, white slippers, white everything. Then she cooks a white meal – mashed potatoes, steamed fish, cauliflower, chablis. Murray wears a white suit. Then they get drunk and go to it.'

'That doesn't sound so odd,' I said. She was not lying, but repeating a lie.

'They also have a Black Night, Red Night. Or Indian Night. She puts on a sari, cooks a curry, they burn incense and run through the *Kama Sutra*.'

'Tell me about Eskimo Night. Do they rub noses?'

'Be serious, will you? Murray was telling me about it – we were in his living-room. As he was describing these dressing-up games I noticed he was filling my glass. This little squirt was trying to get me drunk! I was feeling pretty rotten, and he was annoyed that I wasn't drinking fast enough. So he pulled out some pot and rolled me a joint. I once tried some in K L, but it wasn't anything like this. My brain turned into oatmeal. Then I looked around and didn't see Charlie. I was panicky. "Where's Charlie?" I said. Murray looked at me. "Oh, he's with Sue."

' "Where are they?" I said.

'He pointed to a door – the door was closed. I said, "I've got to talk to him" – I don't know why I said it. Maybe it was that stuff I had just smoked.

'Murray said, "Don't go in there. They don't want you to."

' "How do you know what they want?" I said. He sort of chuckled. I said, "Hey, what's going on?"

'He had a really evil look on his face. He said, "You really want to know?"

'Then I knew. I wanted to cry. I said, "My husband's in that room with your wife!" He said something like, "So what?" and put his arm around me. I pushed him away and stood up. He got mad at me – he was really peeved. He tried to grab me again, and I hit him. He said, "Hey, what's wrong with you?"

'What's wrong with *me*? This man's a cultural affairs officer in the United States embassy. He's supposed to be a diplomat, he gives lectures, he makes statements to the press, he writes reports – or whatever they do. And he's peeved because I won't cooperate with his wife-swapping! It was too much. After an hour or so, Charlie and Sue came out looking pretty pale and pushing their clothes back in place. We all had a drink and talked about – Jesus, we talked about Jimmy Carter and the budget cuts. The next day we left. Charlie wouldn't talk about the other thing – the monkey business.'

Lois was silent for a while. Then she turned over on to her side, her back to me. I got up on one elbow and, seeing that she was crying, I put my arm around her to comfort her.

She said, 'Hold me tight – please.' I did. She murmured, 'That's nice.'

What now? I thought.

She said, 'Charlie never pays any attention to me.'

'I can't help liking him,' I said.

Lois said, 'I'm married to him,' and then, 'Don't let go.'

'I feel a bit silly,' I said. 'Should we be doing this?'

'I get nothing,' she said. 'Nothing, nothing. This isn't a life.'

'You're going to miss your tennis.'

She twisted away from me and heaved her legs up.

'What are you doing, Lois?'

'Getting these damn shoes off.'

I said, 'I'm supposed to be having lunch with Charlie. I couldn't face him. Please don't take your shoes off.'

'He doesn't care,' she said.

Another lie: for all his frenzy and occasional deceit, there was no man who would have cared more about his wife's infidelity. Remember, they had no children to encumber their intimacy, so they were like children themselves – such couples so often are.

'That seems worse,' I said, resenting her ineptness.

She pressed her back against me, moving her skirt sinuously on my thighs; and still facing away she uttered a despairing groan.

'Then just hold me,' she said. 'I'll be all right in a minute.'

When she got out of bed her pleated skirt was crushed and her socks had slipped down. She brushed herself off, adjusted her socks, and tucked in her jersey. She looked as if she had just played her match and been defeated.

She said, 'I feel very virtuous.'

'I don't,' I said. Then she was out of the door. I thought: *She is insane.*

Charlie was late for lunch. When he arrived, I looked for indications of the craziness Lois had attributed to him. But there were none. She needed to believe he was crazy, in order to make excuses for herself.

He said, 'Do you really have to go to Düsseldorf after the lecture?'

'The lecture was your idea,' I said. 'If it wasn't for that I'd be on the train now.'

'You're welcome to stay as long as you like. Lois was hoping you would.'

I said, 'I don't think there's much I can do for her.'

'Fair enough.' He seemed gloomy and almost apologetic, as if he had guessed at what had gone on that morning between Lois and me. I did not want to upset him further by telling him her wild stories. He said, 'I'd leave this place tomorrow except for one thing. This is the first place Lois can live a normal life. I'm staying for her sake. Believe me, it's a sacrifice. But there are good doctors here. The best medical care. That's what she needs.'

'I understand.' I could not say more without revealing that I pitied him.

'You'll like Düsseldorf. Goldsack's a live wire. A very bright guy – he's got a big future in the foreign service. He'll make ambassador as sure as anything. His wife's fun, and I think I should tell you – she's an easy lay.'

That was the first clue I had that Lois might not have been completely wrong about Charlie. And it made me all the more eager to meet the Goldsacks. I left immediately after my lecture, and two days later was in Murray Goldsack's office.

'Flint cabled me that you were coming,' he said. 'I've been looking over your bio. It's really impressive.' Goldsack was small and dark, in his early thirties, and he looked me over closely, giving me the strong impression that I was being interviewed and appraised. He said, 'I wish I had your Southeast Asia experience. My wife keeps saying we should put in for a tour there.'

'You might be disappointed.'

'I'm never bored,' he said, and made it sound like a reproach. 'Flint said you might be available as a volunteer speaker.'

'Other people do it so much better,' I said.

'Give us a chance to entertain you at least,' he said. 'We'd like to have you and your wife over for a meal. I hope you'll both be able to make it.'

'If my bio says I'm married, you've been misinformed.'

Goldsack laughed. 'What I mean is, I'd rather you didn't come alone.'

I said, 'I know an antique dealer in town. He's a lovely fellow. Now, he's someone you might like to consider as a volunteer speaker.'

'Wonderful,' said Goldsack. He jumped up and shook my hand to signal the meeting was over. 'I'll leave a message at your hotel with the details.'

That was the last I saw of Goldsack. There was no message, which was just as well, because there was no antique dealer. I thought: *Poor Lois*.

★2★
RECEPTION
★

The best telegram I ever had said this: CALL ME TOMORROW FOR WONDERFUL NEWS. I had twenty hours to imagine what the news might be. And I delayed for a few hours more. I wanted to prolong the pleasure. I loved the expectation. How often in life do we have the bright certainty that everything is going to be fine? Months later, I told someone about the telegram. She said, 'It would have driven me crazy with impatience!'

I was more than patient. I was almost fulfilled. I could have waited a month. After all, a reliable witness had assured me that it was wonderful news.

Travelling alone through Europe, I had just left Germany for Holland, where the telegram awaited me. I liked the Dutch. They were sensible; they had been brave in the war. They still tried to understand the world, and their quaint modernism had made them tolerant. They behaved themselves. It was a church-and-brothel society in which there were neither saints nor sinners, only at worst a few well-meaning hypocrites. Vice without passion, theology without much terror; they were even idealistic in a practical way. They were unprejudiced and open-minded without being naïvely enthusiastic. They had nice faces. Their pornography was ridiculous, and I think it embarrassed them, but they knew that left to its impotent spectators and drooling voyeurs it was just another sorry prop in sex's sad comedy.

In Amsterdam, where I could have chosen anything, I chose to be idle. I smoked a little hash, talked to Javanese in their own language and was reminded again how 'colonial' and 'bourgeois' are full of the same worthy illusions, like the solidity and reassurance of plump upholstered armchairs in a warm parlour. I sat and read. I ate eastern food and slept soundly in a soft Dutch bed. Each night I dreamed without waking – it had never happened in Ayer Hitam, where nights were racketty and hot.

It was winter. The canals froze. Some people skated, as they did in the oldest oil paintings on earth – moving so fast that the swipes of the speed-skaters' blades made a sound like knives being sharpened. Gulls dived between the leaning buildings and gathered on the green ice. The small frosty city smelled of its river and its bakeries, and beer. I went for long ankle-twisting walks down cobblestone streets.

At last, almost sad because it meant the end of a joyous wait, I made my phone call. The telegram had been informal – a friend in the State Department. I had tried to avoid guessing the news: expect nothing and you're never disappointed.

She said, 'You've got London.'

This was London, this reception. A month had passed since the telegram. The party invitations had my name on them (*'To welcome . . .'*) The guests had been carefully selected – it was pleasure for them, a night out. For us, the embassy staff, it was overtime. I did not mind. I had wanted London. In London I could meet anyone, do anything, go anywhere. It was the centre of the civilized world, the best place in Europe, the last habitable big city. It was the first city Americans thought of travelling to – funny, friendly, and undemanding; it was every English speaker's spiritual home. I had been intending to come here for as long as I could remember.

And this was also a promotion for me: from FS-5, my grade as Consul in the Malaysian town of Ayer Hitam, to FS-4, Political Officer. My designation was POL-1, not to be confused with POL-2, the CIA – 'the boys on the third floor', as we called them at the London embassy. I was only a spy in the most general and harmless sense of the word.

It had been a mistake to walk from my hotel to this reception. My hotel was in Chelsea, near the Embankment; the party was at Horton's, Briarcliff Lodge, in Kensington. London is not a city. It is more like a country, and living in it is like living in Holland or Belgium. Its completeness makes it deceptive – there are sidewalks from one frontier to the other – and its hugeness makes it possible for everyone to invent his own city. My London is not your London, though everyone's Washington, DC, is pretty much the same. It was three miles from my hotel to Horton's, and this was only a small part of the labyrinth. A two-mile walk through any other city would take you inevitably through a slum. But this was unvarying gentility – wet narrow streets, dark housefronts, block upon block. They spoke of prosperity, but they revealed nothing very definite of their occupants. They were sedate battlements, fortress walls, with blind windows, or drawn curtains. I imagined, behind them, something tumultuous. I had never felt more solitary or anonymous. I was happy. The city had been built to enclose secrets, for the British are like those naked Indians who hide in the Brazilian jungle – not timid, but fanatically private and untrusting. This was a mazy land of privacies – comforting to a secretive person, offering shelter to a fugitive, but posing problems to a diplomat. It was my job to know its secrets, to inform and represent my government, to penetrate the city and make new maps.

That walk through London humbled me. I began to feel less like an adventurer – a grand cartographer – than someone in a smaller role. I played with the idea that we were like gardeners. We were sent to maintain this garden, to keep the grass cut and the weeds down; to dead-head the roses, encourage the frailer blossoms. We could not introduce new plants, or alter it. We watched over it, kept it watered; we dealt with enemies and called them pests. But our role was purely custodial. Each of us, in time, would go away. It was an image of a harmless occupation.

But of course in London there was a difference. It was a city without front yards. This was not America, with a low-maintenance lawn around every house. The garden was not a boasting acre here to advertise prosperity to passers-by. In London, all gardens were behind the houses. They were hidden. Plots was the word.

Briarcliff Lodge had once belonged to a duke. It rose up from its surrounding hedge, a graceful monument of creamy floodlit walls and tall windows. What an earlier age had managed with stone, we had with light – floodlights, spotlights, bulbs behind cornices and buried in the ground, wrapped in vines and under-water. It was beauty as emphasis, but it also afforded protection. Inside and out, Everett Horton had restored Briarcliff Lodge at embassy expense. He had hired six waiters tonight, and two front-door functionaries. I handed the first my raincoat – apologizing for its being wet – and gave my name to the second man. But I was not announced. I was early and, after all, I was the guest of honour.

'Mr Horton will be down shortly.'

'Excuse me, where's the –?'

'Just behind you, sir. One flight up.'

In such circumstances the British are telepathic.

Then I heard a child's voice from the upper floor.

'Are the people here yet, Dad?'

'Not yet, but they will be soon. Better make it snappy.' It was Horton's voice. He cleared his throat and said, 'Now do you want to do a tinkle or a yucky?'

I began to back away.

'Both,' the child said.

'All right,' the diplomat said patiently. 'Take your time.'

All happy families have a private language. The Hortons' was just about as useful and ludicrous-sounding as any other. But if Horton could be that patient with his child, I had little to worry about; and if he was happy he was more than human.

The rooms in this house were enormous – a gym-sized drawing-room (perhaps once the ballroom), a library, the dining-room to the right, and behind it the morning room and conservatory. A foyer, a cloak room, a wide staircase. And this was only the ground floor. It was ducal splendour, but Horton was no duke. He lived, I knew, with his wife and child in an apartment on the third floor, at the back of the house. Servants' quarters, really – their little yellow kitchen, microwave oven, dishwasher, toaster, Bloomingdale's furniture, their TV and five telephones. Horton had not taken possession of the house – he was its custodian. He lived like any janitor, like any gardener. Such is the fate of a career diplomat.

Some minutes later, he came downstairs.

'We've got rather a mixed bag tonight,' he said. He was formal, a bit stiff-faced. He had a reputation for affecting British slang, and it was hard for me now to think of him as the same man who had just said *a tinkle or a yucky*?

The front door thumped shut.

'Mr and Mrs Roger Howlett,' said the functionary from the hall. There was both dignity and strain in his announcing voice.

'The publisher,' I said.

'Good show,' Horton said. 'I'm glad you had a chance to swot up the guest list.'

He was being tactful – I had done little else for the past week. It had been, so far, the whole of my job, that guest list with its fifty names, and more – occupations, ages, addresses, and (if

24

applicable) political leanings. It was a comprehensive list, like 'Cast of Characters' at the opening of a Victorian novel. Learning it was like cramming a vocabulary list for a language exam. The only danger at such a reception was in knowing too much – startling the innocent guest by seeming over-familiar with him.

Until then, my overseas experience had been in Uganda and Malaysia. Prudence, but not much subtlety, had been required of me in those places. Uganda wanted money from us, Malaysia wanted political patronage; both deviously demanded that we be explicit and suspected us of being spies. Here in London we were regarded as high-living and rather privileged diplomats, a bit spoiled and unserious. But in fact every officer at the London embassy was in his own way an intelligence gatherer. There were too many secrets here for any of us to be complacent. This garden was not ours and it contained some strange blooms. And maybe all good gardeners are at heart unsentimental botanists.

Horton's drawing room was soon filled. I stood at the door to the foyer. In this, the most casual setting imaginable, no one could be blamed for thinking that mine was the easiest job in the world. But every American in that room was hard at work and only the British people here were enjoying themselves. Once again it struck me how cooperative party guests were – it was perhaps the only reason embassy receptions were ever given, to enlist the help of unsuspecting people, to find out whether the natives were friendly, to take soundings, to listen for gossip.

I entered the room – penetrated London for the first time – and set to work.

'Hello. I don't think we've met,' I said to a young woman.

It was Mrs Sarah Whiting, second wife of Anthony Whiting, Managing Director of the British subsidiary of an American company which made breakfast cereal. Whiting himself was across the room talking to Margaret Duboys from our Trade Section. The Whitings had no children of their own, though Mr Whiting had three by a previous marriage to an American woman still resident in Britain and still referred to, by Vic Scaduto, our CAO, as 'Auntie Climax'. Sarah Whiting was something of a mystery to the embassy; she had only been married a year to the Managing Director. She was still full of the effortful romance of the second marriage – or so it seemed. I got nowhere by inquiring about her

25

husband's business. Second wives are usually spared the details: the husband's affairs were determined by another woman long ago. Anyway, I knew the answers before I asked the questions.

She said, 'You're an American.'

'How did you guess?'

'You look as if you belong here.'

'Seeing as how I've only been here a week, I'm deeply flattered.'

'Then you must be the guest of honour,' she said. 'Welcome to London.'

We chatted about the weather, the high price of apartments – I told her I was looking for a place – and the décor of this room. She spoke knowledgeably about interior decoration ('I would have done that fascia in peach') and when I complimented her, she said she was interested 'in a small way'. I was soon to find out how small.

'I make furniture,' she said.

'Design it or build it?'

'I do everything.'

I was impressed. I said, 'You upholster it, too?'

'Not much upholstery is necessary,' she said. 'Most of my furniture is for dolls' houses.'

I thought I had misheard her.

'You mean' – I measured a few inches with my fingers – 'like this?'

'It depends on the house. Some are smaller, some bigger. I make cutlery, as well.'

'For dolls' houses?'

'That's right,' she said.

'Very tiny knives and forks?'

'And spoons. And tea strainers. Why are you smiling?'

'I don't think I've ever met anyone in your line of work.'

She said, 'I quite enjoy it.'

'Your children' – yes, I knew better, but it was the obvious next remark – 'your children must be fascinated by it.'

'It's not really a child's thing. Most of the collectors are adults. It's a very serious business – and very expensive. We export a great deal. In any case, I don't have any children of my own. Do you have kids?'

'I'm not married,' I said.

'We'll find you a wife,' she said.

I hated that – it was the tone of a procuress. I may have showed a flicker of disapproval, because she looked suddenly uneasy. Maybe I was queer! Bachelor means queer!

I said, 'Please do.'

She turned to the woman next to her and said, 'Sophie – this is the guest of honour,' and stepped aside to make room.

'Sophie Graveney,' Sarah Whiting said, and introduced us.

Miss Graveney, thirty, was an Honourable, her late father a lord. Her brother had succeeded to the title. We knew little about her, except for the fact that she had spent some time in the States.

I said, 'We were just talking about dolls' houses.'

'Sarah's passionate about them.'

'If things go on like this, I'll have to get Sarah to rent me one to live in.'

'You're looking for a place, are you?'

'Yes. Just an apartment – a flat.'

'What area?'

'I'm near the river at the moment, near Chelsea Embankment. I think I'd like to stay down there.'

'Chelsea's very nice. But it's pricey. You might find something in Battersea. It's not as fashionable, but it's just across the Bridge – South Chelsea, the snobs call it. There are some beautiful flats in Prince of Wales Drive, overlooking the park.'

'I'll consider anything except the sort of place that's described as "delightfully old-fashioned". That always means derelict.'

'These are lovely,' she said. 'Do you jog? Of course you don't, why should you?' And gave me an appraising stare. She had soft curls and wore lip gloss and I could see her body move beneath her loose black dress. She was also very tall, and had large feet. Her shoulders were scented with jasmine. 'I do jog, though. For my figure. I do a little modelling. I jog around Battersea Park every morning.'

Sarah Whiting laughed and said, 'Tell him your story about that man.'

'Oh, God,' Sophie said. 'That man. Last summer I was out jogging. It was about seven in the morning and I'd done two miles. I was really mucky – pouring with sweat. An old man stepped in front of me and said, "Excuse me, miss, would you care for a drink?" I thought he meant a drink of water. I was out of breath and

27

sort of steaming. I absolutely stank. I could barely answer him. Then he sort of snatched at my hand and said, "I've got some whisky in my car." '

Her eyes were shining as she spoke.

'Do you get it? There I am in my running shoes and track suit, drenched with sweat, my hair hanging in rat-tails, and this foolish old man is trying to pick me up! At seven o'clock in the morning!'

'Incredible!' Sarah said.

'Then he said, "I want to be your bicycle seat," and made a hideous face. I jogged away,' Sophie said innocently. 'I didn't fancy him one little bit.'

'If I get a flat near Battersea Park I can watch you jogging,' I said.

'Yes. If you get up early. Isn't that thrilling?'

A waiter passed by with a tray of drinks. Sophie took another glass of white wine and, seeing that I did not take any, she looked somewhat disapproving.

'Oh, God, are you one of these people who doesn't drink?'

I said, 'I'm one of these people who's cutting down.'

'Oh, God, you don't smoke either – how boring! I smoke about two packs a day.'

'Do you?' I said. 'Now that's really interesting.'

'Is that funny?' she said, and blinked at me. 'I never know when people are joking.'

There was a dim suspicion in her voice and a moment of stillness, as if she had just realized that I was a perfect stranger, who might be mocking her. She looked around and smiled in relief.

'Terry!' she said, as if calling for help.

She had seen a friend. She introduced him to me as Lord Billows though he insisted I call him Terry. I recognized him from the Guest List – he ran a public relations firm, which had a New York office. We talked for the next ten minutes about smoking, its hazards and pleasures: he represented a tobacco company and was very defensive about its sponsorship of mountain climbing competitions – teams of climbers racing up mountainsides, a sport I had never heard of. To change the subject, I told him I had spent the past two years in Malaysia. He said he knew 'Eddie Pahang'. Very chummy: he was referring to the Sultan of Pahang.

Lord Billows said, 'Your ambassador in K L gave marvellous parties.'

'So they said. I seldom got to K L. I was in Ayer Hitam, with the stinking durians and the revolting rubber-tappers. You've never heard of it. Nobody has. On the good days it was paradise.'

'Who was your sultan?'

'Johore.'

'Buffles – I knew him well. Buffles was a real old trooper. A magnificent polo player in his time, you know. And a greatly misunderstood man.'

'He used to come to our club once a year,' I said. 'One of his mistresses was in the drama society. She was a Footlighter. That's what they called themselves. They loved being in plays.'

Lord Billows had been grinning impatiently at me through all this. Then he said, 'I'm going to ask you a very rude question,' and fixed his face against mine. 'But you probably won't consider it rude. You Americans are so straightforward, aren't you?'

'That is rather a rude question,' I said.

Lord Billows said, 'That's not the question.'

'Ask him,' Sophie said. 'I'm all ears.'

'The question is, are you in fact a member of a club in London?' Lord Billows turned aside to Sophie and said, 'You see, in the normal way one would never ask an Englishman that.'

I said, 'I think the Ayer Hitam Club has a reciprocal arrangement with a London club.'

'I doubt that very much,' Lord Billows said. 'I have three clubs. The Savile might suit you – we have some Americans. I'm not as active as I'd like to be, but there it is. I put your chap Scaduto up for the Savile. I could do the same for you. Let me give you lunch there. You could look it over. I think you'd find it convivial.'

'Is it delightfully old-fashioned?' Sophie asked.

'Exactly,' Lord Billows said.

Sophie said, 'He'll detest it.'

'When applied to houses delightfully old-fashioned means a draughty ruin. When applied to clubs it means bad food and no women.'

'The Savile has quite decent food,' Lord Billows said. 'And most of the staff are women.'

'I was in a club like that once,' I said.

'In London?'

'The States. When I was eleven years old,' I said. 'No girls. That was the rule.'

Lord Billows stared at me for several seconds, as if translating what I had said, and then he said coldly, 'You'll excuse me?' He walked away.

'You shouldn't have said that to him,' Sophie said. 'Why make a fuss about men's clubs? I don't object. I hate all this women's lib stuff, don't you?'

She had not addressed the question to me, but to Mrs Howlett – Diana – wife of Roger, the publisher, who was standing next to her. The two women began laughing in a conspiratorial way, and Roger Howlett told me several stories about Adlai Stevenson, and I gathered Horton had briefed him about me because Howlett finished his Stevenson stories by saying, 'Adlai was enormously good value – single, like yourself.'

'Meet Walter Van Bellamy,' Roger Howlett said, and tapped a tall rangy white-haired man on the arm. 'One of your fellow-countrymen.'

Bellamy showed me his famous face and celebrated hair, but his eyes were wild as he said, 'You and I have an awful lot in common, sir.' Then he moved away, pushing through the crowd with his arms up, like a sleepwalker.

'He won all the pots and pans last year,' Howlett said. 'And here is one of our other authors.' He took hold of a large pink man named Yarrow.

'I've only written one book for Roger,' Yarrow said. 'It was political. About Land Reform. I was a Young Communist then. You didn't blink. That's funny – Americans usually do when I say that. It was a failure, my literary effort.'

'I've found,' Howlett said, 'that some of my authors actually get a thrill when their books fail. I've never understood it. Is it the British love of amateurism?'

I knew from the Guest List that Yarrow was a Member of Parliament, but to be polite I asked him what his business was.

He hooked his thumb into his waistcoat pocket and sipped his drink and said, 'I represent a squalid little constituency in the West Midlands.'

The way he said it, with a smirk on his smooth pink face, and a glass in his hand, and his tie splashed – he had sloshed his drink as he spoke – I found disgusting. If he meant it, it was contemptuous; if he had said it for effect, it was obnoxious.

I said, 'Maybe you'll be lucky and lose your seat at the next election.'

'No fear. It's a safe Tory seat. Labour haven't got a chance. The working-class don't vote – too lazy.'

'I want him to do me a book about Westminster,' Howlett said.

'Europe – that's the subject. We're European,' Yarrow said. 'That's where our future is. In a united Europe.'

'What actually *is* a European?' I asked. 'I mean, what language does he speak? What flag does he salute? What are his politics?'

'Don't ask silly questions,' Yarrow said. 'I must go. There's a vote in the Commons in twenty minutes. Rather an important bill.'

'Are you for it or against it?'

'Very much against it!'

'What is the bill?'

'Haven't the faintest,' Yarrow said. 'But if I don't vote there'll be hell to pay.'

He left with two other M Ps. Howlett went to the buffet table and I walked around the room. I saw Miss Duboys talking to Lord Billows, and Vic Scaduto to Walter Van Bellamy, the poet. A black American, named Erroll Jeeps, from our Economic Section, looked intense as he stabbed his finger into the transfixed face of a woman. Jeeps saw me passing and said, 'How are you holding up?'

'Fine,' I said.

'This is our main man,' Jeeps said, 'the guest of honour.'

I said, 'I'd almost forgotten.'

'It's a very jolly party,' the woman said. 'I'm Grace Yarrow.'

'I just met your husband.'

'He's gone to vote. But he'll be back,' she said.

'The Third Reading of the Finance Bill,' Jeeps said. 'It's going to be close.'

'You Americans are so well informed,' Mrs Yarrow said.

Horton stepped over and said, 'I'm going to drag our guest of honour away,' and introduced me to a *Times* journalist, an antique dealer named Frampton, and a girl who did hot-air ballooning. The party had grown hectic. I stopped asking for names. I met the director of a chain of hotels, and then a young man who said,

'Sophie's been telling me all about you' – as if a great deal of time had passed and I had grown in reputation. A party was a way of speeding friendship and telescoping time. It was a sort of hot-house concept of forced growth. We were all friends now.

Someone said, 'It rains every Thursday in London.'

'We bought our Welsh dresser from a couple of fags,' someone else said.

The man named Frampton praised one of Horton's paintings, saying, 'It's tremendous fun.'

At about eleven, the first people left, and by eleven-thirty only half the guests remained. They had gathered in small groups. I met a very thin man who gave his name as Smallwood and could hardly match him to the man on the Guest List who appeared as Sir Charles Smallwood. And I assumed I had the wrong man, because this fellow had a grizzled, almost destitute look and was wearing an old-fashioned cutaway coat.

Edward Heaven, a name that appeared nowhere on the Guest List, was a tall white-haired man with large furry ears who vanished from the room as soon as he told me who he was, on the pretext of giving himself an insulin injection in the upstairs lavatory. 'Puts some people off their food, it does,' he said, but he made for the front door and the next moment he was hurrying down the street in the drizzle, without a coat.

The party was not quite over, I thought. But it was over. Of the nine people remaining in the room, seven were embassy people, and when the last guests left – the *Times* man and the antique dealer – Horton said to us, 'Now, how about a real drink?'

He then went out of the room and told the hired help they could go home. In his dark suit, and carrying a tray, Horton looked like a waiter. On the tray was a bottle of whisky and some glasses. He poured himself a drink, urged us to do the same, and said, 'Please sit down – this won't take long.'

I assumed this was one for the road. But it occurred to me, sitting among my embassy colleagues, that I had said very little to them all evening. In a sense, we were meeting for the first time. Their party manner was gone, and although they were tired – it was well past midnight – they seemed intense, all business. This impression was heightened by the fact that Debbie Horton, Everett's wife, had disappeared upstairs in the last hour of the party. Neither Miss Duboys nor I was married, and none of the others' wives was present. We had all come to the reception alone.

Horton sat in the centre of the circle of chairs, like a football coach after an important game. Scaduto had told me that he liked to be called 'coach'. He looked the part – he was a big fleshy-faced man, who used body-english when he spoke.

He said, 'To tell the truth, I didn't expect to see Lord Billows here tonight. We were told he was going through a rather messy divorce.'

'They've agreed on a settlement,' Al Sanger said. Sanger had dark hair and a very white face and a bright, almost luminous, scar on his forehead. He was, like me, a political officer, but concerned with legal matters. 'His wife gets custody of the children.'

Miss Duboys said, 'What happens to her title?'

'She stays Lady Billows,' Erroll Jeeps said. 'If she remarries, she loses it.'

'Find out what she's styling herself now,' Horton said to Jeeps. 'We don't want to lose touch with her. If we do, there goes one of our most persuasive strings.' He turned to me and said, 'I noticed our guest of honour chatting up Lord Billows. Did you make any headway?'

'He wanted to put me up for a club,' I said.

'Jolly good,' Horton said.

'I told him I wasn't interested.'

'That was pretty stupid,' Sanger said. 'He was trying to do you a favour.'

I could tell from Horton's expression that he was in sympathy with Sanger's remark.

Sanger still faced me. I said, 'So you approve of discrimination against people on the grounds of sex?'

'It's a London club,' he said.

'They don't allow women to join.'

Sanger said, 'Are you afraid they'll turn you down?'

Horton and the others looked shocked, and Margaret Duboys said, 'I don't want to get drawn into this discussion.'

I said, 'Tell me, Sanger, is that remark characteristic of your tact? Because if it is, I'd say your mouth is an even greater liability than your face.'

'Gentlemen, please,' Horton said, in his coach's voice. 'Before this turns into a slanging match, can we move on to something less controversial? I need something on Mrs Whiting – the second Mrs Whiting. Did anyone have a word with her?'

Scaduto said, 'I didn't get anywhere.'

'She makes furniture,' I said. 'Very small furniture. For dolls' houses.'

Sanger said, 'You dig deep.'

'And cutlery,' I said. 'Very tiny forks and knives. If you wanted to stab someone in the back' – here I looked at Sanger – 'I don't think you'd use one of Mrs Whiting's knives.'

Horton smiled. 'Debbie wants her on a committee. We had no idea what her interests were. That's useful. What about our MPs?'

Jeeps said, 'The Finance Bill passed with a Government majority of sixteen. I've just had a phone call. There were eight abstentions.'

'Good man,' Horton said. 'Were any of those abstentions ours?'

'Six Labour, two Liberal. The Tories were solid.'

Miss Duboys said, 'Derek Yarrow filled me in on the anti-nuclear lobby. It seems to be growing.'

Jeeps said, 'I did a number on Mrs Yarrow.'

'What did you make of Mr Yarrow?' Horton asked me, and I realized that in spite of the crowded party my movements had been closely monitored.

'Blustery,' I said. There was no agreement. 'Contemptuous. Probably tricky.'

'He's given us a lot of help,' Sanger said.

'He seemed rather untrustworthy to me. He described his constituency as "squalid". I didn't like that.'

'That's a snap judgement.'

'Precisely what I felt,' I said, and Sanger scowled at me for deliberately misunderstanding him. 'He's a born-again Tory. He lectured me on Europe. You realize of course that he was a Communist.'

'That's not news to us,' Scaduto said.

'I intend to read his book,' I said.

Sanger appeared to be speaking for the others when he said, 'Yarrow doesn't write books.'

'He wrote one. It didn't sell. It was political. Howlett published it.'

'Yarrow's a heavy hitter,' Sanger said.

'Thank you,' I said, scribbling. 'I collect examples of verbal kitsch.'

Horton said, 'Do me a memo on Yarrow's book after you've read it.' Then, 'Was Sophie Graveney alone?'

'Yes,' Steve Kneedler said. It was his one offering and it was wrong.

'No,' Jeeps said. 'She left with the BBC guy – the one with the fake American accent. I think she lives with him.'

'That would be Ramsay,' Horton said.

'She doesn't live with Ramsay,' I said.

'How do you know that?' Jeeps said.

I said, 'Ramsay's address is given as Hampstead. Sophie Graveney doesn't live in Hampstead.'

'Islington,' Jeeps said. 'It's not far.'

'Then why is it,' I said, 'that she jogs around Battersea Park every morning?'

The others stared at me. Horton said, 'Maybe you can put us in the picture. If she's living with someone there, we ought to know about it.'

Scaduto said, 'Her mother's Danish.'

'So was Hamlet's,' Sanger said.

'I've just realized what it is that I don't like about the English aristocracy,' Scaduto said. 'They're not English! They're Danes, they're Germans, they're Greeks, Russians, Italians. They're even Americans, like Lady Astor and Churchill's mother. They're not English! My charlady is more English than the average duke in his stately home. What a crazy country.'

Margaret Duboys said, 'The Greek Royal Family is Swedish,' and this seemed to put an end to that subject.

But there was more. The Guest List was gone through and each guest discussed so thoroughly that it was as if there had been no party but rather an occasion during which fifty British people had passed in review for us to assess them. Miss Duboys said that she had found out more on the Brownlow merger, and Jeeps said that he had more on his profile about the printing dispute at *The Times*, and Sanger said, 'If anyone wants my notes on export licensing, I'll make a copy of my update. Tony Whiting gave me a few angles. He's got a cousin in a Hong Kong bank.'

I said, 'No one has mentioned that fidgety white-haired fellow.'

'Howlett,' said Scaduto.

'No. I met Howlett,' I said. 'The one I'm talking about said his name was Edward Heaven. He wasn't on the Guest List.'

'Everyone was on the Guest List,' Horton said.

'Edward Heaven wasn't,' I said.

No one had any idea who this man was; no one had spoken to him or indeed seen him. But there was no mystery. Before we left Briarcliff Lodge, Horton called the embassy and got the telex operator, a new man named Charlie Hogle. Hogle took the name Edward Heaven and had the Duty Officer run it through the computer. The reply came quickly. Two years previously, Edward Heaven had been Horton's florist. He was probably still associated with the florist and had found out about the party because of the flowers that had been delivered. Mr Heaven had crashed the party. Horton said that he would now get a new florist and would try to tighten security. You couldn't be too careful, he said. They were kidnapping American diplomats in places like Paris.

'I think we can adjourn,' he said, finally. 'It's been a long day.' At the door, he said, 'You look tired, fella.'

'I'm not used to working overtime,' I said.

'You've been spoiled by the Far East,' he said. 'But you'll learn.' He clapped me on the shoulder. 'I know it's expecting a lot – after all, you're new here. But I like to start as I mean to go on.'

NAMESAKE
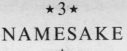

Erroll Jeeps was a great talker, and lively company; but his jokes could be savage. It was he who first told me the story about the truck with the load of bowling balls that overturns on the expressway outside Chicago. The police arrive and see a Polish workman slamming the bowling balls with a hammer and breaking them into pieces. They ask him what he's doing and he says, 'I'm trying to kill some of these niggers before they hatch!'

He told these stories with the best of humour, but I could not repeat them without feeling guilty and bigoted. In any case, I saw a lot of Jeeps. Every day after lunch, which was usually a cheese sandwich in the embassy cafeteria with him, I went for a walk in Hyde Park. They were long walks, but I timed them: I could quick-march down Rotten Row or around the Serpentine and be back at my desk in under an hour. When Jeeps came along, I took longer – I could justify it. Wasn't this part of my job?

He said that being black he was treated as if he had an affliction. He had been at the London embassy for three years and knew everyone. Some people behaved towards him as if he was an invalid – they were solicitous; others acted as if he had something contagious.

'Then there's people who think they understand me because they just spent four years in Mozambique!' He deliberately mispronounced the name: 'Mozam-bee-que,' he said. It rhymed with 'barbeque'.

'You've got high visibility, Erroll,' I said.

'There's all kinds of names for it,' he said. 'I used to be coloured, right? Then I was a Negro. And then I turned into an Afro-American. After that, I was just a member of a Minority Group. Now, I'm black. Listen, when I joined the Foreign Service everyone figured I'd put in for Africa – that's where blacks are supposed to go – like people with names like Scaduto angle for the Rome embassy.'

'My first overseas post was Kampala,' I said.

'Better you than me. They've got tails there. I asked for New Zealand. I did my graduate work in economics – the effects on the labour force in depressed capital-intensive economies. New Zealand's a good model – it's going broke. I figured I could get some research done. Instead, I was posted here. England's a good model, too. Three million unemployed, galloping inflation – hey, this place is mummified!'

It was March, but spring comes early to London. The daffodils looked like flocks of slender-necked ducks in pale poke-bonnets, and the crocuses, bright as candy, dappled the ground purple and white. The sky was clear – bluer than any in Malaysia. Girls in frock coats and black velvet riding hats trotted along the bridleway.

Hyde Park is a series of meadows, big enough so that the habitual park-users – dog-owners, kite-flyers, lovers and tramps – have plenty of room. They need it. There was heavy traffic in Kensington Road; I mentioned to Jeeps that in three weeks I had yet to hear anyone sound his horn here.

'They know it's no use,' he said. 'Look at all those cars. It's worse than Chicago. And the price of gas! Those people are paying almost four bucks a gallon to sit there in that jam. Hey, life can be kind of abrasive here. I wouldn't stay, except that from an economist's point of view this is the front line. This is where all the casualties are.'

'You'd hardly know it here. It's very peaceful.'

'People have been mugged in Hyde Park,' Jeeps said. He spoke with satisfaction and now he had a spring in his step.

We had walked along the margin of the park. Jeeps had pointed out the Iranian Embassy at Princes Gate, where the siege had taken place; he had shown me the scorch marks on the windows. We walked farther. At the Albert Memorial he stopped. He smiled at me.

'Hey, some people have had even worse experiences.'

'Killed?'

'Maimed for life,' he said.

He was still smiling.

'That's hilarious,' I said. But my sarcasm had no effect on him.

'I'm thinking of a particular case,' he said, and went on chuckling. Then he turned to the Albert Memorial – the exaggerated grief in the monument, and all that expensive sculpture, only cheapened it and made it more pompous. I looked at it – it was a frantic gazebo – and thought of money.

Jeeps was saying, 'England is a terrible place for Anglophiles. This post attracts snobs, you know. They end up so disappointed.'

I said, 'I've never known a snob who wasn't also a liar.'

'Right,' he said. 'Baldwick was a liar.'

'Baldwick – is that a name?'

'Baldwick is *only* a name. He was CAO before Vic Scaduto took over. It was the only interesting thing about him – his name. He was really proud of it. It was an old English name, he said one of the great English families, the Baldwicks of Somewhere – he wasn't sure where. He was about forty-five or so, he'd been posted around the world. He kept asking for London and getting a negative. Like these people who want Africa so they can find their roots – he wanted to find his roots in England. Someone – was it his grandfather? – anyway, someone had told him there was a family estate, a castle, property, shields, suits of armour, all the rest of it. The Baldwicks were in the Domesday Book, the old man said, only where do you find the Domesday Book? Certainly not in Dacca, which was Baldwick's first post. Not in La Paz, not in Addis, not in Khartoum – his other posts. All he found were telephone books.

'That was it, see. Wherever he went, even if it was Baltimore, he picked up the telephone book and looked for his name. It's probably not so strange. I've done it myself. But the world is full of people called Jeeps – although you might not think so – and it is not exactly crawling with Baldwicks. He never found one! He found Baldwins and Baldicks and even Baldwigs – I love that one – but he couldn't find Baldwick. Was he discouraged? No, sir – it made him real proud, because this meant he was the only claimant to the family fortune.

'And it also made him a little obsessive. He wanted to find another Baldwick, but he didn't want to hear that there were a million of them running around the place. He kept looking in telephone books wherever he was posted. No luck – but he had hopes. After all, the Baldwicks were supposed to be in England. By this time he had worked himself up to Public Affairs Officer. It was a pretty glorious job for a guy who wasn't very bright and whose field was visual-aids. But that's what happens when you go to Dacca and Khartoum.

'He was finally posted to London. In order to swing it, he took a cut in salary and agreed to be demoted to CAO. Was he eager, or what? They say his wife threatened to leave him, but this was what he had always wanted. At last, a chance to climb the family tree! His wife never forgave him. She was the one who told me this story. She was really bitter – she didn't leave anything out.

'The first thing Baldwick did in London was to get a telephone book. He looked up his name, and bingo! He found one – only one, so that was perfect. It was a John Baldwick, living in some armpit in east London. But then, having found the name, he really didn't know what to do. Should he tell him he was a long-lost relative? The man might not believe him. And what if the family fortune was in dispute? What if the will was being probated? He figured they might make it tough for him – cut him out of it altogether. And the last thing he wanted to do was reveal that he – one of the noble Baldwicks – was doing a fairly humdrum job at the American Embassy.

'He knew he had to get his act together. He decided to pose as a tourist. He would say that he was just passing through and that, seeing as how this fellow and he had the same unusual name, would he be interested in meeting for a drink? Completely innocent, see. Very casual.

'He phoned the number and got no answer. He kept trying. One day he got a funny noise – not a busy signal but something that sounded like a bumblebee. He phoned the operator and was told that the line had been disconnected.

'A few weeks went by. He considered writing a letter. Do tourists passing through London write letters to people in London? Baldwick didn't think so. He stuck to the casual approach. He called again. It rang this time. It was the other Baldwick! The guy had a funny accent – probably upper-class, he thought. I mean, upper-class accents are really strange, hardly English at all, German or 'mew-mew' or a bad case of adenoids. Half of these so-called aristocrats sound like they have sinus trouble.

'Baldwick barely understood his namesake. This pleased him – the guy was genuine! He did his routine. Just passing through. Same name. Wonder if you'd care for a drink? The guy was a little leery – wouldn't you be? – but it worked. They agreed to meet. Now, here's the interesting part. Being new to London, Baldwick didn't know where to meet him. The man didn't invite him to his house – English people never do until they've known you about ten years. So our Baldwick says, "Let's meet in Piccadilly Circus."

'Would a New Yorker say, "I'll meet you in Times Square?" You know he wouldn't, but Baldwick had every hope of actually finding this guy in Piccadilly Circus in the middle of June. "By the fountain," he said. "Six o'clock."

'Naturally, it didn't work. There were hundreds of people there. Baldwick paced up and down for an hour and then went home. Later, he called the guy. "Why weren't you there?" he says. The other man swore he had been there, but how could he find him with a thousand people milling around?

' "What about a quieter place?" our Baldwick says. "What about a pub?" The other guy says okay and the place they fixed on was The Bunch of Grapes in Knightsbridge. Baldwick said he was staying at a hotel nearby. Actually he had an apartment near there, in Egerton Gardens, but he didn't want the guy to know.

'The night they agreed to meet, there was something doing here in Hyde Park – one of those free-for-all races. And The Bunch of Grapes, which usually wasn't very busy, was packed with people. And yet Baldwick had arrived early. He sat by the main door in the Saloon Bar and watched every person come in. Every single one. He stared at each one, but no one came up to him and said, "Mr Baldwick – my name is Baldwick, too!" He sat there until closing time. He got pretty drunk, because by now he figured the other guy had his number – suspected him of trying to horn in on the family fortune. Here's this lousy American claiming to be a member of this great English family – castle, swords, paintings, suits of armour, etcetera. Before he left the Grapes he looked into the Public Bar, stared in each man's face. No takers. He went home.

'The next day he called the guy again. The guy was furious and so was he. Each accused the other of having let him down, each one said it was a pretty rotten trick, a waste of time, and what did he think he was trying to pull? They argued for a while, and then it came out. Our Baldwick said he had been in the Saloon Bar, the other guy had spent the whole evening in the Public Bar. "I always use the Public Bar," the guy says.

'Our Baldwick didn't know the difference. If he had, he might have left it there. He might have hung up and stopped looking for his long-lost relatives. He might have just quietly sized the whole thing up and stopped chasing around for his namesake. I'll tell you one thing – if he had stopped looking then, he would have died a happy man. Not fulfilled, but happy. Aren't people better off with an illusion? The truth is pretty awful sometimes, and illusions can make a nice pillow.

'Baldwick told him he had looked into the Public Bar, but he admitted that by then he had been in a hurry. The other guy started arguing again. Our Baldwick said he had to leave London in a few days and that he would probably never be back. It was now or never. "And I've got a little present for you." He had to say that. Things were getting a little spooky.

'The other Baldwick cheered up. But still he did not offer our man an invitation to drop in for tea. Somehow, this made our man imagine an even greater house, an even grander estate, even shinier armour, and a fat legacy. He says, "Do you know the Albert Memorial?"

'The other guy says, "No." *No!*

'Our Baldwick still isn't suspicious. "It's near the Albert Hall," he says. "Across the street."

' "Oh, I went to a boxing match there once," the guy says. They actually have boxing matches in that beautiful building. It's a kind of bull-ring! Incongruous, isn't it? But listen, here is our man, Baldwick, explaining to the Londoner where the Albert Memorial is, and if that's not incongruous I don't know what is.

' "I'll meet you on the top platform of the Albert Memorial at exactly two o'clock tomorrow," our man says. "We'll be the only people there. It's foolproof. And then I can give you the present I mentioned."

'It was right here,' Jeeps said.

We were on the steps of the Albert Memorial – he had walked as he had told the story – and now it was just before two o'clock. I wondered whether Jeeps had planned all this – rehearsed the story, dramatized it for my benefit, so that it was the right place and time. We were alone at the monument. The traffic flowed towards Kensington Gore and streamed through the park.

Jeeps said, 'Baldwick came from down there,' and pointed past the Albert Hall. 'He walked to one of those archways and waited until about one minute to two. At exactly two, he saw a guy running across the road, dodging cars, coming lickety-split. Up the walkway, up all these steps, to here –'

Jeeps had been walking up the stairs. He stopped, he stood still, he squinted at the path.

I said, 'Then what happened?'

'Our Baldwick almost cried. He stayed right where he was, over there at the Albert Hall. I mentioned he was a snob. He was a roaring snob. The kind you want to punch in the face. But, now, all his dreams about his old family and his name –'

'Was the other guy wearing old clothes?'

'No, he was fairly well-dressed – even carried an umbrella.' Jeeps had an umbrella. He tucked it under his arm and went on squinting. 'He was completely respectable. So that wasn't the matter. That wasn't why our Baldwick turned away and hid behind a pillar and went home to his wife.'

'He went home?' I said. 'He didn't talk to this guy, after all that trouble?'

'Nope.'

'I don't understand why, Erroll. They could have been related!'

'Look. Stand down there a little, and look.'

I moved down the stairs and did so.

'What our Baldwick saw, you see now. The other guy was right here, at just this time of day. Get it?'

'His namesake was where you are now,' I said.

'Right. But that's all they had in common, that funny name. The rest was what you see. Look! If your name was Jeeps would you think you were related to me?'

He began laughing very hard in a mocking way, as if jeering at me for not having guessed sooner about Baldwick's namesake. His laughter was humourless. It was merely a harsh noise, challenging me to look at his black face.

★4★
AN ENGLISH UNOFFICIAL ROSE
★

The fashion in London that year was rags – expensive ones, but rags all the same. Women wore torn blouses and patched jeans, and their shoes were painted to make them look scuffed and wrongly paired. Their hair was cut in a raggedy way – front hanks of it dyed pink and green and bright orange and blue. They wore plastic badges and safety pins, and they called themselves punks. The idea was for them to seem threadbare. It was a popular look, but it was not easy to achieve. It took imagination, and time, and a great deal of money for these spoiled wealthy girls to appear down and out.

But Sophie Graveney wore a smooth blouse of light silk the texture of skin and a close-fitting skirt slit all the way to her hip, and steeply pitched spike-heeled shoes. The weather was uncertain, but most days were warm enough for a jacket. Sophie's was bottle green velvet, with two gold clasps where there might have been buttons. She said she could not bear to be mistaken for someone poor, and was willing to risk being called unfashionable for her rich clothes. Styles change, but beauty is never out of fashion – I told her that. And no one expected this rag business and coloured hair to last very long. People stared at Sophie. She was no punk. Horton, my boss at the London embassy, had called her 'an English rose'.

I find it impossible to see a well-dressed woman without thinking that she is calling attention to her charms. Isn't that lady with the plunging neckline and that coin-slot between her squeezed breasts – isn't she declaring an interest? Certainly that attractive woman in the tight skirt is making a general promise. At the same time, such women are betraying a certain self-love. Narcissism is necessary to that kind of beauty. It is the aspect that maddens lovers, because it is unreachable. Sophie's self-possession was a kind of inaccessible narcissism. In her beauty there was both effort and ease. Her hair had been softly curled, her eyes and mouth delicately painted, but beneath her make-up and under her lovely clothes was a tall strong girl in the full bloom of thirty, who jogged four miles before breakfast. She was healthy, she was reliable, she dressed as if she was trying to please me. I was flattered, and grateful. So far, I had no friends in London who weren't connected with the embassy. I liked the promises of her clothes. I needed someone like Sophie.

After a month here I had a routine. It was a bachelor's consolation – my job, my office, my hotel-room – and I hated it. It made everything serious and purposeful, and I suppose I began to look like one of those super-solemn diplomats, all shadows and monosyllables, who carry out secret missions against treacherous patriots in the (believe me) laughably false plots of political thrillers. It seemed pointless, this austerity, and I did not believe in my own efficiency. I wanted to break free of it, to prove to myself that my job did not matter that much. I hated the implied timidity, the repetition, the lack of surprise in this routine. In a poor country – a Hardship Post – I could have justified these dull days by telling myself that I was making a necessary sacrifice. It is some comfort, when one is braving tedium, to know that one is setting a good example. But in London? I wanted to live a little. I knew I was missing something.

No longer: Sophie and I were dining at 'Le Gavroche', having just seen a spirited *Hamlet* at the Royal Court. She smiled at me from across the table. There was a flicker of light in her eyes, a willingness to agree, good humour, a scent of jasmine on her shoulders, and a certain pressure of her fingers on my hand that offered hope and a promise of mildly rowdy sex. I was happy.

She talked the whole time, which was fine with me. By habit and inclination I never discussed my work with anyone outside the embassy. I listened gladly to everything she said; I was grateful that I did not have to ask my ignorant questions about London. And yet, though she talked mostly about herself, she revealed very little. She told me her plans – she wanted to travel, to see Brazil ('again') – she had friends in Hong Kong and New York. She was vague about what she was doing at the moment. She seemed surprised and a little annoyed that I should ask.

' "What do you do for a living?" ' Her accent was the adenoids-and-chewing-gum American drawl that the British put on when they are feeling particularly skittish, which, thank God, is seldom. She went on, 'It's not a question people ask in England.'

'It wasn't my question. I didn't say, "What do you do for a living?" I said, What are you doing at the moment?'

'I know what you meant, and you shouldn't have asked.'

'I wonder why.'

'Because it's bloody rude, that's why,' she said softly, and seemed pleased with herself. 'Anyway, why should one do anything? I know plenty of people who don't do anything at all – absolutely nothing.'

'You like that, do you?'

'Yes, I think there's something really fantastic about pure idleness.'

' "Consider the lilies of the field", etcetera, etcetera.'

'Not only that. If a person doesn't really do anything, you have to take him for what he is rather than what he does. Your asking me what I'm doing is just a cheap way of finding out what sort of person I am. That's cheating.'

I said, 'I don't see why.'

She shrugged and said, 'Daddy didn't do much, but Daddy was a gentleman. You probably think I'm a frivolous empty-headed girl who sits around the house all day varnishing her nails, waiting for parties to begin.' She worked her tongue against her teeth and said, 'Well, I am!'

'It's been the ruin of many a Foreign Service marriage – I mean, the wife with nothing to do but advance her husband's career. All that stage-managing, all those tea parties, all that insincerity.'

'I'd love it. I wouldn't complain. My headmistress used to say, "Find a husband who'll give you a beautiful kitchen, and lovely flowers to pick, and lots of expensive silver to polish." That sort of thing's not fashionable now, is it? But I don't care. I like luxury.'

And although this was only the second time I had seen her, I began seriously to calculate the chances of my marrying her. She was glamorous and intelligent; she was good company. Men stared at her. She had taste, and she was confident enough in her taste so that she would never be a slave to fashion.

I was turning these things over in my mind when she said, 'What do I do? A bit of modelling, a little television, some lunchtime theatre. You probably think it's all a waste of time.'

'You're an actress,' I said.

'No,' Sophie said, 'I just do a little acting. It's not what you'd call a career. Everyone criticizes me for not being ambitious. Crikey, of course I spend time, but I don't waste time – are you wasting time if you're enjoying yourself?' She did not wait for my reply. She said, 'I'm enjoying myself right now.'

'Shall we do this again some time?'

'Again and again,' she said slowly in a kind of heated contentment. 'Would you like that?'

'Yes,' I said, 'I really would.' .

She reached over and touched my face, brushed the aroma of jasmine on my cheek – it was the most intimate, the most disarming gesture – and said, 'It's getting late –'

I kissed her in the taxi going back to her house. She did not push me away. But after a few minutes she lifted her head.

'What's wrong?'

'This is Prince of Wales Drive,' she said. 'Aren't those mansion blocks fantastic?' She kissed me again, then she took my arm and said, 'Wouldn't you like to live there?'

They were not my idea of mansions, but I found myself agreeing with her: yes, I said, and looked through the taxi window at the balconies. It was as if we were choosing a location for a love-nest. Sophie squeezed my arm and said, 'That one's fun.'

I saw dark windows.

'Wouldn't it be super to live here?' she said. And it seemed as if she was speaking for both of us.

I said, 'It sure would.'

'Are you looking for a place to rent? Your hotel must be rather cramped.'

'I'm moving the first chance I get. I'm going to buy a place – renting is pointless, and anyway I've got two years' accumulated hardship allowance to spend.'

She kissed me then, and we were still kissing as the taxi sped on, turned into a side street, and came to rest on Albert Bridge Road in front of a tall terrace of narrow houses. I paid for the taxi, then walked with her to the front gate.

She said, 'Your taxi's driving away.'

'I've paid him. I told him to go.'

'That was silly. You'll never get another one around here – and the buses have stopped running.'

I said, 'Then I'll walk,' and clung to her hand, 'Although I don't want to.'

'It's not far to your hotel.'

'I didn't mean that. I just meant I'd rather stay here with you.'

'I know,' she said. 'You're sweet.'

The English are frugal. They can economize on words. Sophie gave nothing away. She planted a rather perfunctory kiss on my cheek, and when I tried to embrace her she eased out of my grasp and said comically, 'Do you *mind*?' and took out her door-key.

'You're beautiful,' I said.

'I'm tired,' she said. 'I must get some sleep. I have a big day tomorrow – a screening – and I have to be up at the crack of dawn.' She gave me another brisk kiss and said lightly, 'Otherwise I'd invite you in.'

I said, 'I want to see you again soon.'

'I'd like that,' she said.

I was half in love with her by then and in that mood – half-true, half-false – I strolled home whistling, congratulating myself on my good luck. London is kind to lovers – it offers them privacy and quiet nights and spectacles. Albert Bridge was alight. In the daytime it is a classic bridge, but at night all its thousands of yellow light-bulbs and its freshly painted curves give it the look of a circus midway suspended in the sky. The lights on its great sweeps are very cheering at midnight over the empty river.

The next day I wanted to call her, but a long meeting with Scaduto held me up. It was eight o'clock before I left the office. Scaduto furiously preened himself in the elevator mirror as we descended to Grosvenor Square. He said he had called his wife to tell her he'd be late. She had screamed at him.

'Get this,' he said. 'She says to me, "You never listen." That's interesting, isn't it? What does it mean, "You never listen"? Isn't it a paradox, or some kind of contradiction? Tell me something – has anyone ever said that to you? "You never listen"?'

I said no.

'Right. Because you're not married,' Scaduto said. 'You've got to be married to hear things like that. Isn't that terrible?' He began to laugh, and said, 'You wouldn't believe the things married people say to each other. You can't imagine the hostility. "You never listen" is nothing. The rest is murder.'

'Awful things?'

'Horrendous things,' he said. 'What are you smiling for?'

'What does it matter what people say, if you never listen?'

Steam came out of Scaduto's nose – the sound of steam, at any rate. Then he said, 'I've seen guys like you – nice, happy, single guys. They get married. They get ruined. Unhappy? You have no idea.'

I was indignant at this because I took everything he said to be a criticism of Sophie. His conceited and miserable presumption belittled her. I thought: *How dare you* – because his cynicism was about life in general, the hell of marriage, the tyranny of women. He was cheating me out of my pleasant mood, the afterglow of having met someone I genuinely liked and wanted to be with. I hated his sullen egotism: his marriage was all marriages, his wife was all women, he and I were brothers. *Ain't it awful* was the slogan of this fatuous freemasonry of male victims.

I said, 'I pity you.'

'Keep your pity,' Scaduto said. 'You'll need it for yourself.'

His voice was full of fatigue and experience – and ham. The married man so often tries to sound like a war veteran, and the divorced one like a man discharged because of being wounded in action.

I met Sophie for a drink a few days later. We went out to eat again the following week. On our first date I had wanted to go to bed with her. That desire had not passed, and yet another feeling, a deeper one, like loyalty and trust, asserted itself. It was compatible with lechery – in fact, it gave lechery an honourable glow.

And now she called me occasionally at work. She had a touching telephone habit of saying, 'It's only me –' What could be easier or more intimate? She liked to talk on the phone. It was fun, she said, whispering into my ear.

About two weeks after *Hamlet* she called and said, 'Are you free this evening?'

'Yes,' I said, and thought of an excuse to dispose of the appointment I had – a journalist that Jeeps had urged me to meet. I could meet him anytime, but Sophie –

'It's a flat,' she said.

What was she talking about?

'Just what you've been looking for,' she said. 'Bang on Prince of

Wales Drive. Overstrand Mansions. It's at the front with that lovely view.'

'That's wonderful – shall we meet there?'

'I'm afraid I can't make it. I've got a screening on. But you should go. I'll give you the owner's number. It's a friend of a friend.'

'I was hoping to see you,' I said, interrupting her as she told me the price. 'What about going with me tomorrow?'

'This flat might not be available tomorrow,' she said.

'I'll look at it this evening then.'

'Super.'

'Will you be available tomorrow?' I said.

'Quite available.' She said that in what I thought of as her actress's voice. Whenever she said anything very serious or very definite, she used this voice, and sometimes an American accent.

I went to see the flat. Its balcony was the brow of this red brick mansion block, and from it I could see my own hotel beyond the park and the river. This pleased me – my own landmark, in this enormous city, among the slate roofs and steeples and treetops.

The flat was larger than I wanted, but I thought of Sophie and began to covet it for its extra rooms. The owner, a friendly German, offered me a drink.

He said, 'As you probably gathered, my wife and I decided to split up.'

I told him I had gathered no such thing, that it was none of my business, but the longer I sat there trying to stop him telling me about his divorce (it seemed to cast a blight on the place), the more I felt I was sitting in my own room, enclosed by my own walls, the crisp shadow spikes of my balcony's grille-work printed on my own floor.

'She is now back in Germany,' he said. 'She is an extremely attractive woman.'

Because I felt it was already mine, and because I knew it was a sure way of getting him off the subject of his wife, I said, 'I want it – let's make a deal.'

Later I gave him the name of the embassy lawyer and said I wanted to move quickly. By noon the next day my deposit was down and a surveyor was on his way to Overstrand Mansions. Within a week papers were examined and contracts exchanged. It was the fastest financial transaction I had ever made, but I was paying cash – my accumulated hardship allowance from my Malaysian post, and the rest of my savings. It was my first property deal, but I felt in my heart that I was not in it alone and not acting solely for myself.

I had called Sophie the day after visiting the flat. I was, I realize, intent on impressing her. Would she want me if she saw I was powerful and decisive? When I finally found her, she was pleased but said she couldn't meet me. 'Quite available' meant busy. She had a 'sitting' or perhaps a 'shooting' or a 'screening' or a 'viewing' or an 'opening' or a 'session'. What did she mean? I had never come across these obscure urgencies before. Language is deceptive; and though English is subtle it also allows a clever person – one alert to the ambiguities of English – to play tricks with mock precision and to combine vagueness with politeness. English is perfect for diplomats and lovers.

Some days later I was making Sophie a drink in my hotel room – a whisky. I had the bottle in my hand.

'It should be champagne,' I said. 'We're celebrating – I've exchanged contracts.'

'Whisky's warmer than champagne,' she said, and sat down to watch me.

'How do you like it?'

'Straight,' she said. She was not looking at the glass. 'As it comes.'

'How much?'

'Filled,' she said, and showed me her teeth.

'How many inches is that?'

'Right up,' she said, and sighed and smiled. She had said that in her actress's voice.

There was no hitch, the survey encouraged me, and Horton – as if praising my on-the-job initiative – said that London property was a great investment. I was more than hopeful; I had, mentally, already begun to live at Overstrand Mansions. In this imagining Sophie was often standing at the balcony with a drink in her hand, or in her tracksuit, damp with dew and effort (running raised her sexual odours, the mingled aroma of fish and flowers), and she was laughing, saying 'Do you *mind*?' as I tried to hold her, and driving me wild.

I had to be reassured that she needed me as much. We had not so far used the word love. We pretended we had an easy-going, trusting friendship. I think I joked with her too much, but I was eager – foolishly so. Instead of simply saying that I wanted to see her and making a date with her, I said, 'Sophie, you're avoiding me.'

It was facetious. I could not blame her for missing the feeble joke. But, unexpectedly, it made her defensive. She took it as an accusation, and explained carefully that she had very much wanted to see me but that she was busy with – what? – a 'shooting' or a 'viewing'. Then I was sorry for what I'd said.

The arrival of my sea-freight a day later gave me an excuse to call her. She was excited. She said, 'You've got the key!'

'Not yet.'

She made a sympathetic noise. She sounded genuinely sorry I hadn't moved in. And then, 'What if something goes wrong with the deal?'

'I'll find something else.'

'No, no,' she said. 'Nothing will go wrong. Actually, I can quite see you there in Overstrand Mansions –'

She didn't say us, she excluded herself; but this talk of me and my flat bored me. And I was a little disappointed. I listened dimly, then hung up having forgotten to tell her my real reason for calling – that my sea-freight had passed through customs and was at the warehouse.

It was furniture, my Malaysian treasures, my *nat* from Burma, a temple painting from Vietnam, Balinese masks, *wayang* puppets and my Buddha and the assortment of cut-throat swords and knives (a *kris* from the Sultan, a *kukri* from the DC) I had been given as going-away presents. I had bought the furniture in Malacca. It was Chinese – an opium-smoker's couch, and a carved settee with lion's head legs. The bed had carved and gilded panels and four uprights for a mosquito-net canopy. And I had teak chests with carved drawers, and polished rosewood chairs, and brassware and pewter. These and my books. I had nothing else – no plates or dinnerware, no glasses, no cooking pots, nothing practical.

I wanted Sophie to see my collection of Asian things. I knew she would be impressed. She would marvel at them, she would want me more. I longed to leave my small hotel room on Chelsea embankment and spread out in Overstrand Mansions. I yearned to be with her.

She had picked out the flat, and in buying it I had never acted so quickly, so decisively. I was glad. She had made me bold. But I tried not to think that I had bought it for us, because it was too early – she was not mine yet. I hoped she knew how badly I wanted her. I could not imagine that a desire as strong as mine could be thwarted. At times it seemed simple: I would have her because I wanted her.

I thought: If only she could see these treasures from Asia! And I tried to imagine our life together. It was a wonderful combination of bliss and purpose, and it made my bachelor solitude seem selfish. What was the point in living alone? Secretly, I believed we were the perfect couple.

All this happened in the space of three weeks – the exchanged contracts, the arrival of my furniture, the numerous phone calls. I did not see Sophie in the third week, and it was frustrating because now it was Sunday. The German had given me the key yesterday; I was moving in tomorrow.

I moved in. She had led me here. I was grateful to her that morning as the men carried my tea-chests of Asian treasures upstairs (and they called their moving van a 'pantechnicon' – I had never heard the word before and it pleased me). There was space for everything. This was the apartment I needed. She had known that, somehow, or guessed – another indication that she understood me. I was delighted because Sophie had made this her concern. But where was she?

I called her but got no answer. I tried again and managed, by speaking slowly, to leave a message with her charlady who was exasperated at having to write it down. She read the message back to me with uncertainty and resentment.

That night I woke up and was so excited to be in a place of my own I got out of bed and walked up and down, and through all the rooms and finally on to the balcony. I was so pleased at this outcome I vowed that I would send Sophie a case of champagne. I lingered on the balcony – I liked everyone out there in the dark.

My roaming in the night made me oversleep. I did not get to the embassy until after eleven, and my desk was stacked with pink

While You Were Out ... message slips. Scaduto had called and so had Horton's secretary, and there was still some paperwork to do on my apartment – insurance and some estimates for painting it. But most of the messages were from Sophie. Five slips of paper – she had been ringing at twenty-minute intervals.

My happiness was complete. It was what I wanted most, and it seemed to me as if I had everything I wanted and was in danger of being overwhelmed by it. The phone-calls were the proof that she wanted me. I would send her the case of champagne, of course; but that was a detail. She could move in with me anytime. We would do what people did these days – live together, see how we got along. It was a wonderful tolerant world that made such arrangements possible. I would have a routine security check done on Sophie, but if Horton questioned the wisdom of our living together I could always reply that I had met her at his house and that he had a share in creating this romance.

The phone rang. Sophie's voice was eager. 'You've moved in – that's super.'

'You've been a great help,' I said. 'When can you come over to look around?'

'My life's a bit fraught at the moment,' she said. Her voice became cautious and a bit detached. But she had rung me five times this morning! Then all the eagerness was out of her voice and with composure she said, 'I expect I'll be able to manage it one of these days. I'm not far away.'

'We could have a drink on the balcony. The way you like it. Right up.'

'Yes,' she said, with uncertainty. She had forgotten.

Then I felt awkward and over-intimate. Had I said too much?

'It's a very nice flat,' I said.

'I'm so glad for you. I knew you'd like it.'

I wanted to say, *Come and live with me! There's enough room for both of us! I won't crowd you – I'll make you happy in my Chinese bed!*

We worked at the London embassy with the doors open. I could see Vic Scaduto just outside my office, talking to my secretary. He was impatient and held a file in his hand that he clearly wanted to show me. He made all the motions of wanting to interrupt me; he made his impatience look like patience. At times like this Scaduto tap-danced.

I said, 'Sophie, I have to go.'

'There was something else,' she said.

'I'll call you back.'

'I've rung you half a dozen times this morning. Please. I've got so much else to do.'

She sounded irritated, and I could see Scaduto's feet – shuffle-tap, shuffle-tap – and the flap of the file as he juggled it.

I said to Sophie, 'What is it?'

'You've moved in – you've got the flat. So it's all settled.'

'I'm going to buy you a case of champagne,' I said. 'I'll help you drink it. I know a place –'

'That's very sweet of you,' she said. 'But two per cent is the usual commission.'

I waited for her to say more. There was no more.

I said, 'Are you joking?'

'No.' She sounded more than irritated now. She was angry: I was being wilfully stupid.

'Is that why you've been ringing me this morning – for your commission?'

'I found you a flat. You had an exclusive viewing. You bought it for a reasonable price –'

I said, 'Did you fix the price?'

But she was still talking.

'– and now you seem to be jibbing at paying me my commission.'

Scaduto put his head into my office and said, 'Have you got a minute?'

'Write me a letter,' I said, and still heard her voice protesting in the little arc the receiver made, the distance between my ear and the desk.

Scaduto smiled. He said, 'For a minute there you looked married.'

Because Sophie's letter was delivered by hand and arrived at the front door of the embassy it was treated as if it contained a bomb or a threat or an explosive device. It was X-rayed, it was passed through a metal detector, it was sniffed by a trained dog. I complained to the Security Guard about the delay, but in the event I wished that the letter had never come.

It could not have been more businesslike or broken my spirit more. It was one chilly paragraph telling me that I had moved in, that she had been instrumental in finding me the flat – 'following your instructions' – and that in such a situation two per cent was the usual commission.

It was not a great deal of money, the equivalent of a few thousand dollars – not enough to be really useful, only enough to ruin a friendship. I could have paid her immediately, but I didn't want her to be my agent – I wanted her love.

Instead of writing what I felt, I wrote logically: I had not given her an order to find me a flat; she had not negotiated the price; she had not been present when I reached agreement with the owner; she had played no part in the contract or any subsequent negotiations. Hers had been an informal, friendly function. If I had known that the fee was going to be two per cent I would have taken it into account and adjusted my offer. She was, I said, presuming.

Then I contemplated tearing up the letter. I had either to destroy it or send it – I didn't want it around.

Sophie rang me two days later. She said, 'How dare you! Don't write me letters like that. What do you take me for?'

I said, 'I thought you were an actress.'

She turned abusive. She swore at me. Until that moment I had marvelled at how different her English was from mine. and then, with a few blunt swears, she lost her nationality and became any loud, crude, bad-tempered bitch spitting thorns at me.

I sent her the champagne. She did not acknowledge it. And she dropped out of my life.

I learned one thing more. One day I found an earring in the kitchen. I called the German, who now lived in a smaller place in Pimlico. He came over and had a drink. He was grateful – it had belonged not to his wife but to his mother. He showed no signs of wanting to leave. My whisky made him sentimental. He said that we were both foreigners here in London. We had a lot in common. We ought to be friends.

To get him off the subject, I asked him about Sophie.

'She brought us together, you and me,' the German said. 'She charged me two per cent. But it was worth it. Here we are, drinking together as friends.' He glanced around the flat. He said, 'These English girls – especially the ones with money – can be very businesslike. And did you notice? She is very pretty. She lives with an Iranian chap. They all want Iranians these days.' The German laughed out loud. 'Even if you call them Persians they still seem boring!'

And then, to my relief, he began telling me about his ex-wife.

★ 5 ★

CHILDREN
★

'Vic's got this theory. Parents owe their children everything, but children don't owe their parents anything. Why should they? They didn't ask to be born. People tell their kids, "You treat this place like a hotel." My father used to tell me that! It's funny, because family homes are exactly like hotels – where you've been brought. No kid ever checked in of his own free will, did he? And Vic says if the parents keep their part of the bargain – I mean, discharge their responsibility and do everything they can for their kids, they'll never have a problem. Hey, it's amazing how irresponsible most parents are. Some of these embassy people you just would not believe –'

Marietta Scaduto's voice was dropping to a whisper: Vic was on his way back to the room with his children and some other people's children. They were all boys – even Vic, come to think of it.

'I don't know why I'm bothering to tell you this – you don't have any kids,' Marietta said.

'Or parents either,' I said. 'Does Vic have a theory about orphans? I only ask because I lost my parents in an air crash when I was five. But you do get over these things, you know. I had a happy childhood – I suppose, it's a bit like being blind from an early age. I adapted. The kind of orphan I was – bright, solitary, with my trust fund from the insurance money – it was like being privileged, inheriting a title early. And I seem to have managed. I'm not looking for a mother figure. Maybe that explains why I'm not married.'

I had said too much. It was then that she gave me a look of pure murder.

This conversation came later, over coffee, after she had told me about her poems and said she was unhappy and – rolling her lower lip down sourly – 'I know your type.'

But Vic had a theory! She made him sound serious. The man's wife – when she's angry or incautious – can reveal such surprising secrets. And so can the man expose the wife. And the children most of all. But who would have thought that man sat around theorizing?

Vic Scaduto – 'Skiddoo' to the office – all gestures, all heel-clicks on the corridor tiles, shooting his pink cuffs, tugging at his earlobe, pinching his face at his reflection in the elevator mirror, tap-dancing as he talked and as his bubblegum snapped, saying, 'The Royal facility in Kensington has a really spacious function room,' then interrupting himself with 'I've got a stack of cables waiting' and 'I'm one of these rare people who has a nose for detail,' neighing his hideous laugh – 'It's my Italian blood,' he explained, and he was never breathless. He had teeth like piano keys and spit flew out of his mouth when he talked.

More than anything he wanted a good post in Italy – running a bi-national centre in Florence or Palermo, or being Public Affairs Officer in Rome. Some of his relatives still lived in Sicily, farming an acre of thorns and procrastinating about selling the pig, so he said.

'It's not that I'm bucking for a promotion – it's just that with my cultural background I think I deserve Italy.' It was a sure sign of his Italian-ness that he mispronounced it, giving it two syllables and making it sound even more like an adverb: 'It-lee'.

He had been interviewed for the transfer, he had taken the language proficiency exam, he was waiting for his report.

'I think they were impressed.' He meant the pair of assessment officers from Washington. Scaduto had invited them to his house. 'I didn't just invite them – I threw the place open to them.'

He had arranged it so that the assessment officers could spend a whole day with his family – Marietta and the three boys.

'I wanted to show them what cultural enrichment really means.'

I said, 'Is that Italian job so important?'

'Not to me, but to my parents. If you've got immigrant parents you'll understand. They left Italy' – *It-lee* – 'with nothing and came to America. They spent Christmas on Ellis Island in 1922.'

'They must be proud of your success,' I said.

'That's just it – my success is the only thing that matters to them. They left home, left their house, gave up their country and abandoned their own parents for their children, my sister and me. They ran off and got married. My parents were bad children!

They put me through college, they lived poor, they're still poor. No one thinks about that, but it's funny – some people who used to be poor are still poor, living where they always lived and dying in the same place. My folks live in an old row-house in Queens, with planes going overhead all day – some people in the neighbourhood are on Disability the noise is so bad. My father is over seventy. He hasn't retired! He cuts fish. You should see his hands. *His* father probably had hands like that, in Caccamo. Then I get this London job. It's a terrific job. I offer to pay his fare over here so he can have a vacation, and what happens? Does he come to visit? No. "Why don't they give you Italy? Ain't you good enough?" He gives me *braciol'* until my head hurts. My mother's worse. She drives me nuts with her phone calls. I mean, both of them sit in Long Island waiting for me to take them back to Italy. Proud of me? Not on your life! I'm disloyal – this isn't the way children are supposed to treat their parents. Hey, children have obligations, don't you know that? But I'll get Italy.'

It-lee: waiting for him to say the word made me inattentive.

'They've got this image in their minds,' he was saying. 'They're on a plane. Jumbo jet, transatlantic flight. Someone in the next seat asks them where they're going. They say, "We're visiting our son. He's got this job at the American Embassy in Roma. Hey, he's doing all right. Me, I put him through school – working nights, working weekends. My wife and I, hey, we're going home. We're from Italy –"'

It-lee again, but Scaduto had started to object.

'It's a fantasy! Listen, old people are really stubborn about their fantasies. You got no idea! Ask Marietta.'

Scaduto had not said anything about his parents to the assessment officers, and yet he had done all he could to emphasize that he was overdue for a post in Italy. Such officials often visited foreign service personnel at home – the crowded party, the powerful drinks, the bonhomie and 'My family's flexible' – but it was rare for them to spend an entire day at the house. Scaduto wanted to impress them with his complete honesty, his willingness to admit strangers to the privacy of his house. It was a considerable risk, but Scaduto said he was sure it would pay off. Anyway, he said, he liked having visitors – so did Marietta and the boys. Hey, wasn't that the point about being in the Foreign Service?

Hey, if you didn't like people you were in the wrong job! So he said.

I was interested when he made the same offer to me, of spending the whole day with him, from just after breakfast until just after midnight. He lived far enough from the centre of London for such a long visit not to seem absurd. His house was in Putney, but the western part, near Roehampton Vale and Richmond Park. It took him over an hour to get to work in the morning by car.

American couples, I discovered, lived in Notting Hill and Islington and Chelsea, and they especially favoured Hampstead. But when they wanted to breed, and exchange their two-bedroom apartment for a four-bedroom house, they crossed the river. The larger the family the farther they penetrated into the suburbs – and all the real suburbs were in the south and west. North was distant and dull – 'the country'; but all the south was London. Vic and Marietta Scaduto and their three boys lived in a leafy street off the Upper Richmond Road, on the 37 bus route.

The house was large – probably six bedrooms, something like a turret on the left, and (the rarest of features in London) a driveway. The wistaria at the front had a stem the thickness of a human leg and (it was now May) was in hanging bloom. The rooms were furnished with treasures Vic had picked up in his previous posts. You could tell where an officer had been by looking at his living room or his bookshelf. Vic had brassware and carpets from Turkey, tables with ivory inlay from Pakistan, Kamba carvings and Kikuyu shields from Kenya. He was not a specialist in anything: he went where he was sent. (So many of us can be described, accurately, as travelling salesmen!)

In a poor country, objects – such as the ones Scaduto had in his living room – often look like treasures. But the farther they get from home the less marvellous and exotic they seem. In a middle-class London house, these looked cheap and vulgar and badly-made. Bazaar merchandise does not travel well, and most of it is so hard to dust it grows fur.

There was a smell – dusty, pollenous, knife-wounds on wood, hair and feathers: curio stink – in the room where we were all now seated. I had just arrived – by bus, quite a novelty, and certainly a conversation-piece, but I was a student of London's bus-routes and told them how I had transferred at Clapham Junction from the 19, which ran near Overstrand Mansions, to the 37. Vic said I was in time for coffee, and Marietta showed me into the conservatory – it was her word for the glassed-in patio area. Vic made a show of arranging chairs around a small table, and then grinding the coffee noisily – the sound made my head spin – and then explaining how he made coffee the real Italian way, before bringing it in on a little rattling table on wheels which Marietta was quick to call a trolley.

'The boys are very anxious to meet you,' Vic said. 'The older two have been studying about the Dyaks. I told them you were in Malaysia. They'll be full of questions.'

'Most Dyaks are in Sarawak, Vic,' I said. 'I never went there.'

'You were near enough,' he said. 'God, the things they learn in geography class. A far cry from my junior high. "Coffee production in Brazil", "Lumbering in Murmansk", "Eskimos on the Mc-Clintock Channel". They're not called igloos, by the way. They're *igluviga*. They wear *mukluks*. They light their *igluviga* with oil-lamps called *koodlies*. Are these kids getting an education or what? English schools are awesome. Latin, French, science, Scripture. No fingerpainting, no bull sessions, no Little League. Hey, they learn the basics!'

Scaduto was not merely proud of his children – he was respectful in a way that suggested that these children had taught him new things about the world, and given him fresh ideas, and surprised him with his own ignorance.

'So they don't go to the American school,' I said.

'Or to the state school either,' he said. 'No, all three of them are at P.L.'

I smiled inquiringly at Marietta Scaduto. My smile was a request for information – and she understood.

'Prince's Lodge,' she said.

'It's a prep school,' Vic said. 'A really fine one. Where are the kids, honey?'

'Upstairs.'

Vic said to me, 'They've got some school friends over.' He winked – it was a gesture of helpless admiration for his children: Scaduto had the Italian gift of being able to wink meaningfully, and he had as many winks as other people had smiles. 'I'll get them,' he went on. 'They're amazing. You won't understand a word they say. I mean, they're incredibly bright.'

He was infatuated. That was touching, but I saw no reason why in order to praise his children's intelligence he had to belittle mine.

He said, 'You can ask them anything!'

I said, 'Can I tell them anything?'

He frowned, and I wished I had kept my mouth shut.

While Vic was out of the room, Marietta said, 'I wrote a poem.'

I did not know what to say. I had just spoken a bit unwisely to Vic. So I hesitated, and that was my mistake. It made her defiant.

She said, 'You think it's a waste of time.'

She had black hair which hung in long lank strands, and large dark eyes. Her eyebrows were bushy, her face and arms thin, covered with hair that made her skin appear almost grey. Vic was too fat and too bald and too silly for his age, which was about forty-four; she was very thin – spider-like and brittle. She held herself straight in the chair and, instead of moving her eyes, turned her whole head stiffly at me.

'No, that's marvellous,' I said. 'Do you write many poems, or was that the first one?'

She said nothing. Had she heard?

'I've always loved poetry,' I said, and felt ridiculous. But she had thrown me. Marietta Scaduto was one of those people who can say, 'I just wrote a poem' and make it sound like, 'I just flushed the canary down the toilet' – like the maddest, most irrational act on earth.

Her eyes did not register my stupid remark ('I've always loved poetry') or even that I had spoken. She was staring trancelike at my forehead as if trying to guess my age.

She said, 'I got the idea at Kennedy Airport. You know those signs above the escalator telling you about the rest-rooms and the gates and the baggage and all that? "Men, Women, Telephones"? That's what gave me the idea. That's what it's called.'

' "Men, Women, Telephones",' I said. 'It's nice – it's got drama!'

I wished then that I had stayed home. Today, this Saturday at the Scadutos', was my fortieth birthday. I had always resisted birthday celebrations – cakes, candles, presents. It is all forced and false and embarrassing, and the song 'Happy Birthday To You' – monotonous and excruciating – has driven me out of restaurants. I had not wanted anyone to know that this was my birthday, I hadn't wanted a party. This day with Vic and Marietta was the best possible alternative, I had thought. I could leave the birthday at home, be anonymous here and, somehow, wake up forty tomorrow morning. I had considered it an event of no importance, but now I regretted that I wasn't at Rule's or Leith's or the Connaught with a woman and getting a little drunk and telling her, 'It's my birthday.' I thought that because I had just realized that I could never mention my age or anyone's age to Marietta Scaduto.

She was still staring at me.

She said, 'You won't like this poem. It's a woman's poem. It's about women's problems.'

I tried to protest. She didn't hear.

'You could write a whole book about those signs,' she said. '"Customs", "Refreshments", "Food", "Handicapped Exit", "Ramp", "Concourse to Ground Transportation", "Way Out". Signs can be poetry. Listen, this is nineteen eighty-one! I could write a book. Men write books. Why shouldn't women?'

I said, 'But women do write books, Marietta, and some of them are awfully good' – why was I saying these idiotic things? I suppose I was afraid of the childish resentment in her eyes – 'why, look at George Eliot and Emily Dickinson and Edna Millay –'

'They're always putting us down,' she said.

'Who do you mean?'

'Vic,' she said.

'Vic puts you down?'

'Constantly.'

'But isn't that different from people like Edna –'

'That's why I wrote my poem,' she said.

'"Men, Women, Telephones"? That one?'

'And "Rest-Rooms – Women and Handicapped",' she said. 'And "Customs". And "Children". I think that's one of my best, "Children", based on the sign. I mean, there's more honest pain in it – I hope you don't think I'm being pretentious or that

I talk about my poems all the day, because I don't. In some states, the sign "Children" is a boy. You've seen it a million times – everyone has. It's like a stencil. It's from about nineteen twenty-two. He's running – his legs are all over the place, and he's smiling. He's wearing these old-fashioned knickers. "Children".'

'It sounds –' I couldn't finish, I didn't know how.

'You're smiling.'

'No!' But, protesting, I began to smile.

'You're just like Vic.'

They called him 'Skiddoo', he tap-danced, he wanted a post in Italy, he complained about his parents, he boasted about his children, he bitched about this sad crazy woman he was married to.

I said – and didn't know why I was being so polite – 'You hardly know me.'

'I know your type,' she said.

Why hadn't I stayed home – This was my birthday!

'Judgemental. You think I'm wasting my time. You're completely absorbed by your job and do nothing but talk about the embassy, as if the embassy's so god-damned important and there's going to be World War Three if you're late for work or you miss a party. You're probably worse than Vic, you're probably like my father – he used to say that education was wasted on a girl –'

Being with her was like reading a letter to a stranger, chosen at random from the Dead Letter Office. It was, at once, both meaningless and embarrassing – you were embarrassed to be holding these sentiments in your hand. Who was she talking to? I did not know her. I was not even moved, and I should at least have pitied her.

It was perhaps more like a glimpse of poor bare flesh – not the beauty of nudity but the wobble of nakedness.

She was still talking – was her father the link? – and then, 'Vic's got this theory –'

Parents owed their children everything, but children did not owe their parents anything; and then that business about how irresponsible most parents were.

Then I told her I was an orphan, and Vic entered with the six boys and said, 'I'm glad to see you two are hitting it off.'

*

We managed to get through lunch. Marietta did not mention her poems again, or the signs, or her father. Like Vic, she was devoted to her children and she tolerated their friends. In the role of hostess, serving lunch, she was mute and efficient and wholly unlike the mad poetess I had seen over coffee. The boys did not eat with us.

But I still wanted to leave – not stay for dinner, not have to face whatever plans Scaduto had made for the afternoon. I wanted to go back to Overstrand Mansion and turn forty alone.

The married couple believe – unreasonably – that when the single person is on his own he is lonely. I am usually happier alone than in company, and I felt trapped at this house. I can be contented in the narrowest space – but there is a kind of social claustrophobia that afflicts me, the persistence of uncongenial people, who crowd a room and make it airless and give me actual physical discomfort: I wanted to go.

And, because I had no excuse for going, I gave myself a reason for staying. Scaduto had mentioned his parents, how they had married young and left their parents in Italy – 'My parents were bad children!' His grandparents had stayed in Sicily. He had told me his theory – and she had griped about her father. Vic had then promised that I would be impressed with his boys. I forced myself to be interested in these generations of children. At last, after lunch, Vic brought the boys out to meet me properly. I was fascinated and horrified and instructed, and I would not have left that house for anything.

He had suggested a walk in Richmond Park – spending the afternoon there, and then back to the house for dinner. Each of his three boys had a friend. We set off for the park, the eight of us, like the Beaver Patrol – boys ahead, scoutmasters behind. After about a mile, the Upper Richmond Road entered East Sheen, and we turned into the genteel streets that fringed the park, passing brick and mock-Tudor villas and the trim rose gardens and the well-washed milk bottles that are the very emblem of the Tory suburbs.

Scaduto said, 'Their school is on the next street. It's one of these completely anachronistic schools. They sing hymns loud and out of tune, they're forced to run cross-country in the rain, they do Latin and Scripture –'

'And – was it *lumbering*?' I said.

' "Lumbering in Murmansk." One of their topics, and if you don't know it backwards and forwards you get a hundred lines – "I must remember to do my homework thoroughly." Their matron's a hag. They have to sit in the corner if they misbehave. They get beaten – it works! They put on old-fashioned plays and eat disgusting food. And that's not half of it.'

'It would age me twenty years,' I said.

'It's good for them,' Vic said. 'What do you know? You don't have any kids.'

We had entered the park at Sheen Gate. The boys were waiting for us and walked with us across the meadow towards the deer – thirty or forty deer, placidly cropping grass. Vic had told them earlier, when we were introduced, that I had been in Malaysia. Now he reminded them of that and said that if there was anything they wanted to ask me this was the time.

'My father was born in Malaysia,' one of the boys said. 'He still owns part of a tea estate there. My uncle owns the rest of it, but my uncle does all the work. They have thousands of workers – Indians, mostly.'

'They grow lots of tea in Malaysia,' I said.

'My father shot a tiger in the Cameron Highlands,' the boy went on. 'We've got the skin on the wall of our billiard room. My father shot him in the eye. That's why there aren't any bullet-holes in the skin.'

This impressive fact – the tiger shot through the eye – silenced the rest of the boys for a while, and the boy called Jocko, who had told the story, marched ahead like a brigadier.

'My father was born in India,' another boy said. This was Nigel. He was Mario Scaduto's friend. He was tall and had a rather debauched-looking face. 'They've got more tigers in India than they know what to do with. But they've been wiped out in Malaysia. Jocko's father probably killed the last one. My parents say that most blood-sports are nothing more than vandalism.'

'You've been to India, haven't you, Dad?' Scaduto's youngest son looked pleadingly at him to verify the fact, and then glanced at his school-friend, a mouse-faced boy the others called Littlefair.

'Lots of times,' Scaduto said. 'We had a facility right near the border in Pakistan. I used to pop over all the time.'

'We went out there last summer for a holiday,' Jocko said.

'India?' Scaduto asked.

'Hong Kong.' Jocko, I noticed, had a moustache, though he could not have been more than eleven or twelve.

'That's nowhere near India,' Nigel said. 'Jocko's confusing Hong Kong with India.'

'The place is full of ruddy Indians,' Jocko said, facing the others and setting his brigadier's jaw at them. 'Indians own shops there. They're in competition with the Chinese. The Chinese work jolly hard, but they're sneaky. The Indians are arrogant – most of them lie worse than that little git Norris in Form Two, the one they call Ananiarse.'

'We saw some Indians in Trinidad last summer.' This was Littlefair. He was small and bent-over and watchful in a rather elderly way. He was mouse-faced even to the twitching of his pointed nose. 'They were having a Hindu festival. They made a hell of a racket.'

'That's the trouble with England,' Jocko said. 'Too many coloured people.'

'Too many Scotsmen is what I say! Send them all back to their rotten old backward villages –' Nigel stopped speaking suddenly and turned to Mario Scaduto. 'Crikey, I'm sorry! I hope you're not Scottish!'

'They're Italian,' Jocko said. 'Scaduto's an Italian name.'

'Smart boy,' Vic said. And he whispered to me, 'They have this fantastic awareness about language.'

'Our maid's Italian,' Jocko said.

Littlefair said, 'We've got two, a husband and a wife. They're Spanish. You can hear them arguing at night. All Spaniards argue after work.'

'We're not Italian,' Mario Scaduto was saying. 'We're American. We've got this huge house in Silver Springs, Maryland.' But Mario's accent, and its nervous urgent tweet, was English.

'We went to Trinidad on a yacht my father chartered,' the mouse-faced boy called Littlefair was explaining.

The word 'yacht' was heard by the others, who began to listen.

'We were in a hurricane. We almost sank. We had to put ashore in such a hurry the captain ran the yacht aground and completely smashed the hull. That was after we left Trinidad. Then we went to

Jamaica. The coloured people standing by the road, when they saw our car going by to take us to the hotel, they gobbed on it.'

Nigel said, 'I'm going to camp this summer.'

'I hate camp,' Jocko said. 'It's worse than school.'

'This camp's in Switzerland.'

I walked abreast of Vic, just behind the boys, whose voices were raised, as if they intended for us to hear them clearly. Vic looked at me and said, 'Aren't they unbelievable?' I agreed; I said they certainly were; it was the very word for them. But he was praising them. And the boys were still talking.

'My mother says it's not that they can't find jobs, it's that they just don't want to work. They'd rather draw their dole money.'

'Some of these people make a hell of a lot on the dole – twenty or thirty pounds a week. That's more than we pay our maid.'

'If you have masses of children you can make a ruddy fortune on the dole. That's what all these Pakistanis do.'

'Some of them work hard. They take jobs that English people refuse. Ever see them at Heathrow? They're the ones who clean the bogs.'

'They work all night, too. Our plane came in at three o'clock in the morning and there were Pakistanis all over the place with mops and buckets.'

'There's a Pakistani round our way. His shop is open even on Sunday. He never closes!'

'That's the trouble with them – they're just interested in making money.'

Scaduto's children mingled with their friends. It was impossible to tell them from the others in this chorus of voices. All the accents were the same to my unpractised ear, like the cries of 'My father says' and 'My mother says'. After holidays, and the Far East, and immigrants, and Welfare, they discussed work – the best jobs – and schools – the best schools.

'How old are your children, Vic?'

'Eight-fifteen, nine-forty-five and twelve-thirty,' he said, as if reciting a timetable. 'Mario's twelve-thirty. He starts public school next September. If we go to Italy he can be a boarder.'

'Radley's a brilliant school,' one of the boys was saying. 'They did that television series about it.'

'My father says they put too much emphasis on books. I'm going to Ardingly. They've got sailing.'

Littlefair said, 'I'm going to Marlborough,' and when no one commented he became even more mouse-like, and twitched his nose, and said, 'My grandfather gave them a library.'

'My father's an old boy of Saint Paul's.' This was the Scottish boy they called Jocko. 'That's why I want to go to Westminster.'

'American schools are rubbish,' another boy said. He was dark-haired. He was, I realized, one of the Scaduto boys.

'Tony,' Vic said sharply.

'Oh, you know they stink, Dad,' the boy said in a jeering way. 'The kids carry knives. They take drugs. There's no discipline. Half the teachers can't even read.'

'Flipping Norah!' Nigel said.

'They smoke marijuana in the bogs,' Tony Scaduto said. 'The teachers go to discos with their girl students and get them pregnant.'

'Gordon Bennett!' Jocko said, and in spite of myself I laughed out loud at the exclamation.

'I'm really impressed with English schools,' Vic said. 'But just because you like English schools doesn't mean you have to run down American ones. Compulsory free education is an American idea.'

The boy called Nigel said, 'American schools are brilliant at sports,' and then smiled patronizingly at the Scadutos.

'What does your father do?' the Littlefair boy was asking the youngest Scaduto, whose name was either Frankie or Franny.

'He works in the West End,' Mario said, helping his brother out.

'He has an office in Mayfair,' Tony said.

It was a highly imaginative way of describing Vic Scaduto's job as Cultural Affairs Officer at the American Embassy in Grosvenor Square. Vic heard and gave me a pained and apologetic look. Then, in an attempt to set the record straight, he cleared his throat and spoke loudly.

'I'm with the American Embassy, on the cultural side.'

'Hussein – that coloured boy in Form Three they call "turd-head" – his father's with the Saudi Arabian Embassy,' Jocko said.

70

'He has TV cameras in his drive – for security reasons. And an armed guard. That weed Beavis went to a birthday party there. Hussein's father weighs about twenty stone! Beavis said he looks like a chucker-out.'

'Princes come to visit him, Beavis said' – this from Littlefair.

'Not real princes,' Nigel said. 'Coloured ones, wrapped in blankets, with towels over their heads.'

Mario Scaduto said, 'The coloured ones are just as good as the real ones.'

Nigel smiled and said, 'There are three thousand members of the Royal Family in Saudi Arabia. It's because they have all those wives. They have billions of children. Everyone you meet is a prince, even the people who do the washing-up. It doesn't mean a thing.'

The smallest Scaduto said, 'I don't believe you!'

'My father's company's got an office in Jeddah,' Nigel said. This seemed to settle the argument. He added, 'My father goes there in Concorde.'

'Concorde doesn't go to Jeddah,' Jocko said.

'It goes to Bahrein,' Nigel said. 'He changes planes there.'

We had walked across the park, from Sheen Gate to the woods on the hill to the south, passing the deer which hardly noticed us, and older people with dogs on leads, who never took their eyes off us and seemed to listen to the boys yelling and boasting.

'The last time we were here it was awful bleak,' Vic said.

The last time: he meant when the assessment officers had spent the day with him.

We were surrounded by azaleas and tall and tumbling rhododendrons which grew in the high shade of the woods.

'These are really pretty,' he said.

'We've got lots of these at home. My mother grows them. She's entering some in the Chelsea Flower Show.'

Oh, shut up, I thought, and walked on ahead. But I could still hear them.

'Richmond Park is famous. I'll bet you don't have parks like this in America.'

'They used to. They've all been ruined by vandals. That's what my father says.' Was this one of the Scadutos?

'I've been to America lots of times.' I turned. This was Nigel.

'So have we.' Littlefair.

'We never go to America,' Tony Scaduto said. 'We prefer it here.'

Jocko said, 'You're American.'

'I don't feel American,' Mario Scaduto said.

'Neither do I,' Tony said.

'But you are!' Littlefair said. 'Your parents are American, so that means –'

Vic had caught up with me, and he had abandoned the boys, given up on their conversation – they were screaming at each other now, and he looked sheepish.

He said, 'I'll get that job in Italy. Then everyone will be happy. My folks will come over and visit. They'll be proud – it's what they always wanted. I think I'll put these kids in the American school in Rome. You don't have to tell me they need it. I know. They won't like it, but they'll get used to it. A job like this can be hell on a family – you have no idea.'

My last memory of that day at the Scadutos' was the dinner itself – not Vic asking where the lemon for the fish was and Marietta saying, 'Get it yourself!' and not Vic (who quickly became drunk) defending the death penalty for child molesters, joined by his three boys who said that they were in favour of capital punishment not only for murder but also stealing; it was the memory of Marietta leaning over and telling me at great length that in spite of what people said about parents teaching their children, the truth was that children taught their parents. Children, Marietta said, sort of raised their parents and helped them grow up and if it wasn't for her three she would probably never have taken up poetry. It wasn't the children who belittled women writers – it was the adults. And wasn't it a shame that I did not have any – especially here in London where there were so many opportunities for kids? I remembered that – as a consolation – because Vic Scaduto ('All parents are children' – he wouldn't leave the topic!) of course never got the job in Italy.

★6★
CHARLIE HOGLE'S EARRING
★

There is something athletic, something physical, in the way the most successful people reach decisions. The businessmen who plot takeovers, the upstarts who become board chairmen, the master-minds of conglomerates – they are often jocks who regard more thoughtful men as cookie-pushers, and who shoulder their way into offices and hug their allies and muscle in on deals. They move like swaggerers and snatchers, using their elbows when their money fails. And when they are in command they are puppet-masters.

Everett Horton, our Number Two, prized his football photo-graph (Yale '51) as much he did his autographed portrait of the president. Here was another of him, posed with a Russian diplo-mat, each in white shorts, holding a tennis racket and shaking hands across a tennis net. And others: Horton golfing, Horton fish-ing, Horton sailing. Horton had interesting ears – slightly swollen, and gristlier than the average, and they did not match: 'Wrestling,' someone said. It seemed innocent vanity that Horton thought of himself as a man of action. I suppose he was a man of action. He worked hard. He succeeded where Ambassador Noyes often failed.

Erroll Jeeps used to say, 'Watch out for Horton's body-english.'

He could have sent me a memo, or phoned me, or we might have had lunch. But he had not become Minister by sending memos. He was a hugger, a hand-shaker, a back-slapper – body-english – and when something important came up he tore down-stairs and interrupted whatever I was doing and said, 'You're the only one around here who can straighten this out. You've been in the Far East, not in Washington, among the cookie-pushers!'

Today he hugged me. His sweet-whisky fragrance of after-shave lotion stung my eyes. A file folder was tucked under his arm.

'Is that the problem?'

'That's his file,' Horton said.

I tried to catch a glimpse of the name, but he tossed the file on to a chair and kicked my office door shut.

'Let me tell you about it. That'll be quicker than reading this crap.' He sat on the edge of my desk and swung one heavy thigh over the other.

'Do you know Charlie Hogle, the telex operator?'

'I saw him once at your house,' I said. 'I don't go down to the telex room.'

'You let your *pyoon* do it, eh?' It was the Malay word for office-lackey, and he was mocking me with it. He said, 'You should get around more – you'd be amazed at some of the things you find.'

'In the telex room?'

'Especially there,' Horton said. 'This fellow Hogle – very gifted, they say, if you can describe a telex operator in that way. Very personable. Highly efficient, if a bit invisible. He's been here almost three years. No trouble, no scandal, nothing.' Horton stopped talking. He stared at me. 'I was down there this morning. What do I find?' Horton watched me again, giving me the same dramatic scrutiny as before. He wanted my full attention and a little pause.

I said, 'I give up – what did you find?'

'Hogle. With an earring.'

Horton sighed, slid off the desktop and threw himself into a chair. He was remarkably agile for such a big man.

I said, 'An earring?'

'Right. One of those gold . . . loops? Don't make me describe it.' Horton suddenly seemed cross. 'I don't know anything about earrings.'

'Was he wearing it?'

'What a dumb question! Of course he was.'

'I thought you were going to tell me that he stole it – that you found it on him.'

'He's got a hole in his ear for it.'

I said, 'So he's had his ear pierced.'

'Can you imagine? A special hole in his ear!'

I said, 'What exactly is wrong, coach?'

He had encouraged us to use this ridiculous word for him. I had so far refrained from it, and though I felt like a jackass using it today, it seemed to have the right effect. It calmed him. He smiled at me.

'Let's put it at its simplest. Let's be charitable. Let's not mock him,' Horton said. 'An earring is against regulations.'

'Which ones?'

'Dress regulations. The book. It's as if he's wearing a skirt.'

'But he's not wearing a skirt. It's jewellery. Is there a subsection for that?'

'Sure! In Muslim countries, Third World countries –'

'This is England, coach.'

'And he's a guy! And he's got this thing hanging off his ear!'

'You're not going to get him on a technicality,' I said. 'All you can do is ask him to remove it. "Would you mind taking off that earring, Mr Hogle?"'

Horton did not smile. He began lecturing me. He said, 'You act as if there's nothing wrong. Did you know there's no law against lesbianism in this country? Do you know why? Because Queen Victoria refused to believe that women indulged in that sort of behaviour!'

'Hogle's earring is hardly in that category,' I said.

'Bull! It's precisely in that category. That's how serious a violation it is. It's unthinkable for a man to turn up at work wearing an earring, so there's no legislation, nothing in the rule-book for earrings *per se*. But there's a paragraph on Improper Dress –'

'That covers lewd or suggestive clothes.'

'What about Inappropriate Accessories?'

'Religious or racial taboos. Cowhide presents in Hindu countries, pigskin suitcases in Muslim countries, the New York Philharmonic touring Israel and playing Wagner.'

'What has Wagner got to do with Accessories?'

'You know what I mean. Earrings don't figure.'

'There's something,' Horton said. He came over to me and jerked my shoulder, giving me a hug. 'It doesn't matter.' He grinned. He was a big man. He hugged me sideways as we stood shoulder to shoulder. 'There's always something – just find it.'

'Why me?' I said. 'You could do it more easily.'

His eyes became narrow and dark as he said, 'I'll tell you why I can't.' He looked at the door suspiciously, as if he was about to bark at it. Then, he made an ugly, disgusted face and whispered, 'When I saw Hogle with that thing in his ear, and the hole, and the implications, I felt sick to my stomach.' He glanced darkly at the door again. 'He's a nice clean-cut guy. I'd lay into him – I'd lose my temper. I know I would, and I want to spare him that. You'll be more rational. You know about these nutty customs. You've been in the Far East.'

'Doesn't Hogle have a Personnel Officer?'

Horton gave me a disdainful look. His expression said I was letting him down, I was a coward, a weakling.

He said, 'You don't want to do this, do you?'

'What I want is of no importance,' I said. 'I do what I'm told.'

'Excellent!' he said. Horton stood up straight. The muddy green was gone from his eyes – he was smiling. 'Now get down there and tell Hogle to divest himself.'

I said, 'That's his file, right?'

'Ignore the file for now. When you've settled this problem, stick a memo in here and hand it back to me. I also want to know why he's wearing it – that's important. And, by the way, this is strictly confidential, this whole matter – everything I've said.'

I made a move towards the file.

'You don't really need that,' he said.

'Maybe not,' I said. 'But I think I'll take it home and blow on it.'

I had thought *Why me*? But of course Horton was testing me as much as he was gunning for Hogle. He was trying to discover where my sympathies were: would I give him an argument, or would I obey? Perhaps I was a latent earring-wearer? Horton's own reaction seemed to me extraordinary. He felt sick to his stomach. That may have been an exaggeration, but the fear that he would lose his temper was almost unbelievable in someone whose temper was always in check. Everett Horton – he wanted to be called 'coach'! – was a man of action. I could not understand his reticence now, unless I was right in assuming that I was the real subject of the inquiry.

I was new here – less than four months on the job. I had to play ball. And I must admit I was curious.

The file was thin. Charlie Hogle had come to us from the Army under a programme we called 'Lateral Entry'. He had been in the Communications unit of the Signal Corps, running a telex office in Frankfurt. He was twenty-nine, not married, a graduate – German major – from the University of Northern Iowa in Cedar Falls. He had been born and raised in nearby Waterloo, Iowa. His annual job evaluations from the State Department fault-finders were very good. In fact, one suggested – as a black mark – that Hogle had experienced 'no negative situations'. In other words, he was such a happy fellow he might prove to be a problem. I did not buy that naïve analysis. Hogle was a well-adjusted, middle-level technician with a spotless record, and after looking through this worthy man's file I regretted what I had been ordered to do.

Lunch with him was out: it was both too businesslike and too friendly. Anyway, I hated lunch as unnecessary and time-wasting. Lunch is the ritual meal that makes fat people fat. And dinner was out – too formal. I kept telling myself that this was a small matter. I could send for him. I pictured poor Hogle, clutching his silly earring, cowering in my office, awkward in his chair.

There was only one possibility left – a drink after work. That made it less official, less intimidating, and if I got bored I could plead a previous engagement and go home.

I met him at a large over-decorated pub called The Audley, on the corner of Mount and South Audley Streets, not far from the embassy. Hogle, whom I spotted as American from fifty feet away, was tall even by generous standards of the mid-west. He was good-looking, with a smooth polite face and clear blue eyes. His blond eyelashes made him look completely frank and unsecretive. His hands were nervous but his face was innocent and still. His voice had the plain splintery cadences of an Iowa Lutheran being truthful. I took him to be a muscular Christian.

'I kind of like these English beers,' he was saying now. (Earlier we had talked about his Sunday school teaching.) 'They're a little flat, but they don't swell you up or make you drunk like lager. Back home –'

As he spoke, I glanced at his earring. It was a small gold hoop, as Horton had said, but Horton had made it seem like junk jewellery, rather vulgar and obvious – and embarrassing to the onlooker. I was surprised to find it a lovely earring. And it was hardly noticeable – too small to be a pirate's, too simple for a transvestite. I thought it suited him. It was the sort of detail that makes some paintings remarkable; it gave his face position and focus – and an undeniable beauty. It was the size, and it had the charm, of Shakespeare's raffish earring in the painting in the National Portrait Gallery.

Charlie Hogle was still talking about beer. His favourite was the California Coors brand, because it was made from –

This was ridiculous. We were getting nowhere. I said, 'Is that an earring you're wearing?'

His fingers went for it. 'Yes,' he said. 'What do you think of it?'

'Very nice,' I said. He smiled. I said, 'And unusual.'

'It cost me twenty-two pounds. That's almost fifty bucks, but it included getting my ear pierced. I figured it was worth it, don't you?'

Was he trying to draw me?

'You've just,' I said, 'got the one?'

'One earring's enough!'

I said, 'I'm not sure –'

'You think I should have *two*? Don't you think that'd be pushing it a little?'

'Actually,' I said, and hated my tone of voice, and dreaded what was coming, 'I was wondering whether one earring might be pushing it, never mind two.'

'You said it was nice.' He looked at me closely, and sniffed. He was an honest fellow for whom a contradiction was a bad smell. 'What do you mean "one earring might be pushing it"?'

'It *is* very nice,' I said. 'And so are these split skirts the secretaries have started to wear. But I wouldn't be very happy about your wearing a split skirt, Mr Hogle.'

He smiled. He was not threatened: he saw a joke where I had intended a warning. He said, 'I'm not wearing split skirt, sir.'

'Yes,' I said. 'But you are wearing an earring.'

'Is that the same as wearing a skirt?'

'Not exactly, but it's the same *kind* of thing.'

'What – illegal?'

'Inappropriate,' I said. This was Horton's line, and its illogicality was hideously apparent to me as I parrotted it. 'Like coming to work in your bathing suit, or dyeing your hair green, or –'

I couldn't go on. Hogle was, quite rightly, smiling at the stupidity of my argument. And now I saw that Horton's objection was really a form of abuse.

Hogle said, 'I know those things are silly and inappropriate. I wouldn't come to work dressed like a slob. I'm no punk. I don't have green hair.'

'Yes, I know.'

'I've got a pretty clean record, sir. I got a commendation from the consul in Frankfurt for hanging on and keeping the telex room open during a Red Army Faction riot. I'm not bragging, sir. I'm just saying I take my job seriously.'

'Yes, it's mentioned in your file. I know about it.'

'You've been looking in my file,' he said. His face became sad, and his attention slackened. He had let go of his earring. 'I get it – my ass is in a crack.'

'Not yet.'

'Sir, I could have bought a cheaper earring – one of those silver dangly ones. Instead I saved up. I bought a nice one. You said so yourself.'

'I also said it's rather unusual.'

'There's nothing wrong with "unusual", is there?'

'Some people think so.'

He looked at me, with his lips compressed. He had now seen the purpose of this innocent drink. I had led him here on a false pretext; I had deceived him. His eyes went cold.

He said, 'Mr Horton, the Minister. It's him, isn't it?'

'It's the regulations,' I said lamely.

'He was staring at me the other day, like the second louies used to stare at me when I was in the army. Even though he was about fifty feet away I could feel his eyes pressing on my neck. You can tell when something's wrong.' Hogle shook his head in a heavy rueful way. 'I thought he used to like me. Now he's yanked my file and sent you to nail me down.'

Hogle was completely correct. But I could not admit it without putting Horton into a vulnerable position and exposing him as petty and spiteful – after all, Horton's was the only objection to the earring. But Horton was boss.

I said, 'Everyone thinks that it would be better if you dispensed with your earring.'

'I still don't understand why.'

'It's contrary to dress regulations. Isn't that obvious?'

He touched the earring, as if for luck. He said, 'Maybe they should change the regulations.'

'Do you think it's likely they will?'

He made a glum face and said no.

'Be a sport,' I said. 'I'm telling you this for your own good. Get rid of that thing and save yourself a headache.'

Hogle had been staring at his glass of beer. Without moving his head, he turned his eyes on me and said, 'I don't want to seem uncooperative, sir, but I paid good money for this earring. And I had a hole punched in my ear. And I like it, and it's not hurting anyone. So – no way am I going to get rid of it.'

'What if we take disciplinary action?'

'That's up to you, sir.'

'You could be suspended on half pay. What do you say to that?'

'I wouldn't like it much,' Hogle said.

'Mr Hogle,' I said, 'does that earring represent anything? I mean, is it a sort of symbol?'

'Not any more than your tie-clip is a symbol. You don't see many tie-clips these days – and I think yours is neat. I think this earring is neat. That's the only reason. Don't you think that's a pretty good reason?'

I wished he would not ask me these questions. They were traps, they incriminated me, they tore me in two. I said, 'What I think doesn't matter. I'm an employee. So are you. What you think doesn't matter either. There is nothing personal about this, there's no question about opinion, or tolerance, or flexibility. It's strictly regulations.'

Hogle replied in a sort of wounded whisper. 'I'd like to see the regulations, sir,' he said. 'I'd like to see in black and white which rule I've broken.'

'It's a very general regulation concerning appropriate dress,' I said. 'And we can make it stick. We're going to give you a few days to decide which is more important to you – your earring or your job.'

I had lapsed into 'we' – it is hard to use it and not seem cold and bullying: it can be a terrifying pronoun. And yet I had hoped this meeting would be friendly. It was, from my point of view, disastrously cold. His resentment made me officious; my officiousness made him stubborn. In the end I had simply pulled rank on him, using the scowling 'we' and given him a crude choice. Then I left him. He looked isolated and lonely at the table in the pub, and that saddened me, because he was handsome and intelligent and young and a very hard worker. His earring distinguished him and made him look like a prince.

The next day I went to Horton's office. Seeing me, he rushed out and gave me a playful shove. He then helped me into the office with a hug, all the while saying, 'Get in here and tell me what a great success you've been in the telex room.'

I hated this fooling. I said, 'I've had a talk with Hogle.'

'With what result?'

'He's thinking about it.'

'You mean, it's not settled? You let him *think* about it?'

I freed myself from his grasp. I said, 'Yes.'

'It's not a thinking matter,' Horton said. 'It's an order – didn't you tell him that?'

'I didn't want to throw my weight around. You said yourself there's no point making an issue out of it if it can be settled quietly.'

Horton gaped at this. He became theatrical, imitating shock and incredulity with his exaggerated squint, and there was something of an actressy whine in his voice when he said, 'So he's still down there, wearing that *thing* on his ear?'

I let him rant a bit more. Then I said, 'I didn't want to put pressure on him. If he hasn't got the sense to see that our displeasure matters, then he's hardly any use to us.'

'That's a point – I don't want any passengers in this embassy, and I certainly won't put up with freaks.' Horton's phone was ringing; it had the effect of sobering him and making him snappish. 'I'll expect that file back by the end of the week – and I want a happy conclusion. Remember, if you can't get this chappie' – Horton wiggled his head on the word – 'to remove his earring you can hardly expect me to have much faith in your powers of persuasion.'

'I'd like to drop the whole damn thing,' I said.

Horton paused, and he peered at me with interest in spite of his nagging phone. 'And why is that?'

'I don't see the importance of it,' I said.

'It is very important,' he said. 'And of course I'm interested in your technique. You see, in this embassy one is constantly trying to point out that there is a sensible, productive way of doing things – and there is the British way. Tactful persuasion is such an asset, whether one is dealing with a misunderstood aspect of NATO, or an infraction of the dress regulations by a serving officer – I mean, Hogle's earring. I hate even the word.'

'I'll do it,' I said. 'But my heart isn't in it.'

'That is precisely why I want you to do it,' Horton said. 'If nothing else, this should teach you that feelings have nothing to do with this job. Now, please, get it over with. It's starting to make me sick.'

I chose the pub carefully. It was in Earls Court and notoriously male; but at six-thirty it was empty and could easily have been mistaken for the haunt of darts players and polite locals with wives and dogs. Hogle was late. Waiting there I thought that he might not turn up at all, just to teach me a lesson. But he came with an excuse and an apology. He had been telexing an urgent cable. Only he had clearance to work with classified material after hours, and the Duty Officer – Yorty, a new-comer – had no idea how to use a telex machine. So Hogle had worked late. As an ex-Army man he understood many of the military cables, and he had security clearance, and he was willing; I knew from his file that he didn't make mistakes. His obedience had never been questioned – that is, until Horton spotted the earring. I began to see why this detail worried Horton so much: Hogle, in such a ticklish job, had to be absolutely reliable.

He said, 'I've been thinking over what you told me.'

He looked tired – paler than he had three days ago. It was not the extra work, I was sure – he was worrying, not sleeping well. Perhaps he had already decided to resign on a point of principle, for in spite of his wilted posture and ashen skin, his expression was full of tenacity. I suppose it was his eyes. They were narrow, as though wounded, and hot, and seemed to say, 'No surrender.'

I said, 'Don't say anything.'

He had been staring into the middle distance. Now he looked closely at me. He winced, but he kept his gaze on me.

I said, 'I've managed to prevail. I took it to the highest possible level. I think everyone understands now.'

'What do you mean, "understands"?' There was a hint of anxiety in his voice.

'Your earring,' I said.

'What's there to understand?'

'You've got nothing to worry about. We don't persecute people for their beliefs any more. If that were the case I wouldn't be in the Foreign Service.'

'Wearing an earring,' Hogle said. 'Is that a belief?'

'It depends on how naïve you are,' I said. 'But be glad it doesn't matter. Be glad you live in a free society, where you can dress any way you like, and where you can choose your friends, whether they're British or American, white or black, female or male –'

Hogle became very attentive.

I said, 'I'm grateful to you. It's people like you who break down barriers and increase our self-awareness.'

'I don't want to break down any barriers,' he said. 'I'm not even sure what self-awareness is all about.'

'It's about earrings,' I said. 'The other day I told you your earring was nice. I was being insincere. Can I call you Charlie?'

'Sure.'

'Charlie, I think your earring is fantastic.'

His hand went to his ear. He looked wary. He did not let go of the earring or his earlobe. He sat fixedly with his fingers making this plucking gesture on his ear.

'It's a very handsome accessory,' I said. His fingers tightened. 'A real enhancement.' They moved again. 'An elegant statement –'

I thought he was going to yank his ear off. His hand was trembling, still covering the earring. He said, 'I'm not making a statement.'

'Take it easy,' I said, giving him the sort of blanket assurance of no danger that convinces people – and rightly – that they're in a tight spot. 'You've got absolutely nothing to worry about!' He looked very worried. 'You can relax with me.' I ordered him a drink and told him there was no point discussing the earring.

'I'm certainly not making any kind of statement,' Hogle said. The word worried him. It had implications of being unerasable and hinted of hot water. 'I got the idea from one of the delivery men – an English guy. He wasn't making any statement. It looked neat, that's all.'

'It looks more than neat,' I said. 'It has a certain mystery. I think that's its real charm.'

He winced at this, and now he was pinching his earlobe. He lowered his eyes. He did not look up again.

'I feel funny,' he said.

'Be glad you work with people who say yes instead of no.'

I gave him a friendly punch on the shoulder, the sort of body-english Horton would have approved. It made me feel uncomfortable and mannered and over-hearty. It amazed me then to realize that Horton was always punching and hugging and digging in the ribs. Hogle was unresponsive, not to say wooden. His eyes darted sideways.

The night's clients had started to arrive in the pub – men in leather jackets, with close-cropped hair, and heavy chains around their neck, and tattooed thumbs, and sunglasses. Some were bald, some devilishly bearded, one wore crimson shoes, another had an enormous black dog on a leather strap. All of them wore earrings.

'Have another drink,' I said.

Hogle stood up. 'I have to go.'

'What's the hurry?'

He was breathing hard. A man encased in tight black leather was hovering near us and staring at Hogle. The man had silver chains with thick links looped around his boots and they clanked as he came closer.

'No hurry,' Hogle said. Now he was reassuring me in the way that I had reassured him earlier, giving me hollow guarantees as he backed away. 'Hey, I had a good time.' He stepped past the clanking man whose leather, I swear, oinked and squeaked. 'No kidding. It's just that' – he looked around – 'I told this friend of mine, this girl I know that I'd – I don't know, I'd give her a call.' He looked desperate. 'Hey, thanks a lot. I really appreciate everything you've done!'

Then he left, and then I removed my earring. That was easy enough to do – just a matter of unscrewing the little plunger and putting the foolish thing into my pocket. And I hurried out of the pub hearing just behind me clanks and squeaks of reproach.

In my report for Charlie Hogle's file I recorded the earring incident as a minor infraction – Inappropriate Dress. I left it vague. What was the point in explaining? I noted the two meetings, I described Hogle as 'compliant' and 'reasonable'. There was no innuendo in my report. I spared him any indignity. It sounded no worse than if he had come to work without a necktie.

Indeed, it was no worse than if he had come to work without a necktie. I had had no objection to the earring, nor had any of Hogle's co-workers in the telex room. Horton had made it an issue; Horton was Minister, so Horton was obeyed. And Hogle did not wear his earring again.

'It's for his own good,' Horton said later, and he squeezed my arm. I was the team member who had just played well; he was the coach. He was proud of me and pleased with himself. He was beaming. 'I feel a thousand times better, too! That really annoyed me – that kid's earring. I used to go down to the telex room a lot. I realized I was staying away – couldn't stand to look at it!'

'Aren't you being a little melodramatic?'

'I'm completely serious,' he said. 'That situation was making me sick. I mean sick. I got so mad the first time I saw that thing on his ear' – Horton turned away and paused – 'I got so mad I actually threw up. Puked! That's how angry I was.'

'You must have been very angry,' I said.

'Couldn't help it. We can't have that sort of thing –' He didn't finish the sentence. He shook his head from side to side and then said, 'You were too easy on him in your report. That kid had a problem. Incredible. I took him for a clean, stand-up guy!'

I said, 'He may have feelings of which he's unaware. It's not that uncommon.'

'No,' Horton said. 'I'll keep an eye on him.'

'Fine,' I said. 'Anyway, everyone's safe now, coach.'

He smiled and smacked my arm and sent me back to my office.

In the following weeks I saw scores of young men Hogle's age wearing earrings. They were English, and all sorts, and I was ashamed that I had been a success. It was not merely that I had succeeded by deceiving Hogle, but because I had made him think that there was something dangerous and definite in this trinket decorating his ear. And he never knew just how handsome that trinket made him. Hogle would be all right. But, after what he had told me, I was not so sure about Horton.

★ 7 ★

THE EXILE

★

Everyone knows Ezra's Pound's funny name, but no one can quote him. This was also the case with the American poet, Walter Van Bellamy, who – like Pound long ago – lived in England. Nearly everyone knew what Bellamy stood for, but I had never met a person who could quote a single line he had written. I wondered sometimes whether the people who bought his books actually read them. Certainly they went to his readings and listened to him reciting his poems. He did so in a whisper, but it was an amazing one. Most people whisper in a monotone; Bellamy could whisper over an octave and a half, a characteristic he shared with the best actors.

His subjects were love, nature, humanity, and war. He also wrote frankly of how he had once lost the balance of his mind. That was the phrase he used. I liked 'lost the balance' very much, as if he lost the little that remained and had none left. This confession of a recent bout of lunacy made him greatly sought-after as a party guest, and it also conferred on him glamour and respectability. His poem 'I am Naked' was about these very paradoxes.

Inevitably, his poems concerned politics. His readings had the flavour of political meetings and some had the heat and unanimity of religious get-togethers. That was what the clippings said in his embassy file, which was all I knew at the beginning. (I had met him once at an embassy reception and had found him deaf on gin – we got nowhere.) To a large extent, Bellamy's audience could best be described as believers, and they were charmed by his music. He was famous for the sounds in his poems, what he called 'my throbs and gongs'. It was possible that people were so persuaded by him beforehand there was little need afterwards for them to remember anything. Still, it surprised me that no one could quote his poems. His presence was memorable, though: a broad chest, eyes as blue as gas flames, a stern bony Pilgrim Father's face, and enormous hairy hands. He was also very tall – my height, about six-three. He walked with a slight stoop, cringing posture that had probably evolved out of a fear of banging his head.

His strong, distinctly radical views were well-known – his position on South Africa, nuclear disarmament, NATO, and even such rarefied issues as the exploitation of non-union labour in the wine-growing region of northern California. He had led peace marches in the 1970s, when he had been regarded as the soul of propriety in his dark grey three-piece suit and hand-knotted bow-tie and gold watch-chain. You might have taken him for a Tory politician, or a banker, or an Episcopal preacher. He had a copper-bottomed look of authority, of solidity and trustworthiness; he had a good old name. The ragged, angry protest movements of the Sixties needed his respectability and they were probably surprised by how vocal he was on their behalf. He had the appeal of John Kennedy – in fact, the two men had been classmates at Harvard. His 'Elegy on the Death of J F K' was celebrated for its intimate and unexpected details of the two men's friendship. Within very few years of this poem, Bellamy became a public figure, who stumped around the United States reading his poems and giving encouragement to the anti-Vietnam protesters. He was noted for his willingness to share a platform with a folk-singer, a jailbird or whoever. Most people agreed that he was the conscience of his generation. Bellamy seemed to have no fire, but that was not so surprising. A conscience does not shout – it murmurs.

What else? Yes, he looked wonderfully well-fed. This alone was an amazing characteristic in a poet, but he was a most unrepresentative figure. The more I found out about him the more bewildered I was. He had a large following, but he was not only a poet. He was like a spiritual leader, like one of those bearded domineering Indian gurus; but for Bellamy poetry was the medium of instruction. His humility was so conspicuous and challenging it was like arrogance; but his sense of certainty, and the preachiness of his poems – and his physical size – attracted many people to him. He had considerable influence, and I was very glad it was for the good. His followers were a peaceful and romantic bunch on the whole – the college crowd – who perhaps trusted and liked this well-dressed father-figure more than the middle-aged men who also wrote poems and carried banners and played to the gallery, and who dressed like chicken-farmers and long-distance truckers, and who could be pretty embarrassing in the cold light of day.

Bellamy had the strange privacies also of a spiritual leader. There were no rumours and stories of his excesses but there were resonant and suggestive silences. To look like a banker and to be known for his nervous breakdown – that was what made him. And his marriages had also given him fame. He had been married three times. But he was no philanderer – he had been victimized and thrown into confusion by these messy affairs. Each of his wives had been extremely rich.

It was some measure of his fame that he was known as a writer to people who did not read him, and a great writer to those who did not read at all. He was all the more celebrated for not living in America. When Walter Van Bellamy came to England from New York in the early Seventies he was called an exile. It did not seem the right word to describe a man who was often on television telling lively stories, or else doing something public and political before a crowd. I thought of exiles as gaunt silent men with red eyes, pacing the rocky foreshores of barren islands; or else unshaven men in hot overcoats who spoke in thick accents and slept on sofas. Bellamy did not fit my stereotype. And were you still an exile if you occasionally flew home First Class in a jumbo jet to attend a New York party? I did not think so. Some years he taught at Harvard. He had money. His rich wives had been sympathetic. They were more patronesses than wives. He was lucky. He had always lived well – he was in his way a socialite, a party-goer, if a somewhat reluctant one. He had a house in the depths of Kent and an apartment in Eaton Square. Perhaps the most unusual thing about him was that, as a poet, he made money. People bought his books even if they didn't read them. The books were symbols or tokens of belief. Buying them was a political act, an affirmation that you were on his side – whatever side he was boosting at that moment.

I had been introduced to him at Everett Horton's house, when he was drunk and deaf. I was eager to meet him again, because I had read him at school. He too had been to Boston Latin, and his books in the school library and the thought that he had sat under these same windows, this whiff of literary history, fuelled my own ambition to write, until I drifted into the State Department. I had wanted to talk to him. It is a natural desire to want to meet a writer and size him up. But I did not see him again until the Poetry Night of the London Arts Festival, where he was reading.

His poems that night were dense and full of his personal history, but his reading was vigorous and gave life to what seemed to be little more than spidery monologues about his domestic affairs – how he had cleaned out a sink and swept a room and ordered a pint of milk and so forth – modern poetry, as a lady behind me said out loud. There is a personal tone in some poetry that is so intimate it gives nothing away – so private it sounds anonymous. Bellamy's was a sort of general confession of practical untidiness with which any youngster might identify. I say 'youngster' because Bellamy seemed to be addressing younger people, implying that he understood them and offering them reassurance. This restrained snuggling was a popular approach. The audience clamoured for more, and that was when I noticed how lonely he looked in the spotlight – how solitary and anxious to please.

As an encore that night he read a long poem, called 'Londoners', about Americans in London, starting with Emerson and Hawthorne and ending with himself. In between, there were references to Mark Twain, Stephen Crane and Henry James. The personal note was struck in such sentences as 'Tom Eliot told me –' and 'Cal Lowell used to drawl –'. Afterwards, he said the poem was about language and culture. With a characteristic flourish, he added, 'And schizophrenia.'

What I have written so far will not be news to anyone who has followed the career of Walter Van Bellamy. He was a public man, the facts are well known – but wait: it is the public men who have the darkest secrets. They have the deepest cellars and hottest attics, and they are consoled by blindness and locked doors. It is impossible to guess at what truly animates these people whose surfaces we seem to know so well, and there is nothing in the world harder to know than the private life of a public man.

The London embassy had tried to cultivate Bellamy. We needed him. He had a powerful eminence among the writers in London – partly for being American and partly because his present wife was a patroness. She was an irascible Englishwoman who, for tax reasons (ah, the resourceful English aristocracy!) held an American passport.

In the previous ten years Bellamy had signed petitions condemning our intervention in Vietnam and our arming small Central American countries; about our decision to build a neutron bomb – and more: public matters. Of course we needed his criticism, but it was unhelpful, not to say humiliating, to get publicly. I had told Horton that I hoped there was a friendly way of gaining Bellamy's confidence. It occurred to me at the poetry reading that in another age a man like Bellamy might have chosen to be a diplomat – even today the French, the Spanish, the Portuguese, chose poets as their cultural attachés, and the Mexicans had recently sent one of their most distinguished writers to be Ambassador to France. Bellamy could, I thought, teach us a great deal. There were too few men at the London embassy who were willing to criticize policy decisions – they felt their jobs were at stake. That sort of thing wouldn't bother Bellamy. He had a reputation as a humane poet-philosopher; he also had a private income. I felt that someone like Bellamy might keep us from making stupid mistakes. And it would certainly be a very good thing for our image in Britain if Bellamy chose to associate himself with us, for there was no question but that British intellectuals regarded our London embassy as a stronghold of corrosive philistines, reactionaries, anti-communists and America-firsters – a nest of spies. Bellamy would be a good corrective.

True, he was a little unpredictable. He had been something of a prodigy, he had published while still very young and had attracted the notice of the really eminent – Robert Frost, and Eliot, and Pound. He had gained laureate status while still in his forties. Now at sixty-three, and nearly always in the public eye – 'the most visible poet since Yeats,' he had been called – he qualified as a bard. He was a complicated man – confused, vain, too many sleeping pills, too much wine, but he wrote like an angel. I was sure of it. I could never understand why no one remembered the lines of his poems – I don't know why I was unable to recall a single line. But, then, who can quote Ezra Pound?

When the reading – this Poetry Night – was over, Bellamy walked off the stage and was mobbed by people asking for autographs. I noticed that few people addressed him directly. They stood shyly, offering him his books which were open to the flyleaf. He signed them without saying a word. The group around him was reverential. Out of politeness – but it might have been fear – they kept their distance and even averted their eyes as, not speaking, Bellamy scrawled his name in various editions of his books. When he was finished he saw me.

Our height was all the introduction we required. Tall people often find themselves talking to perfect strangers, merely because the stranger is also tall. Tallness is like a special racial attribute.

Bellamy spoke over the heads of his admirers, 'I think we've met before.'

'At an American Embassy reception,' I said. 'Months ago.'

'Yes,' he said and came over and shook my hand, 'I remember you well.'

His eyes were unsteady and his hair had the look of having been combed by someone other than himself. In his wincing, round-shouldered way he seemed wounded or drunk, but he was more likely just very tired after two solid hours on the stage.

'How is your wife?' he said.

'I think you have someone else in mind,' I said. 'I'm not married. I'm the man from Boston. Excuse me, that didn't sound right!'

Bellamy said, 'Is she still writing poems?'

He had not heard me, and he had mistaken me for Vic Scaduto, whose wife wrote poems – or at least she said she did.

'Not married,' I said, shaking my head.

'So am I,' he said. 'I was just leaving – why don't you come along?'

His tone was neutral, but this was the strangest thing about Bellamy. At a distance he was very friendly, but the closer you got to him the cooler he became. Giving a lecture or a reading Bellamy had a very warm intimate tone; in public he was relaxed; but face-to-face, like this, he was deaf and almost completely indifferent. This I am sure will be news to many of his fans.

I followed him outside, not certain that I was really wanted.

He said, 'Have you eaten?'

'No.' But I was not particularly hungry. 'I don't want to intrude. We can meet some other time. You must be tired after your reading.'

'Time to eat,' he said. He waved a taxi towards us. 'You haven't eaten. You might as well come along. After you.'

It was off-hand, as plainly-spoken as I have written it, not really an invitation but rather a nod to the inevitable. We rode in silence for a while.

I said, 'I don't feel right about this.'

'It's dinner-time,' Bellamy said. 'Too bad about your wife.'

The wife-business had taken hold of him, but I had no idea what he was imagining. It seemed a ludicrous trip in this taxi, for the fact was that I did not want to go with him, and he probably did not want me along either – and yet here we were on our way to a restaurant. I wasn't even hungry!

It was Wilton's in Bury Street – expensive, English, dark-brown, and joyless. Emma, Bellamy's wife – the third – was waiting for him at the table inside the restaurant. With her were the Poulters, man and wife. I recognized the name instantly.

'Like the mustard?' I asked.

Poulter's English Mustard had a green and yellow label, and an unforgettable Royal Warrant – *By Appointment to HM Queen Elizabeth The Queen Mother*, with her gold crest. I often stared at this label and tried to imagine the Queen Mother painting Poulter's mustard on a Royal sausage.

Mr Poulter said, 'I *am* the mustard.'

It was clear from the way Poulter had stood up and shown Walter Van Bellamy his chair and called the waiter over for a fresh drinks order, that he was the host. Poulter was paying. I had no business there.

Bellamy said, 'For God's sake, sit down!'

But they were one chair short. They had not expected me.

Poulter was very tactful. He urged me to take his chair. This proved embarrassing. I sat and left Mr Poulter, the host, standing. Every other diner in the restaurant was seated. I quickly stood up again and offered him my seat.

Bellamy turned his back on us. He was drinking wine and – his hand shook badly – spilling it.

Mrs Poulter's hair arrangements were bright mahogany and so shiny and stiff they looked shellacked. She became suddenly flustered and said, 'There seems to be something wrong. There are too many people. Norman, there's one too many!'

And Mr Poulter said, 'No, no. Our friend here' – he beckoned a waiter over – 'will get us another chair.'

The table in the cubby hole was still set for four and, worse, it was designed for four, so throughout the meal the discomfort reminded me that Bellamy had no right to bring me there and make me an unwelcome guest.

Bellamy did not explain my presence to the Poulters. For a time he spoke to the waiter, who did nothing but listen and agree ('That needs saying, sir!'). Emma spoke to Norman Poulter about the treachery of postmen, and I spoke to Mrs Poulter about the weather in Indonesia.

The table jolted – Bellamy was shifting position. He stared at me and said, 'Learn of the green world what can be thy place.'

'I suppose that's good advice,' I said.

'Pull down thy vanity,' he said.

'Excuse me?'

'But to have done instead of not doing,' he said. 'This is not vanity.'

'No –'

'Here, error is all in the not done,' he said, 'all in the diffidence that faltered.'

The others, hearing this, had fallen silent and were watching me. Bellamy was smiling broadly.

'Ezra,' he said.

He was quoting Pound!

At eleven o'clock Bellamy stood up and took Emma by the arm and said, 'We have to go. We're in the country these days and our last train leaves in half an hour.'

I stayed uneasily with the Poulters.

Mrs Poulter said, 'Bingo's going through a rather bad patch.'

'Bingo?'

'Walter Bellamy, of course.' She had lipstick flecks on her teeth. 'Do you mean to say you're a friend of his and you don't even know his name?'

That was as far as I had got with Bellamy, which annoyed me, because I still admired him and we still needed him. A month later we had a request from our Binational Center, 'Amerikahaus' in Berlin, asking whether Bellamy would be available to represent the United States in a seminar called 'Writing East and West'. Everett Horton, our Number Two, told me to take care of it.

I called his house in Kent. A housekeeper answered and said he was in London. I called the Eaton Square number. A tetchy voice said I could not speak to him.

'It's very important,' I said.

'He is very ill.' Was this Emma? 'In any case, he is not here.'

'May I ask where I can get in touch with him?'

'I am not obliged to answer your questions!'

The phone was slammed down.

There were two more cables from Berlin, demanding Bellamy. My secretary tried but failed to discover Bellamy's whereabouts. There was another cable, and then I went to Scaduto. He was the Cultural Affairs Officer, I said; surely it was his job to deal with Bellamy, the literary man, the poet –

'A binational seminar in West Berlin, with writers from both sides of the Iron Curtain, and you call it literary?' He laughed at me.

' "Writing East and West" – that's what it's called.'

'Guys from East Germany,' he said. 'You call them writers?' He tap-danced for a moment, then said, 'Face it – it's political. That's why we need Bellamy to represent us. The Ambassador's going to be there! Bellamy's got the right profile – he's old, experienced, liberal, well-known, active in political protest. Did you know he was arrested in 'sixty-five on a peace march in Washington? Do you have any idea what that buys in terms of credibility with these so-called Marxist writers? Plus, he's well-connected, lovely wife, and he wears these terrific suits.'

'And he's sick,' I said.

'So you say,' Scaduto said. 'It might just be a story – famous men often have people around to protect them. "He's sick" – it might be a euphemism for "Take a hike" or "Don't bother him".'

It was then that I remembered the Poulters and that awkward dinner at Wilton's. I found 'Poulter's Mustard Ltd' in the phone book and called the main office. My telephone technique, to reassure people, was to call very early in the morning and leave the embassy number and my name. They always called back: a call from the American Embassy always seemed important. Poulter was prompter than most. Yes, he remembered me.

I said, 'I know Bingo's very ill. I wonder whether you can tell me where he is – I have something to give him.'

'Doesn't he usually go to The Abbey?' Mr Poulter said.

'In London?'

'Yes,' he said, 'that clinic on the other side of the river.' *Other side* in London always meant south.

I said, 'I wasn't sure, but I can check.'

'I try to avoid The Abbey,' Poulter said. 'I've never liked those places. And anyway, Bingo will be out soon. He never stops long.'

By then, it was too late to ask what was wrong with Bellamy.

'Berlin is still waiting for a reply on that Bellamy request,' Horton said, just before I went home.

I said, 'I feel as if I've been looking for Bellamy my whole life.'

'Then it's about time you found him.'

Back home at my apartment in Overstrand Mansions, I looked up The Abbey in the phone book and discovered that it was not far from me. Its address was Spencer Park, on the 77 bus route in Wandsworth.

I switched off all the lights so that I could think, and sitting in the darkness I reflected on the fact that what I had told Horton was true: I had been aware of Walter Van Bellamy, and seeking him, since my schooldays. Then, to impress us, my English teacher, Mr Bagley, showed us Bellamy's first book of poems, and the jacket-flap that said – *attended Boston Latin School*. We were very proud of Bellamy and, because of him, were proud of ourselves. It seemed possible that we could do what he had done. For me, he was more than a fellow townsman – he was, in fact, like my alter ego; and here we both were in London, not exactly exiles but with certain likenesses and affinities.

I knew no more about him than what I have written here. Some people regarded him as one of the greatest living writers, but my image of him was indistinct – from hearsay and books, from the reception at Horton's, the reading, the terrible dinner at Wilton's. I could not say what he was really like. What was at the heart of my quandary was the suspicion that Walter Van Bellamy was a little like me.

The best news was that this private hospital – its name, The Abbey, said everything – was nearby. It was three miles at most, a fifteen-minute bus ride. I called and was told that Bellamy was indeed a patient, that he could receive visitors, and that visiting hours were not over until nine o'clock. It was now seven-thirty.

I resolved to visit him that night. On the bus, I was amazed at my audacity: here I was visiting one of the most famous American poets. I wondered if I could bring it off. It was like anticipating a hard interview. Would I measure up, and could I get him to agree to the Berlin request? I did not know much about him, but I knew he was human. At the time, I was naïve enough to find that a consolation.

The Abbey was a Victorian house behind a wall, with a tower to one side. Its tall church-windows were heavily leaded. A mock-gothic villa, its rear garden was part of a private park – the most inaccessible park in London – and its Frankenstein-movie façade faced Wandsworth Common, many chestnut trees and a row of bent-over hawthorns. Its sign, in old script, was well lighted, but the building itself was in darkness – the curtains were well drawn, and it was impossible to get a glimpse of anything going on inside. When I rang the bell and entered I saw that it was a very deep house – ahead of me, past the reception desk, was a long corridor.

A nurse took swift squeaky rubber-soled steps towards me, but before I could identify myself I heard a sudden yakking and the rattle of what was almost certainly lunatic laughter.

'Sorry about that,' the nurse said. 'Are you here to see one of the guests?'

'Mr Bellamy,' I said; and I thought: *guests*?

'Is he expecting you?'

My first impulse was to lie and say yes. But I shook my head and said that I had not had time to get in touch with Mr Bellamy on the phone.

The nurse said, 'He can't use the phone.'

'Is he that bad?'

'No, no. He'd be on the phone all day, talking nineteen to the dozen, if we let him. But we have instructions from the family. He's not allowed to use the phone.'

'Poor fellow.'

'They're afraid of what he'll do.' She smiled at me.

'What *will* he do?'

'I mean say.' She smiled again. 'He never gets any visitors.'

'Is it contagious?'

'Being manic?' She nodded with real conviction and said, 'It may sound silly but I honestly think it is. Crazy families! If you promise not to excite him you can see him. But don't stay too long. Have you been here before?'

I said no and she told me to follow her. Bellamy's room was on the top floor. The nurse knocked, there was a grunt from inside the room, and she left me there to go in on my own.

Bellamy lay on the bed. He was fully clothed – overdressed if anything – wearing a jacket and turtle-neck sweater and tweed trousers and thick socks. The room was small and hot and brightly-lit and smelled of cough-remedies: Bellamy also had a cold. On a chair there were books – three were Bellamy's own, including his *Poems New and Selected*. He was reading a small black Bible.

He glanced up. It was a glance I recognized: his nod to the inevitable – not friendly, not hostile. But he was drugged – his lips were puffy and inexpressive, his eyes sleepy-looking.

He said, 'Read that,' and handed me the Bible where a passage was circled in pencil. 'Read it out loud.'

' "I have digged and drunk strange waters, and with the soles of my feet have I dried up all the rivers of besieged places." ' I gave the Bible back to him. Its leather cover was unpleasantly warm where he had been holding it.

'What does it mean?' he said.

I shrugged, and already I felt as if I had failed the interview.

'It's a poem,' Bellamy said. 'It's my poem.'

He tore the Bible page out and opened his mouth to smile. I thought he was going to eat the page. He crushed it into his pocket.

'How do you feel?' I asked.

'I don't sleep.'

'Can't they give you something?'

'That's not it,' he said in a drowsy voice. 'I haven't got time to sleep. Too much work to do. Look.' He picked up a book and said, 'Are you the taxman?'

On the bus I had thought: Will I measure up? Am I bright enough? The anticipation hurt my nerves. I imagined certain questions. But I had not expected this. I felt sorry for him.

I said, 'I'm from the embassy. I have a message for you.'

'I've been getting messages for weeks. Taking them down. I

don't want any more messages.' He showed me the book again, and again he said, 'Look.'

It was *Poems New and Selected*. He flipped the pages. I saw blue ink, a blue scrawl, poems scribbled over and smudged, balloons with words in them, and arrows, and asterisks. You see a person's bad handwriting and you get frightened or sad. It was the sort of book that students kept, full of underlinings and annotations and crossings-out. Now Bellamy was holding it open to a particular page. I could see that he had crossed out nearly all the lines in that poem and had rewritten them. I couldn't judge how good the new lines were – they were scarcely legible. The exclamation marks did not make me hopeful.

'You're rewriting your poems.'

'Improving them,' he said. 'I'm getting messages.'

'But these poems have already been printed,' I said.

'Full of mistakes.' His eyes brightened. He looked desperate, as if he had been tricked and trapped and could only escape through this great labour of rewriting. He looked at his hands. There were ink-stains on them that brought his wrinkles into relief. He motioned to the other books, opened one – it was *Londoners*. It was a mass of blue ballpoint. The handwriting was wobbly and childish and actually frightening to look at. It indicated disorder and mania and big blue obsession. 'And these.'

His head lay to one side, on his shoulder, as if he was trying to read upside-down writing. But when he shut the book his head didn't move.

He said, 'The names of race-horses – they aren't names. They're numbers. Word-numbers. Meaningless.'

I said, 'I had never thought of that.'

'It's true. A Jew thought it up, the names, to confuse people. You can make a lot of money if you know how to confuse people.'

'How do you know it was a Jew?' I said.

'Because the Jews have all the money,' he said. 'What's wrong with you? Sit down.'

I was standing at the foot of his bed. I said, 'I can't stay. I just wanted to make sure you're all right.'

'I'm not all right,' Bellamy said. 'Didn't anyone tell you?'

'You should write some new poems – not rewrite the old ones,' I said, eager to change the subject.

'If your car was rusty, would you paint it or sell it?' he asked.

'I guess I'd fix it,' I said.

'A Jew would sell it,' he said. 'But I'm not selling these rusty poems. I'm fixing them.'

I wanted most of all to open a window. It was stuffy in here – and the smell of Vick and old socks and last week's apples made it stuffier. I looked out through the window bars and saw a blackness: Spencer Park. I sat down.

Bellamy said, 'Tell them I'll have this book fixed pretty soon, and then I'll leave this place.'

'Who shall I tell?'

'The rest of them,' he said. 'Roger, Philippa, all the Howletts.'

Now I was certain that I wanted to leave. He thought I was his publisher. It was a charade – and pathetic. He had no idea who I was. It was unfair and tormenting for him if I stayed longer.

'Here's one,' he said. He took up a piece of paper and cleared his throat. 'They were naked at last and had no pockets to pick.' He smiled. He said, 'The Jews.'

I stood up.

'They knew they had to be purified, an angel gave them the news.' He smiled as before. 'The Jews.'

I said, 'I get the point.'

'Their shoes –'

I could not stop him. He read on. It was a short poem, but it was poisonous, as clumsy as the scribble it was written in. It was demented, it was awful, it was wrong. And the next one he tried to read was an attempt at comedy. Anti-Jewish feeling nearly always tries to pass itself off as humour, because there is a kind of easy freemasonry in anti-semitism, the nudge, the shared joke. And it is worse because it is completely fearless hatred mimicking sanity as it mocks its victims.

I was glad for the knock on the door as he started poem three: 'The Jewnighted States.' The door opened.

'Hello Walter,' the man said. 'Have you taken your pill?'

Bellamy reached for the pill and put it into his mouth and drank his water. Doing this, he became childish again – the way he pulled a face and had a hard time swallowing, the way he gulped his water and wiped his mouth with the back of his hand, the way he drooled and sat forward, working his jaw.

'May I see you for a minute?' the man said to me, and led me into the corridor. 'I'm Doctor Chapman. Are you a friend of Walter's? Family?'

'Not really, no,' I said. 'Just an interested party.'

'Pity. He's doing marvellously well. But he'd do a great deal better if he got more visitors. I'm thinking of releasing him. He needs company.'

'He says some rather wild things. Race-horses. Jews. And he's rewriting his poems. I think he's crazy.'

The doctor smiled at me. 'That's not a word we use here.'

'You use all the others – why not that one?' I said. 'And Bellamy's in there babbling about the beauties of Auschwitz. Why don't you tell him there are certain words, certain ideas –'

The doctor was still smiling. It was a Bellamy smile, of a kind – impatient, patronizing, humourless. He said, 'A famous Jewish writer once said, "All men are Jews," meaning all men are victims. It's not true, you know. The opposite is closer to the truth. All men are Nazis, really. I mean, if all men are anything, which of course they're not. What a depressing subject! But I'm keeping you from Walter. Sorry. I just wanted to find out if you were close to him.'

'I'm from the embassy,' I said. 'We try to keep an eye on our citizens, even if they are determined to be exiles.'

'He's that, all right. Exile – it's a good word for his condition.'

I did not re-enter Bellamy's room. I did not stay. He had no idea who I was. I took a bus home and drafted a cable to Berlin, which I sent the next day, explaining that Walter Van Bellamy could not attend this seminar, or any other.

And of course, for months afterwards, whenever I saw a book of Bellamy's or a newly-published poem, I searched it for signs of madness, or Jew-baiting, or plain stupidity. But there was nothing, nothing, nothing. His poems were serene and unmemorable; they never touched these subjects; and afterwards, when I couldn't remember them, they frightened me.

8

TOMB WITH A VIEW
★

'There's another woman to see you,' my secretary said, giving me an old-fashioned look on 'another'.

It had been a bad morning – I knew she was thinking about Mr Fleamarsh's ashes. Mrs Fleamarsh had come in a few days before. Her husband had complained of chest pains on the train to Salisbury, missed the cathedral, collapsed on the bus, and died at Stonehenge. She insisted on having him cremated, so that she could carry him in her handbag. Is there a more presumptuous statement than 'He would have wanted it this way'? Accompanying his coffin back to Baltimore would have meant her missing the tour of the Lake District, and Stratford was tomorrow. Mrs Fleamarsh gave me to understand that a whole unburnt adult human corpse was a terribly inconvenient thing. 'He bowled a lot,' she said, as if this was all the explanation I needed. And even more obscurely, 'He always had one of those shiny blue jackets.'

I arranged for the cremation, but as Mrs Fleamarsh was in Stratford, the ashes were delivered to me at the embassy. The urn, the size and shape of a white crock of Gentleman's Relish, stood on my desk for most of the afternoon. And it put me in the mood for what happened later that day, though I would willingly have missed it all – Mrs Fleamarsh, the ashes of her husband, and Miss Gowrie and her dark lodger.

Miss Gowrie, the other woman – she had watery eyes and a wind-reddened face – introduced herself as a friend of Sir Charles Smallwood, whom I dimly remembered having met at Horton's reception. Miss Gowrie, I guessed, was nearing seventy. She sat down and planted both her feet on the carpet to steady herself and she began squashing her handbag in her lap.

She said, 'I'm afraid I have a rather shocking story to tell you. I mentioned it to Charlie' – this was the way she referred to Sir Charles Smallwood – 'and he said I should come straight to you.'

I thought she was a bit drunk or having trouble with her

dentures. In fact, she was straining to speak in a dignified way –
she was fighting her cockney accent, and losing. She had a voice
of astounding monotony.

I said, 'Go on.'

'Well' – *wayew* – 'it's about my lodger then, isn't it?'

She looked around the office, she peered at the walls, she
spoke again. She was one of those people who seem – in the way
they whisper and squint – to be addressing eavesdroppers.

'Mind you, I'm not really a landlandy in the normal way. It's just
that I live in Mortlake and the Council put up me rates, didn't
they? Practically doubled them. I had to take in lodgers to pay
the additional. That's Mr Wubb. Coloured.'

'What colour, Miss Gowrie?'

'There's only one colour,' she said. 'Black. One of yours.'

I tried to convey, with silence and cold eyes, that I did not like
this at all.

'And that's why I'm here,' she said.

'Because your lodger is black?'

'Because he's a thief.' *Feef* was what Miss Gowrie said.

'British?'

'Of course not.'

'Before you go any further, I think I should remind you that this
is the American Embassy,' I said. 'Properly speaking, if you have a
problem with your lodger you should go to the police.'

'He's one of yours,' she repeated. 'American. And he's driving
me mental. It's not fair!'

'How do you know he's a thief?'

'He keeps the rubbish under his bed, don't he?'

'Rubbish?'

'Rubbish is what he steals – pots and pans and that. He's driving
me mental.'

As she spoke, I resolved to check the man's citizenship. I didn't
like Miss Gowrie's manner. She behaved as if she was holding me
responsible for this thieving lodger. I hoped I could get rid of her
without becoming involved in her problem. I had had enough that
day dealing with the ashes of Herbert Fleamarsh. The worst
problems in any office arise at roughly four in the afternoon. It
was four-ten, and I wished that I had gone home early.

'Mr Wubb has no right whatsoever to come here and steal

from people. Some college student! I suppose he's studying how to steal. Why don't he stay in his own country and steal?'

'That's a good question,' I said, picking up the telephone. 'Let's see if the police have an answer to it.'

'Oh, please, sir!' she said, and her fear brought forth a terrible tone of respectfulness, almost grovelling. She looked suddenly frightened and small, and I felt genuinely sorry for her. 'Please don't tell them. It would be in all the papers. There'd be talk. It would kill me.'

'That you had a dishonest lodger?'

'That I had a flaming lodger at all,' she said. 'I don't want the rest of them to know.'

'The rest?'

'The street,' she said. 'They don't take lodgers, certainly not black ones. They're awfully decent.'

She was asking me to agree with her. I said nothing.

'He's one of yours,' she said. 'You'll know what to do.'

But he wasn't, and I didn't.

It seemed no business of ours, this light-fingered lodger who might or might not have been American. I checked the files. There was no one named Wubb registered with the embassy – but not every American registered, and would a thief? Miss Gowrie telephoned me the next afternoon. She was desperate, and I had a free evening: the combination often ends badly. But I liked the idea of going upriver to Mortlake, so I visited her, just to look around, and perhaps to find excuses for my curiosity.

'He's rearranged all his furniture, hasn't he?' Miss Gowrie said, letting me into the tall gloomy house. It was just off the Mortlake Road that ran along the river, and the river could be seen – we were mounting the steps to the lodger's room – from Miss Gowrie's upper windows. On this wet black afternoon the river's dampness seemed to penetrate every brick of the house, and the trees dripped grey water from the tips of their boney branches. 'In his room,' she said. 'He's moved everything, every stick.'

She threw his door open, releasing mingled smells, sweet and sour. Miss Gowrie saw me sniffing.

'He does all his own cooking,' she said. 'That pong is all his. It hums sometimes.'

I looked around the room and then turned to Miss Gowrie and said, 'Tell me, does your lodger have a small bump or bruise – a little swelling, say – right here on his upper forehead?'

'Yes – you've *seen* him,' she cried.

'Does he often wake you up in the middle of the night, padding around?'

'All the time! Gives me a fright sometimes. How do you know about his bruise –'

'And have you noticed that he cooks at night – only at night – not during the day?'

'Yes!' she said and clawed her hair straight.

'Your lodger is a very devout Muslim,' I said.

'Musselman?' she said, saying it like 'muscle-man', and frowning. 'I don't know about that. And as for devout –'

'Oh, yes,' I said. 'Muslim certainly, because he rearranged the furniture so that he could face Mecca – over there.'

Miss Gowrie peered in the direction of Mecca and, seeing only Barnes Common, made a face.

'– and taken down those pictures,' I said, examining a pair of framed prints stacked to face the wall: two busty ladies in black lace. 'They hate pictures of human beings.'

'Spanish,' Miss Gowrie said. 'They're the same as blacks!'

'Here's his prayer mat,' I said. 'And he must be devout because he has a prayer-bump on his forehead. The bruise – you've seen it. Also, if he wakes you up at night, he must be saying his prayers five times a day. They bump their heads when they pray.'

'He might not be praying – he might be cooking.'

'Of course. Because this is the Muslim period of Ramadhan. It's like Lent, and it goes on until the end of next month. He can't eat or drink anything until sundown. That's why he eats at, ah' – I had seen a small valise under the bed, and its luggage tag – 'Abdul Wahab Bin Baz. That explains it.'

Instead of looking relieved, Miss Gowrie had become progressively worried by the information I had given her. And then she said, 'Ain't you glad you come over?'

'Miss Gowrie, he's not one of ours,' I said.

'He's black,' she said.

'Arab.' The Saudia Airlines luggage tag said everything: he was a Wahabi, he had flown from Mecca to London. A fanatical traveller?

'Don't split hairs,' she said, and flung herself at me. She grasped my arm and exhaled the smell of bread and fishpaste.

'You know these people and their funny ways. You can help me. You're the only one who can. The police don't know about prayer bumps and eating after sun-down, do they?'

Instead of agreeing I asked her where her lodger was.

'College,' she said. 'It's a sort of night school. He goes out about six and comes back at nine. That's when he starts eating.'

'And praying presumably.'

'I wouldn't know about that,' Miss Gowrie said. 'During the day he just frowsts in here. Studies and that. He's a great reader. Mad about history. That's what he told me. That's all he told me.'

'How long has he lived with you?'

'Two weeks. I only discovered he was pinching things two days ago. He must have been at it all last week. I thought, then, out you go! But I reckoned he might be dangerous, him being a thief. That's why I called Charlie Smallwood, and he give me your name. You'd know what to do – that's what he told me. Only I wish you'd do it.'

'Let's have a look at his loot,' I said.

Miss Gowrie got slowly to her knees, saying, 'I used to have a proper charlady – I used to have staff,' and went on to say that she had discovered her lodger's thievery while she was cleaning out his room. It was under the bed, in a couple of cardboard boxes. She brought out the boxes, spitting with effort as she did so, and showed me the oddest collection of stolen goods I had ever seen.

There were two brass incense burners, properly called thuribles – they could have been a hundred years old. There was a brass lamp of oriental design and a pair of brass candlesticks. There was a metal crucifix and, lastly, a string of about twenty bells – round ones, about the size of golf balls, with a slit in each one. I had never seen any bells like this. Everything was thick with dust and coated with a kind of sour damp rind, as if it had lain on the floor of an underground cave. 'You think it's junk,' Miss Gowrie said, 'then you look closer and you realize it might be valuable. A little Brasso and a dry rag – come up a treat. But, if you get very close, it looks like junk again, and that's what it is. So why go to the police? All they're going to do is laugh and say, "Steady on, love." They won't treat it as a serious matter. But they don't have to live here, do they?'

'Maybe it's not serious,' I said.

'You're joking,' she said. 'This is diabolical. You don't get this in shops or houses. This ain't the kind of thing that fell off the back of a lorry. Go on, touch it.'

I took one of the bells and shook it. It had a dull sound, and no vibration – about as musical as a pebble hitting a coffin.

'Creepy, isn't it? Like from a church. I tell you, some of this stuff gives me the collywobbles, don't it?'

I knew what she meant. They weren't the sort of things that anyone would steal, and yet where could you buy them? So it had to be stolen, probably from a church, from a derelict altar – a Muslim fanatic might do that. But what about those little round bells?

It was too late to do anything that day. I left Miss Gowrie with a promise that I would try to get to the bottom of it, and the next morning, with the aid of a good map, made a list of all the churches near her Mortlake house. There were seven. My secretary phoned each one and asked whether anything had been stolen from them. All had been burgled, but not within the previous two weeks. We tried a dozen more nearby churches: no luck.

I was still not satisfied and so, that same afternoon, I went to the three churches nearest Miss Gowrie's. The Anglican church and Methodist chapel were both securely locked, but the Catholic church was open. I walked through it and into the deep grass of the churchyard.

'Can I help you?' It was a man with a broom, probably the caretaker, but he was suspicious of me and held his broom with the handle forward, like a weapon.

'Hello,' I said brightly, to calm him. 'Are you missing anything from the church – anything stolen? I'm thinking of things like candlesticks or crucifixes.'

'Not that I know of,' he said, and yet he had an undecided look. He wanted to say more – he had something on his mind.

I said, 'You're very lucky then,' to give him an opening.

'Not really,' he said. 'We've lost most of our outside lights – vandals. They broke every blooming one of them.'

He showed me that all the floodlights in the churchyard had been broken, and as it was also a graveyard, the effect on this grey afternoon was sombre, a sort of bleak and muffled violence.

'I'm amazed they could have broken lights that high,' I said. The spotlights were attached to the eaves of the church, thirty feet up.

'They're savages,' he said. 'They use pellets, catapults, blow-pipes.'

'Did you see them do it?'

'No, and I'll tell you something else,' he said. 'I've worked here at St Mary Magdalene's for twenty-two years, and it's the first time this has happened. The past two weeks have been terrible. Broken glass everywhere. It's so dark at night!'

'Two weeks?' I said, and thought of Mr Wahab.

'The first week was shocking. But this week hasn't been so bad. There's no more lights to break!' He looked at me in a disgusted way and said, 'You're an American, aren't you?'

I told him I was.

'You're used to this sort of thing – vandals, villains, queue-jumpers, law-breakers. But this isn't New York or Chicago. This is the quietest part of London. People behave themselves here. At least, they used to.'

We stood in darkness, because of the smashed lights. But this was the early daytime dark of November: it was not yet five o'clock. I decided to stop by the embassy before I went home.

I was at my desk, wondering whether to call Miss Gowrie to tell her I had found out nothing, when my colleague Vic Scaduto appeared. Seeing me examining one of those strange round bells that the lodger had stolen, Scaduto said, 'You've got the craziest things in your office. Last time I was here there was a funeral urn with a tourist's ashes in your Pending Tray. And now you're playing with a camel bell!'

'How do you know that's a camel bell?'

'Used to see them in India. Place is full of camels. My kids bought bells like that at the bazaar. They're sort of ceremonial – they loop strings of them around a camel's neck.'

I said, 'Can you think of any reason why you might find a camel bell like this is an English church?'

'I love it!' he said, and left my office, snickering.

Just before I went home, the phone rang. It was Miss Gowrie.

'Can you come over straightaway?' she breathed. 'He's just gone out.'

'Is there anything wrong?'

She said, 'There's another parcel, isn't there? He brought it back last night, then, didn't he? The dirty devil!'

'Don't open it. Don't touch it. I'll be right over.'

She was waiting for me by the door, her hands knotted in her apron. She told me to hurry, and started upstairs. Twice she called him a *dir'ee devoo* – 'And he might be back any minute.'

Mr Wahab's room was the same as before – very neat, the prayer mat facing Barnes Common and Mecca, a slight aroma of stale spice in the air, the pictures turned to the wall. After Miss Gowrie unlocked it, she stepped into the hallway to stand sentry duty while I opened the parcel under the bed. It was a pillowcase, its top twisted and held fast with a length of wire. It gave off the same dusty underground odour as the candlesticks and the crucifix and the camel bells. It seemed to contain sticks of wood and broken pottery wrapped in newspaper. I removed them and saw at once that they were bones – old, yellow, spongy, woody bones – and the cracked bowl of a skull, and a jawbone, and a number of loose human teeth.

'More of the same,' I said so as not to frighten her. And I wrapped them and returned them to the innocent-looking pillowcase.

'You'll help me, won't you?'

'I'll do my best,' I said.

I was relieved that she had not seen the contents of that new parcel, for I had always thought of myself as being fairly unshockable, and yet when I remembered those yellow bones and teeth and incense burners and camel bells under the bed of the Arab in that wet suburb of London, I got the shudders.

It was no longer a trivial, speculative matter about a troublesome lodger. The man from Mecca was, quite simply, a grave robber. Mr Wahab was a ghoul. Why hadn't I thought of it before? Though they looked like ecclesiastical items they could not have come from a church. But tombs, especially the larger ones, were often a kind of underground chapel, and had an altar furnished with candlesticks, and an incense burner and crucifix.

It was almost certainly a Catholic tomb – the crucifix said that. An old tomb – this stuff had lain undisturbed for a century. A large tomb, big enough to hold an altar, and one that could be entered through a door – if there had been digging it would have been seen and reported. The tomb was probably above ground. But what sort of a tomb contained camel bells?

This part of London was full of cemeteries – we had cremated Herbert Fleamarsh in nearby Kew. There were five important cemeteries not far from Miss Gowrie's house, and every church had a walled-in graveyard beside it. But only one of these churches interested me: it struck me that a grave-robber needed darkness to hide him, and if he did not have it he might break the sort of lights I had seen smashed at St Mary Magdalene's. But no theft had been reported there.

I did not want to see the caretaker again. He would wonder why I was back; he would be suspicious; he would ask awkward questions. I had no answers. So I let a day pass, and then I waited for the five o'clock darkness, and I entered the church-yard of St Mary's wearing a black coat and black gloves and looking left and right. I crept towards the vaults, the flat-topped granite huts with iron doors or sealed with stone blocks. They were unmarked, they were sadly neglected and overgrown with high bushes. Some were hidden in grass, others had almost burst from the ground or been yanked aside by the roots of the trees. I was behind the church and fighting my way through a tangle of bushes when I saw the tent.

It was a sort of oriental tent, perhaps Arab, with a slanting roof and high steep sides flowing from neatly scalloped eaves. I thought for a moment that I had stumbled upon a group of campers – people often pitched tents by the roadside or in parks (I could see them from the windows of my flat in Battersea) – why not in this graveyard?

But the tent was made of stone. It was white granite or marble, with carved folds, and it bore a tablet with the name *Captain Sir Richard F. Burton*. The explorer's tomb was the strangest I had ever seen.

I went close and tried the door. The putty surrounding the door, a marble slab, had been dug away. But a padlock on a rusty hasp remained. I shook the padlock and it came apart in my hand: it had been sawed through. So he had broken it – I was sure that this was the work of Abdul Wahab Bin Baz. A poem was chiselled into the marble just above the door. I turned my small flashlight on it.

Farewell, dear friend, dead hero, the great life
Is ended, the great perils, the great joys;
And he to whom adventures were as toys,
Who seemed to bear a charm 'gainst spear or knife
Or bullet, now lies silent . . .

What was that? A sound from the churchyard gate.

Crouching, I ran around to the back of the vault. It was not easy – trees grew close to it, and I scratched my face on a branch as I squeezed through.

At the rear of the tomb, overgrown with bushes and partly hidden by the thickness of black branches, was an iron ladder. It was fixed to the stone, it rose to the top of the tent-like roof. More to hide from the caretaker than to see where the ladder went, I climbed the iron rungs, and when I could not go any further I looked down in amazement. I was looking straight into the chamber of the tomb.

This tomb, this stone tent, had a window! It was thick glass and I could see in the narrow beam of my flashlight that it had not been tampered with. But I knew at a glance that the tomb had been plundered. A century of sunlight through this window had faded the stone walls in places and also printed on them the shadows of the objects I had seen in the Arab's room – the lamps, the crucifix, the string of camel bells. Where a thurible had been plucked from the dust a disc-mark remained, of its oval base. Only these shadows were left of what had once been in the tomb, except for the two coffins. They lay on the floor, at either side of a row of footprints. The larger coffin had been opened. Its lid, a fraction lopsided, had a freshly yanked nail at its end and showed a seam of darkness. But if I had not already seen Burton's bones, if I had not tried the lock that seemed so secure, I doubt that I would have noticed that the coffin lid was ajar or suspected any tampering. Even under the penetrating light of my pocket flashlight the tomb was very murky, and only serious scrutiny told me that it had been broken into. It was a terrible little coffin-room, it was dusty, it was cell-like; it gave me a good idea.

The Arab, Abdul Wahab Bin Baz, had to be stopped. Now I knew how.

It was no more than a short stroll, using the foot-bridge over the railway tracks, to a row of shops. In one of these, with a sign saying *Ironmongers*, I bought a large, flat padlock. It was very similar to the one the fanatic from Mecca had cut through in order to enter Burton's tomb.

It was now well after six. The church was shut, the gate was locked. I scaled the brick wall of the churchyard and took up my position at the top of the ladder, where I rested against the slanting window of the tomb. I was completely hidden; the grave-yard was as dark as the bottom of a deep hole. In a doggedly destructive way, by breaking all the churchyard lights, the Arab had guaranteed that I would not be seen.

I thought: What if he doesn't come back?

And yet, Isabel Burton's coffin had not been disturbed.

Later than I expected, after seven, when my knees were about to give out, I heard the thump of feet in the churchyard – someone had come over the wall. There was a swishing sound, of legs moving in brambles and grass. If it was Abdul, and if he entered the tomb, I would see him through the window. I heard nothing for a while, and then there was a slow millstone sound – the marble door being swung open. When he entered the tomb, I ducked, and I did not move again until some seconds later I heard the door being eased shut.

It was not closed entirely. I climbed down the ladder and dashed to the front of the tomb and kicked the door. At that moment there was a cry from the vault, but I was quickly straightening the hasp and clapping the padlock on. There was no sound from inside. The Arab was sealed in. No one would hear him. He had asked for this: and now he was buried alive.

If you knew he was there and you listened carefully you could hear a faint mewing, which was all that was audible of his wild screams through the thick marble walls of the tomb.

*

'I thought it was *him*,' Miss Gowrie said, opening the door and with a look of apprehension still on her face – fright takes a while to fade.

'He won't be back tonight,' I said. 'He may not be back at all.'

'He's out haunting houses, I expect.'

'Not exactly.'

'You come in and have a nice cup of tea,' Miss Gowrie said. 'Put your feet up. Look at the time! It's gone eight – you've had a long day.'

My day was not over. I told Miss Gowrie I had discovered where Wahab had stolen his brassware. I gathered up the objects and put them into a sack. I would return them to their rightful place, I said.

'May I sleep in Mr Wubb's room tonight?' I said.

'What if he comes back?'

'Not a chance,' I said.

'You never know with blackies,' she said.

In his stale bed, in that small room that smelled of carpet dust and prayer sweat, I thought about Abdul Wahab and it occurred to me why he had broken into Burton's tomb. It was simple revenge. Hadn't Burton, the unbeliever, trampled all over Islam? In this Muslim's eyes, hadn't the English explorer violated the sanctity of his religion by dressing up as an Arab and entering Mecca? Burton was no respecter of taboos or traditions – he had plundered the secrets of Islam in his search for adventure.

This was one Muslim's reply: the Arab dressed as an English gentleman, prowling undetected in London – as anonymous as Burton had been in holy Mecca. There was a crude justice in what the disguised Arab had done to Burton's bones in the Mortlake churchyard. This was a civilized country and a different century, but the smell in that bedroom was of dust and bones and the stink of prayer.

I had set my wrist alarm to wake me before dawn. It was still dark when I crept out of Miss Gowrie's house. I liked the thrill – carrying the brassware and camel bells and Richard Burton's bones through the damp chilly streets to the graveyard where the tomb had been opened.

There was no sound at the door of the vault. I went around back and mounted the ladder and shone my flashlight inside.

Wahab lay on the floor, sleeping on his side. He woke when I turned the light on his eyes. This was the first time I had really seen him.

His dark face had a stretched look of panic – the expression certain fish have in fishbowls: trapped and pop-eyed, with fat swollen lips. His eyes were red and puffy, and he was at the last stage of terror. He was limp, making pleading faces at me – or rather at the light, and blinking at the brightness of it. He would have confessed at that moment to being Leon Trotsky.

He clasped his hands and implored me.

I breathed on the window. The vapour condensed, and with my finger I traced a cross in it and shone my flashlight on it. It is the simplest of symbols, but to the man from Mecca it was strange and unwelcome, and I was sure that it made him more fearful than the darkness he had endured in that tomb all night. It was now safe to remove the padlock: I had announced myself as the avenging Christian.

As soon as the hasp was released he pushed the door open, and gasped – gave a whinny of fright – and then disappeared at the far end of the churchyard.

It was still dark. I had plenty of time to replace the thuribles, the lamps, the crucifix, and the camel bells, as well as Burton himself in his ornate and rotting coffin. Then I shut the door of the tomb and locked it. I had left everything just where it belonged in the tomb, as anyone could see.

9

THE MAN
ON THE CLAPHAM OMNIBUS
★

If Sir Charles Smallwood had not sent Miss Gowrie to visit me at the embassy, and if I had not helped rid this Mortlake landlady of her vengeful lodger, I would never had given this gentleman another thought. Miss Gowrie had called him 'Charlie'. She made me curious and she allowed me an excuse to see him.

We knew him vaguely. He was usually invited to our embassy parties and very often to dinners. He was, somehow, on the permanent guest list. But he was seldom a guest. He invariably turned down the invitations. I had seen him once, but only long enough to shake his hand – a damp, slack, small-boned hand. The only other thing about him that I could remember was that he had been wearing evening dress of an old-fashioned kind – bib and stiff collar, white scooped-out waistcoat, starched cuffs, black trousers and tails. He should have looked like a prince; in fact, he looked like a headwaiter, though he was not so poised. It was the functionaries, the waiters and doormen in London, who dressed correctly. The rest of us seldom did. Sir Charles wore his evening dress the way an old veteran wears a uniform for a regimental reunion. He looked uncomfortable in this stiff and slightly ill-fitting suit, and it also looked forty years out of date. I could not remember his face.

His address was in the computer, and his code-number – eight digits – explained why he was repeatedly invited to embassy functions. He was a very high grade of guest, the best English ally, a baronet from an old family.

Al Sanger, from the Legal Department, had shown me which keys to hit on the computer.

'If the British knew the kind of information we had on them in this thing, they'd deep-six every one of us,' Sanger said. 'Great grandfather's birthplace, maiden name, nanny's husband's political preference, criminal record, queerness quotient, shoe size, taste in underwear, magazine subscriptions, credit rating – do me a favour!'

Smallwood's name and code had come up and Sanger was scrutinizing the alignments of file references, the green letters and numbers.

He said, 'I don't even know this guy!'

He seemed angry with himself, so I said, 'It's nothing to be ashamed of. I only met him once.'

Sanger said, 'But there is the kind of guy we're *supposed* to know. It's why we're here!'

'Really?' I wondered if he believed what he had just said.

'Yeah – to meet the opinion-formers.'

'How do you know he's an opinion-former?'

'If you see a guy with a long white beard, wearing a red suit and carrying a bag of toys and saying, "Ho-ho-ho," you'd be pretty stupid if you didn't call him Santa Claus,' Sanger said. 'It's all in the profile. Look at Smallwood's. Look at those ratings. That's a pedigree and a half! Where'd you get his name?'

'From a little old lady.'

'That's funny, you know? We're in the business of information-gathering and you stand there uttering pointless jokes and tiresome evasions. Give me a break. I hate unreliable witnesses.'

'It's no joke. The little old lady's name is Miss Gowrie.'

'Let's find out her bust-size,' Sanger said, and leered at the computer's screen. 'We know everything.' Then, suddenly he shouted, 'He lives in Clapham!'

'What's so funny?'

'The man on the Clapham omnibus,' he said.

It was the first time I had ever heard this picturesque description. It brought to mind the vivid image of a thin-faced man sitting alone in an old double-decker bus – a bowler hat on his head, and brass rails on the stairwell, and posters advertising Players Weights and beef tea pasted on the freshly painted red sides; the man swaying as the bus rattled on hard rubber wheels down an avenue of brown cobblestones.

I said, 'It has a nice sound.'

'It just means "the man in the street" – it's a legal term here. In American law he's called the fair and reasonable man. Didn't you go to law school?'

'I haven't had your advantages, Al.'

'I can see that,' he said. 'Anyway, a lot of Foreign Service people have law degrees. See, they know the subtleties in the law, but how can you expect the man on the Clapham omnibus to know them?' And he grinned. 'See what I mean?'

'The average man,' I said.

'Right. A bloke, as they say here. Only this guy' – he was tapping the display panel of the computer screen, where Sir Charles Smallwood's paragraph was illuminated – 'this guy is no ordinary bloke. One thing's for sure. The Clapham address is a front. Probably a *pied à terre*. Baronets don't live in Clapham.'

He had no phone; or else it was unlisted. I wrote to him in Clapham, at the address shown on the computer, inviting him for a meal. He was prompt in refusing. I invited him for a drink. He replied saying he was tied up: he was going to be in the country for a few weeks. I liked 'in the country' – it meant out of town. I let those weeks pass. I wrote again. Was he interested in a pair of complimentary tickets to the London première of *Up North*, a black folk-opera performed by the Harlem Arts Collective? No, he was not. There was a practised politeness in his refusals – he was good, not to say graceful, even lordly, at declining invitations. His handwriting had a black and spattery loveliness. He was a hard man to raise.

This sharpened my desire to meet him, and in the interval I had discovered something about the Smallwoods. They were English Catholics – it said so on our computer. There is something faintly exotic about Catholics in England, something spooky and tribal and secretive. They worry people. They are like Jews in the United States, and they are seen in the same way, as outsiders and potential conspirators. They are feared and somewhat disliked, and they are always suspected of not supporting the protestant monarchy for religious reasons. The Smallwoods traced their ancestry back to the reign of Henry VIII, when they had been recusant – dissenters – and it was their boast that in four hundred years not a single day had passed without holy mass being celebrated in a secret chapel at Smallwood Park, in Hertfordshire. They were like early Christians: they were persecuted, they hid, they clung to their faith, they remained steadfast; and he was one of them.

He lived within walking distance of my apartment in Battersea –

up the road and just on the other side of Lavender Hill, on Parma Crescent. I walked past the house three times before summoning the courage to knock. The house was one in a terrace of twenty, two-up-two-down, with the shades drawn and two dustbins in the front garden – the other houses had rose bushes or hydrangeas. There was an unwashed milk bottle on the front step. Surely this was the wrong house?

Not seeing a bell or knocker, I rattled a metal flap on the letter slot and waited. After a moment there was a shadow on the glass of the door. The door opened, but only a crack, and from this a hidden face spoke to me, asking me what I wanted. It was the voice of a man muttering into a blanket.

'I'm looking for Sir Charles Smallwood.'

'No admittance on business,' the man said.

What did *that* mean?

'This isn't business,' I said. 'This is a social call.'

'And you are?'

I still could not determine whether the man I was speaking to was Sir Charles Smallwood. I had a feeling that he was some sort of manservant. He was tetchy and suspicious, and over-protective, and even – like some English servants I'd seen – domineering. I told him who I was and gave him my American Embassy calling card, with the eagle embossed on it in gold. It was specially designed by a team of psychiatrists to impress foreign nationals.

'Please wait there,' he said.

He shut the door and left me on the front doorstep, but less than a minute later I heard him shooting the bolt inside, and saw his shadow again on the glass, and the door was opened to me.

There was no hallway. I walked from his front step into his front room in one stride. And I was sorry now that I had come, because clearly this was the man's bedroom. There was a cot, and a chair beside it, and it was heated by an electric fire – the orange coils on one bar. It was not enough heat. On the floor, propped against the wall, was a very good painting in a heavy gilt frame. It was black and incongruous and instead of hinting at opulence it gave the room the air of a junk-shop.

I said, 'I hope I'm not intruding.'

'It is rather awkward – your coming unannounced. Will you have tea?'

'No, thank you. I can't stay.'

'As you wish.'

He wore a torn sweater and paint-splashed trousers and scuffed shoes. He might have been a deckhand, spending some time ashore in this small room. If this was Sir Charles's servant, he was being treated rather poorly. He had hair like pencil shavings, the same orangey woody colour, the same crinkly texture.

He said, 'Perhaps a glass of sherry?'

'I'd love one.'

He left the room and I had a chance to look it over more carefully. It was like a monk's cell; it was not improved by the old radio, the wilted geranium, or the narrow cot. I heard footsteps upstairs, a solid tread that banged against wooden planks in the ceiling. And there was a burring noise, like steam and bells, of a television behind the wall, in the next house. It was a hell of a place for a servant to sit, in this front room. I had the impression that there were a number of other people in the house – it was not only the feet on the floorboards above my head, but voices, and the sound of water humming through different pipes in the wall.

'Sorry I was so long,' the man said, when he returned. He handed me a glass of sherry. 'Couldn't find the right glass.'

It was crystal, with eight sides tapering to a heavy base, and it shimmered with a lovely marmalade glint, even in the pale dirty light of this room. A coat of arms was etched on one narrow plane. It was one of the most beautiful glasses I had ever seen. But I drank from it and nearly spewed. The sherry had a vile taste, like varnish, and its smell was like the fumes of burning plastic. Tears of disgust came to my eyes, and I tried to wink them away as I swallowed.

The man watched me. He was not drinking.

'It's awful to drop in,' I said. The man said nothing. He seemed to agree that it was awful. 'But this was the only address I had.'

'This is the only address. There is no other.'

I felt uncomfortable with him waiting there and watching. I wanted him to announce me to Sir Charles, or else to shuffle away in the direction of the noise – get those noisy fools to pipe down – so that I could empty the remainder of my poisonous sherry into the geranium pot.

Just then there was a shout above our heads. We both looked at the ceiling in time for the even sharper reply – an angry but incoherent complaint.

'They're at it again. Fight like cats.'

'Can't you do anything about it?'

'They wouldn't listen.' He was silent a moment. He tucked his hands under his sweater to warm them in the thickness of the folds. 'No, not them!'

'I don't think I could stand that.'

'You'd get used to it.' He said this in a firm school-masterish way, as if he was telling me something I didn't know but ought to.

I said, 'I wonder.'

'You would,' he said, 'if you had no choice.'

I was put off by his know-it-all tone and thought I had been kept waiting long enough. I had had too much bad sherry and peevish advice. I was going to say, *If you don't mind* –

But before my tongue could make that thought a complete sentence, he said, 'What was it you wanted?'

'I want to speak to Sir Charles Smallwood.'

'But I'm Charlie!'

You say, *Of course, what else?* It seems predictable, even perhaps an anti-climax. But only in hindsight do events seem inevitable. At the time, sitting in that monk's cell of a room under the tramping feet and humming pipes, it was the last thing in the world that I expected.

He saw the shock on my face. He said, 'Shall I explain?'

He told me about a man from an old family with a good name who, in the middle of his life, believed he had a curse on him. The man loved his family, but he felt they were to blame for the curse. It was a kind of hereditary illness – nausea sometimes. He was disgusted when he saw common red-faced wheezing men drink beer; his gorge rose when he saw their vicious hands – some of them seemed to have paws of peeling skin. He glanced at the men in horror. They stared back at him. He could not make friends with people who frightened him and, in his way, he suffered.

119

The things he owned had sentimental value but they were also quite useless. He owned a magnificent portrait of an ancestor, but it was so heavy it could not hang on the wall of his tiny house. He owned a boar's head with curved tusks that had been in the family for generations; various family histories – a shelf of books; some silver plate, a chalice and glassware which, under the terms of the legacy, he could not sell or dispose of (who wanted that family crest, anyway?); some old documents on vellum, and odds and ends of no value – Bibles, photographs, enormous latchkeys, some splinters of saints' bones, and a linen scrap from a martyr's winding sheet.

He had no education, apart from two years at Eton. He still owned some of his Eton clothes, and he was lucky that his tails still fitted him – he had not grown at all after being withdrawn from the school at the age of fifteen. He had worn out his cricketing flannels, but not by playing cricket. He still had some of his tweeds. What clothes he had were various school uniforms. But no occasions arose when these uniforms were suitable – only a party now and then, but that was all, because only the grandest parties required him to wear black tie.

The family collapse had come quickly. The death of his father, and then his mother – within six weeks of each other. There had been no time to make any financial arrangements at all. Tax demands were made, some were met; Death Duties – awful pair of words – remained unpaid. There was no more money. The house had belonged to the family for almost five hundred years. It was sold to an Australian who boasted that he was the great-grandson of a pickpocket who had been transported to Botany Bay.

The children were shocked. Instead of legacies being handed out, debts were apportioned. They had never lived in much style, but now each of the children – there were four – found that he was nearly destitute and owed a considerable amount of money. Everything was gone; there was nothing more to sell. The children felt as though they had been turned into debtors and would soon be hunted down.

They consulted solicitors and were given a certain amount of reckless advice. 'Leave the country at once,' a man said. His name was Horace Whybrow. 'Turn yourselves into a limited company and then declare the company bankrupt,' a Queen's Counsel said.

His name was Dennis Orde-Widdowson. They remembered the names because the advice was so dire, and the solicitors' bills put them further into debt.

The children found that, by separating, living in different parts of London and letting matters drift, they could survive. And yet this man, who was the eldest child, who had inherited his father's title, had also inherited the greatest part of the debts – this man often felt as if there was a tide of debt and disgrace rising around him. He was up to his neck. There was no one who would help him, no one who would understand.

He moved to Mortlake and lived in an upper room of a house which at times seemed to suffocate him. He had black moods. He lived with the blinds drawn. The landlady was kind, but she was no help – she too was down on her luck.

He felt he had to kill himself. He did not want to.

Wouldn't someone else in his position understand? Not exactly in his position, but a member of the aristocracy, the withered part of it, from an old family, with a meaningless title like baronet, and an important title like doctor. He knew that if he did not explain his suffering to someone soon, he would not have to kill himself – he would be too ill to prevent himself from dying.

Then a man was found. He had a small title. He was a member of the Scottish aristocracy, and his name was The Honourable Alastair Colquhoun. He was a National Health doctor. Every person, even an aristocrat, had a right in this country to see a psychiatrist, free of charge.

The doctor was sympathetic to his new patient, who seldom ate and seldom went outdoors. The doctor encouraged him to go to parties, although there were very few parties the man could go to wearing white tie and tails.

'I'm cursed,' the patient said. 'It's a trap.'

The doctor smiled. He had a beautiful, noble face. The patient felt he could have kissed that man without any shame – and he knew he wasn't queer. He felt safe in the doctor's presence.

Doctors are the most practical of men, and psychiatrists the most practical doctors. They deal in the obscure but make it obvious, and they treat it with common sense. They argue on behalf of the patient. They are the friends we all ought to have for nothing. They take their time, they are slower than lawyers, they have a kind of selfish patience. This Doctor Colquhoun listened, saying very little at first. When he did speak he said sensible things, such as, 'There are no curses. There are no traps, except the ones we make for ourselves. Your future is up to you. Don't confuse debts with faults. Life can be messy, but you don't change it by worrying –'

Clichés of that sort had a calming effect.

'My ancestors are in the history books,' the patient said.

'My ancestors wrote those books,' the doctor replied.

'But I'm a lodger in Mortlake!'

'Barnes is right next door to Mortlake.' The doctor lived in Barnes.

The patient talked about his family, his feeling of having lived under a curse – the instincts that went with his title. He was burdened by having to be this person without being able to accomplish anything. He said that sometimes he felt that he was the only man in Britain who did not believe in an hereditary title. It was as silly as a belief in reincarnation! What was this naïve trust in a family name?

But, when the doctor mentioned friends, the man said, 'I have none,' and when he mentioned working-class people, the man said, 'I hate them.' He told the doctor that he could not help feeling the way he did – he had been born like this.

'As if you were born somewhat malformed?'

'No,' the man said, 'as if I was born perfect. As if everyone else was malformed.'

He could see that this shook the doctor a little.

The patient said, 'I've never said these things before to anyone.'

'I've never heard them before,' the doctor said.

'Perhaps they don't matter.'

'Of course they matter!' the doctor said. He was indignant, in a sulking aristocratic way. Some of these Scots were frightfully grand.

'But what can I do about it?'

The doctor said, 'You must tell me everything.'

The rest was bleak. It was the man incapable of making a friend or finding a job or paying the family debts. It was the humiliation of being weak and exposed, like a dream he had of finding himself naked in a public place. He despised people for their common-looking faces and the careless way they spoke. Seeing them eat made him sick. He could not bear to watch anyone eat, he said. And there were sights just as bad – hearing people laugh out loud, watching them blow their nose, seeing their underwear on a clothesline. And he hated seeing their old shoes.

The doctor said, 'I think I know what you mean.'

He told the doctor everything. He felt much better as a consequence. He knew now that he could not change his situation, but talking about it he felt less burdened. It did seem at times immensely complicated; but he was not imagining the curse – there really was a curse on him. It was a curse to have to live like an average man. He felt like a fallen angel, for wasn't this poverty truly like a fall from grace?

These visits to the National Health psychiatrist became his life – the life he had been born to. This was enough society for him. The doctor was, of course, an aristocrat. He was intelligent, he was a model of refinement. The way he smoked cigarettes convinced you he was a deep thinker, and very neat and economical. In a world they knew as squalid and unequal they faced each other as equals, and often at the end of a session the doctor offered his patient a glass of good sherry.

Warmed and made optimistic by the wine, the patient could forget the curse of the family name that had hobbled him so badly. Now it did not seem so cruel that he had been born an aristocrat. He had found a way out of this trap. The doctor was his social equal! And the doctor was excellent company. This wasn't therapy or the confessional feeling of well-being. This was like meeting for drinks.

'We have a great deal in common,' the patient said, and was pleased.

'A very great deal,' the doctor said, after pausing a moment. He seemed reluctant to admit it, and said no more.

'Before I met you, I didn't know which way to turn. I used to think about killing myself!'

'How do you feel now?' the doctor asked.

'I feel I have a friend who understands.'

'None of this had ever occurred to me before,' the doctor said. He went on to explain that he had never thought much about the burden of the past, or upholding the reputation of an old name, or the snobbery-nausea, an instinct which was the worst curse of all.

'I'm glad we met,' the patient said.

The doctor did not reply. In recent weeks he had seemed somewhat inattentive. Now and then he was late for his appointments with the patient. Often he cut the session short; sometimes – though rarely – he did not show up at all.

But it did not matter to the patient that the doctor no longer offered his common sense as advice, or that he fell silent when the patient spoke and remained silent long after the patient had finished. It seemed to the patient like perfect discretion. They really were frightfully grand!

His satisfaction was that, having told the doctor everything, he felt well. It was much better than confession, because each time it had become easier – there was less to confess.

There was no cure, but the humiliation, which was painful, could be eliminated. They had met as doctor and patient on the National Health, but they recognized each other as gentlemen.

The patient's depressions ceased altogether. The following week the session was cancelled. It was one of the doctor's no-shows. He was ill – that was the story.

It was a lie. The doctor was dead.

The *Times* obituary was three inches: *The Hon. Alastair Colquhoun*, it said, *Pioneer in Mental Health*.

'He hanged himself,' Sir Charles Smallwood said. 'And that's why I'm here like this. Under the circumstances, I feel I'm doing rather well, though there are those who doubt it. And sometimes people pity me.'

'Take no notice of them,' I said.

'They don't bother me a bit,' he said. 'Honi soit qui mal y pense.'

★ 10 ★
SEX AND ITS SUBSTITUTES
★

When people said, 'Miss Duboys has a friend,' they meant something sinister, or at least pretty nasty – that she had a dark secret at home. Because we were both unmarried and grade FSO-4 at the London embassy we were often paired up at dinner parties as the token singles. It became a joke between us, these frequent meetings at embassy residences. 'You again,' she would say, and give me a velvet feline growl. She was not pretty in any conventional way, which was probably why I found her so attractive. Her eyes were green in her thin white face; her lips were over-large and lispy-looking, her short hair jet-black, and you could see the rise of her nipples through her raincoat.

It took me a little while to get to know her. There were so many people eager to see us married, we resisted being pushed into further intimacy. I saw a lot of her at work – and all those dinner parties! We very quickly became good friends and indeed were so tolerant of each other and so familiar that it was hard for me to know her any better. I desired her when I was with her. Our friendship did not progress. Then I began to think that people were right: she probably *did* have a secret at home.

The facts about her were unusual. She had not been to the United States in four years – she had not taken Home Leave, she had not visited Europe, she had not left London. She had probably not left her apartment much, except to go to work. It made people talk. But she worked very hard. Our British counterparts treated hard workers with suspicion. They would have regarded Margaret Duboys as a possible spy for staying late all those nights. What was she really doing? people asked. Some called her conscientious, others obsessed.

There was another characteristic Miss Duboys had that made the London embassy people suspicious. She bought a great amount of food at the PX in Ruislip. She made a weekly trip for enormous quantities of tax-free groceries, but always of a certain kind. All our food bills were recorded on the embassy computer, and Miss

Duboys' bills were studied closely. Steaks! Chickens! Hamburg! She bought rabbits! One week her bill was a hundred and fourteen dollars and forty-seven cents. Single woman, tax-free food! She was a carnivore and no mistake, but she bought pounds of fish, too. We looked at the computer print-out and marvelled. What an appetite!

'People eat to compensate for things,' said Everett Horton, our number two, who perhaps knew what he was talking about: he was very fat.

I said, 'Margaret doesn't strike me as a compulsive eater.'

'No,' he said, 'she's got a very sweet figure. That's a better explanation.'

'She's thin – it doesn't explain everything!'

'She's pretty,' Horton said. 'She's living with a very hungry man.'

'Let's hope not,' I said, and when Horton leered at me, I added, 'For security reasons.'

She had completely reorganized the Trade Section; she dealt with priority trade matters. It was unthinkable that someone in such a trusted position was compromising this trust with a foreigner who was perhaps only a sexual adventurer. It is the unthinkable that most preoccupies me with thought. Or was she giving all the food away? Or, worse, was she selling it to grateful English people? They paid twice what we did for half as much and, in the past, there had been cases of embassy personnel selling merchandise they had bought at bargain prices at the American PX: they had been sent home and demoted, or else fired – 'terminated' was our word. We wondered about Miss Duboys. Her grocery bill was large and mystifying.

The day came when these PX print-outs were to be examined by some visiting budget inspectors from Washington.

Horton, who knew I was fond of Miss Duboys, took me aside that morning.

'Massage these figures, will you?' he said. 'I'm sure they're not as lumpy as they look.'

I averaged them and I made them look innocent. And yet still they startled me. All that food! For any other officer it would not have looked odd, but the fact was that Miss Duboys lived alone. She never gave dinner parties. She never gave parties. No one had ever been inside her house.

There was more speculation, all of it idle and some of it rather cruel. It was worse than 'Miss Duboys has a friend'. I thought it was baseless and malicious and, in the way that gossip can do real harm by destroying a person's reputation, very dangerous. And what were people saying about me? People regarded her as 'shady' and 'sly'. 'You can't figure her out,' they said, meaning they could if you were bold and insensitive enough to listen. And there was her 'accident' – doubting people always spoke about her in quotation marks which they indicated with raised eyebrows. It was her hospital 'scare'. Miss Duboys, who was a 'riddle', had been 'rushed' to the hospital 'covered with bruises'. The commonest explanation was that she 'fell', but the general belief was that she had been beaten up by her mysterious room-mate – so people thought. If she had been beaten black and blue no one had seen her. Al Sanger claimed he saw her with a bandaged hand, Erroll Jeeps said it was scratches. 'Probably a feminine complaint,' Scaduto's wife said. When I squinted she said, 'Plumbing.'

'Could be another woman,' Horton said. 'Women scratch each other, don't they? I mean, a man wouldn't do that.'

'Probably a can of tuna fish,' Jeeps said.

Al Sanger said, 'She never buys cans of tuna fish!'

He, too, had puzzled over her grocery bills.

Miss Duboys did not help matters by refusing to explain any of it: the grocery bills, the visit to the hospital, no Home Leave, no cocktail parties, no dinners. But she was left alone. She was an excellent officer and the only woman in the Trade Section. It would have been hard to interrogate her and practically impossible to transfer her without being accused of bias. But there were still people who regarded her behaviour as highly suspicious.

'What is it? Horton asked me. 'Do you think it's what they say?'

I had never heard him, or any other American Embassy official, use the word 'spy'. It was a vulgar, painful and unlucky word, like 'cancer'.

'No, not that,' I said.

'I can't imagine what it could be.'

'It's sex,' I said. 'Or one of its substitutes.'

'One of the many,' he said.

'One of the few,' I replied.

He smiled at me and said, 'It's nice to be young.'

The harsh rumours, and the way Miss Duboys treated them with contempt, made me like her the more. I began to look forward to seeing her at the dinner parties, where we were invariably the odd guests – the unmarried ones. Perhaps it was more calculated than I realized; perhaps people, seeing me as steady, solid, with a good record in overseas posts, thought that I would succeed in finding out the truth about Miss Duboys. If so, they chose the right man. I did find out the truth. It was so simple, so obvious in its way, it took either genius or luck to discover it. I had no genius, but I was very lucky.

We were at Erroll Jeeps' apartment in Hampstead. Jeeps' wife was named Lornette which, with a kind of misplaced hauteur, she pronounced like the French eyeglasses, 'lorgnette'. The Jeeps were black, from Chicago. A black American jazz trumpeter was also there – he was introduced as Owlie Cooper; and the Sangers – Al and Tina; and Margaret Duboys, and myself.

The Sangers' dog had just come out of quarantine. When he heard that it had cost three hundred dollars to fly the dog from Washington to London, and close to a thousand for the dog's three months at the quarantine kennel in Surrey ('We usually visited Brucie on weekends'), Owlie Cooper kicked his feet out and screamed his laughter at the Sangers. Tina asked what was so funny. Cooper said it was all funny: he was laughing at the money, the amount of time, and even the dog's name. 'Brucie!'

The Sangers looked insulted, they went into a kind of sulk – their eyes shining with anger – but they said nothing. You knew they wanted to say something like, 'Okay, but what kind of a name is Owlie?' But Owlie was black and it was possible that Owlie was a special black name, maybe Swahili, or else meant something interesting, which – and this was obvious – Brucie didn't.

Unexpectedly, Margaret Duboys said to Cooper, 'Taking good care of your dog – is that funny? People go to much more trouble for children. Look at all the time and money that's wasted on these embassy kids.'

'You're not serious,' Cooper said. 'I mean, what a freaky comparison!'

'It's a fair comparison,' Margaret said. 'I've spent whole evenings at the Scadutos' listening to stories about Ricky's braces. Guess how much they cost the American taxpayer? Three thousand dollars! They sent him to an orthodontist at the American base in Frankfurt –'

'I'm thinking of going there,' Lornette Jeeps said. 'I've got this vein in my leg that's got to come out.'

'They didn't even work!' Margaret was saying, 'Skiddoo says the kids still call him Bugs Bunny. And Horton's kid, eight years old, and he's got a bodyguard who just stands there earning twenty grand a year while Horton Junior plays "Space-Invaders" at these clip-joints in Leicester Square –'

'It's an anti-kidnap measure,' Erroll Jeeps said. 'It'd be easy as shit for some crack-head in the I R A to turn Horton Junior into hand-luggage –'

And then the two Sangers smiled at each other, and while Margaret continued talking, Al Sanger said, 'We're pretty fond of Brucie. We've had him since Caracas –'

There were, generally speaking, two categories of bore at the embassy dinner parties: people with children, and people with animals. Life in London was too hectic and expensive for people to have both children and animals. When they did, the children were teenagers and the animals disposable – hamsters and turtles. One group had school stories and the other had quarantine stories – and they were much the same: both involved time, money, patience and self-sacrifice.

'You certainly put up with a lot of inconvenience,' I said to one woman with a long story.

'If that's what you think, you completely missed my point,' she said.

She was proud of her child – or perhaps it was a puppy.

Margaret Duboys was still talking!

I said, 'Are we discussing brats or ankle-biters?'

'It's still Brucie,' Tina Sanger said.

'Give me cats any day,' I said, sipping my gin and trying to keep a straight face. 'They're clean, they're intelligent and they're selfish. None of this tail-wagging, no early-morning sessions in the park, no "walkies". Dogs resent strangers, they get jealous, they get bored – they stink, they stumble, they drool. Sometimes dogs turn on you for no reason! They revert! They maul people, they eat children. But cats only scratch you by accident, or if you're being a pest. Dogs want to be loved, but cats don't give a damn. They look after themselves, and they're twice as pretty.'

'What about kids?' Al Sanger said.

'They're in-between,' I said.

Calvin said, 'In-between what?'

'Dogs and cats.'

Margaret Duboys howled suddenly. A dark laboured groan came straight out of her lungs. I had a moment of terror before I realized that she was just laughing very hard.

I had been silly, I thought, in talking about cats that way, but it produced an amazing effect. After dinner, Miss Duboys came up to me and said in a purr of urgency, 'Could you give me a lift home? My car's being fixed.'

She had never accepted a ride from me before, and this was the first time she had ever asked for one. I found this very surprising, but I had a further surprise. When we arrived at her front door, she said, 'Would you like to come in for a minute?'

I was – if the embassy rumours were correct – the first human being to receive such an invitation from her. I found it hard to appear calm. I had never cared much about the embassy talk or Miss Duboys' supposed secrets; but, almost from the beginning, I had been interested in offering her a passionate friendship. I liked her company and her easy conversation. But how could I know anything about her heart until I discovered her body? I felt for her, as I had felt for all the women I wanted to know better, a mixture of caution and desire and nervous panic. A lover's emotions are the same as a firebug's.

There was a sound behind the door. It was both motion and sound, like tiny children hurrying on their hands and knees.

'Don't be shocked,' Miss Duboys said. She was smiling, she looked perfectly serene. In this light her eyes were not green but grey.

Then she opened the door.

Cats, cats, cats, cats, cats, cats –

She was stooping to embrace them, then almost as an after-thought she said, 'Come in, but be careful where you step.'

There were six of them, and they were large. I knew at once that they resented my being there. They crept away from me sideways, seeming to walk on tiptoe, in that fastidious and insolent way that cats have. Their bellies were too big and detracted from their handsomeness. Why hadn't she told anyone about her cats? It was the simplest possible answer to all the embassy gossip and speculation. And no one had a clue. People still believed she had a friend, a lover, someone with a huge appetite, who sometimes beat her up. But it was the cats. That was why she had not left Britain for the duration of nearly two tours: because of the quarantine regulations she could not take her cats, and if she could not travel with them she would not travel at all.

But she had not told anyone. I was reminded then that she had never been very friendly with anyone at the embassy – how could she have been, if no one knew this simple fact about her that explained every quirk of her behaviour? She had always been remote and respectful.

That first night I said, 'No one knows about your cats.'

'Why should they?'

'They might be interested,' I said, and I thought: Don't you want to keep them from making wild speculations?

'Other people's pets are a bore,' she said. She seemed cross. 'And so are other people's children. No one's really interested and I can't stand condescension. People with children think they're superior or else pity you, and people with cats think you're a fool, because their beasts are so much better behaved. You have to live your own life – thank God for that.'

It was quite an outburst, considering that all we were talking about were cats. But she was defensive, as if she knew about her mysterious reputation and 'Miss Duboys has a friend' and all those coarse rumours.

She said, 'What I do in my own home, in my own time, is my business. I usually put in a ten-hour day at the embassy. I think I'm entitled to a little privacy. I'm not hurting anyone, am I?'

I said, no, of course not – but it struck me that her tone was exactly that of a person defending a crank religion or an out-of-the-way sexual practice. She had over-reacted to my curiosity, as if she expected to be persecuted for the heresy of cat-worship.

I said, 'Why are you letting me in on your little secret?'

'I liked what you said at Erroll's – about cats.'

'I'm a secret believer in cats,' I said. 'I like them.'

'And I like you.' She was holding a bulgy orange cat and making kissing noises at it. 'That's a compliment. I'm very fussy.'

'Thanks,' I said.

'It's time for bed,' she said.

I looked up quickly with a hot face. But she was talking to the cat and helping it into a basket.

We did nothing that night except drink. It had got to the hour – about half-past two – when to go to bed with her would have been a greater disappointment than going home alone to Battersea. I made it look like gallantry, I said I had to go, tomorrow was a working day; but I was doing us both a favour, and certainly sparing her my blind bumbling late-night performance. She seemed to appreciate my tact, and she let me know with her lips, and a flick of her tongue, and her little sigh of pleasure that someday soon, when it was convenient, I would be as welcome in her bed as any of her cats.

Cat-worship was merely a handy label I had thought of to explain her behaviour. Within a few weeks it seemed an amazingly accurate description, and even blunt clichés such as *cat-lover* and *cat-freak* seemed to me precise and perfectly fair. Cats were not her hobby or her pastime, but her passion.

I got to know her garden apartment. It was in Notting Hill, off Kensington Park Road, in a white building that had once been (I think she said) the residence of the Spanish Ambassador. Its ball-room had been subdivided into six small apartments. But hers was on the floor below these, a ground-floor apartment opening into a large communal park, Arundel Gardens. The garden, like the apartment and most of its furnishings, was for the cats. The rent was twelve hundred dollars a month – six hundred pounds. It was too much, almost more than Miss Duboys could afford, but the cats needed fresh air and grass and flowers, and she needed the cats.

On her walls there were cat calendars, and cat photographs, and in some rooms cat wallpaper – a repeated motif of crouching cats. She had cat paperweights and cat picturebooks, and waste-baskets and lampshades with cats on them. On a set of shelves there were small porcelain cats. There were fat cats stencilled on her towels, and kittens on her coffee mugs. She had cats printed on her sheets and embroidered on her dinner napkins. Cats are peculiarly expressionless creatures, and the experience of so many images of them was rather bewildering. The carpet in the hall was cat-shaped – a sitting one in silhouette. She had cat notepaper, a stack of it on her desk (two weeks later I received an affectionate message on it).

And she had real cats, six of them. Five were nervous and malevolent, and the sixth was simple-minded – a neutered, slightly undersized one which gaped at me with the same sleepy vacuity as those on the wall and those on the coffee mugs. The largest cat weighed fifteen or twenty pounds – it was vast and fat-bellied and evil-spirited, and named Lester. It had a hiss like a gas-leak. Even Margaret was a bit fearful of this monster, and she hinted to me that it had once killed another cat. Thereafter, Lester seemed to me to have the stupid, hungry – and cruel and comic – face of a cannibal.

There was nothing offensive in the air, none of that hairy suffocation that is usual in a catty household. The prevalent smell was of food, the warm buttery vapour of home-cooking. Margaret cooked all the time, her cats had wonderful meals – hamburg in brown gravy, lightly poached fish, stews that were never stretched with flour or potatoes. Lester liked liver, McCool adored fish, Miss Growse never ate anything but stews, and the others – they all had human-sounding names – had different preferences. They did not eat the same thing. Sometimes they did not eat at all – did not even taste it but only glanced and sniffed at the food steaming in the dish and then walked away and yowled for something else. It made me mad: I would have eaten some of that food! The cats were spoiled and over weight and grouchy – 'fat and magnificent', Margaret called them. Yes, yes; but their fussy food habits kept her busy for most of the hours she was home. Now I understood her huge shopping bills. She was patient with them – more patient than I had ever seen her in the embassy. When the cats did not eat their food she put it into another dish and left it outside for the strays – the London moggies and the Notting Hill tom-cats that prowled Arundel Gardens. Why the other dishes? 'My cats are very particular about who uses their personal dishes!'

I said, 'Do you use the word "personal" with cats?'

'I sure do!'

And one day she said, 'I never give them cans.'

It was the sort of statement that caused me a moment of unnecessary discomfort. I ate canned food all the time. What was wrong with it? I wanted to tell Margaret that she was talking nonsense: Good food, fresh air, no cans! Me and my cats!

No, absolutely no cans – the cats drew the line there – but they were not particular about which chairleg they scratched, or where they puked, or where they left their matted hairs. They sharpened their claws on the sofa and on the best upholstered chairs, and went at the wall and clawed it and left shredded, scratched wallpaper, like heaps of grated cheese on the carpet. The cats were not fierce except when they were protecting their food, or were faced with the London strays; but they were very destructive – needlessly so, and it made me angry to think of Margaret paying so much money for rent and having to endure the cats' vandalism. She did not mind.

I only made the mistake of mentioning this once.

She replied, 'But children are a hundred times worse.'

I said, 'How does it feel to have six children?'

If it seemed that way, she said – that they were like children – then how did it seem from the cats' point of view? I thought she was crazy, taking this line (look at it from the cats' point of view!), but she quoted Darwin. She said that Darwin had concluded that domesticated animals which grew up with people regarded human beings as members of their own species. It was in *The Voyage of the Beagle*, where the sheep-dogs treated sheep in a brotherly way in Argentina. From this, it was easy to see that cats regarded us as cats – of a rather inconvenient size, but cats all the same, which fed them, and opened doors for them, and scratched them pleasantly behind their ears, and gave them a lap to sit on, and pinched fleas from around their eyes and mouths, and wormed them.

'Darwin said that?'

'More or less?'

'That cats think we're cats?'

'He was talking about dogs and sheep, but, yes,' she said uncertainly. With conviction she added, 'Anyway, these cats think I'm one.'

'What about their natural instincts?'

'Their instincts tell them no, but their sympathies and learning experience tell them yes. These cats are sympathetic. Listen, I don't even think of them as cats!'

'That's one step further than Darwin,' I said.

By now I knew a great deal about Miss Duboys' cats, and quite a lot about Miss Duboys. We had spent the past five Sundays together. Neither of us had much to do on the weekends. It became our routine to have Sunday lunch at an Indian restaurant, and after a blistering vindaloo curry to return to her apartment and spend the afternoon in bed. When we woke, damp and entangled, from our sudden sleep – the little death that follows sex – we went to a movie, usually a bad, undemanding one, at the Gate Cinema near Notting Hill tube station. Sunday was a long day with several sleeps – the day had about six parts and seemed at times like two or three whole days – all the exertion, and then the laziness, and all the dying and dreaming and waking.

London was a city that inspired me to treasure private delights. Its weather and its rational, well-organized people had made it a city of splendid interiors – everything that was pleasurable happened indoors, the contentment of sex, food, reading, music, and talk. Margaret would have added animals to this list. When she woke blindly from one of these feverish Sunday sleeps, she bumped me with an elbow and said, 'I'm neglecting my cats.'

She had no other friends. Apart from me (but I only occupied her one day of the week), her cats were the whole of her society, and they satisfied her. It seemed to me that she was slightly at odds with me – slightly bewildered – because I offered her the one thing a cat could not provide. The cats were a substitute for everything else. Well, that was plain enough! But it made me laugh to think that for Margaret Duboys I represented Sex. *Me!* It made life difficult for us at times, because it was hard for her to see me in any other way. She judged most people by comparing them with cats. In theory this was trivial and belittling, but it was worse in practice – no one came out well, no one measured up – no humans that she knew were half so worthwhile as any of her cats.

'I make an exception in your case,' she told me – we were in bed at the time.

'Thanks, Marge!'

She didn't laugh. She said, 'Most men are prigs.'

'Did you say *prigs*?'

'No, no' – but she dived beneath the covers.

Usually she was harder on herself than on me. She seemed to despise that part of herself that needed my companionship. We saw each other at parties just as often as before, because we concealed the fact that we had become lovers. I was not naturally a concealer of such things, but she made me secretive, and I saw that this was a part of all friendship – agreeing to be a little like the other person. Margaret thought, perhaps rightly, that in an informal way the embassy would get curious about our friendship and ask questions – certainly the boys on the third floor would keep us under observation. So we never used the internal embassy phones for anything except the most boring trivialities. There was plenty of time at the dinner parties for us to make plans for the following Sunday. People were still trying to bring us together! When I did phone her, out of caution I used the public phone-box near my apartment, in Prince of Wales Drive. Those were the only times I used that phone-box, and entering it – it was a damp, stinking, vandalized cubicle – I thought always of her, and always in a tender way.

She was cat-like in the panting gasping way she made love, the way she clawed my shoulders, the way she shook, and most of all in the way she slept afterwards, as though on a branch or an outcrop of rock, her legs drawn up under her and her arms wrapped around her head, and her nose down.

I don't think of them as cats – a number of times she repeated this observation to me. She did not theorize about it, she didn't explain it. And yet it seemed to me the perfect reply to Darwin's version of domestic animals thinking of us as animals. The person who grew up with cats for company regarded cats as people! Of course! Yet it seemed to me that these cats were the last creatures on earth to care whether or not they resembled an overworked FSO-4 in the Trade Section of the American Embassy. And, if that was how she felt about cats, it made me wonder what she thought about human beings.

We seldom talked about the other people at work, or about our work. We seldom talked at all. When we met it was for one thing, and when it came to sex she was single-minded. She used cats to explain her theory of the orgasm: 'Step one, chase the cat up the tree. Step two, let it worry for a while. Step three, rescue the cat.' When she failed to have an orgasm she would whisper, 'The cat is still up the tree – get her down.'

From what she told other people at dinner parties, and from embassy talk, I gathered that her important work was concerned

136

with helping American companies break into the British market. It was highly abstract in the telling: she provided information about industrial software, did back-up for seminars, organized a clearing-house for legal and commercial alternatives in company formation, and liaised with promotional bodies.

I hated talking to people about their work. There was, first, this obscure and silly language, and then inevitably, they asked about my work. I was always reminded, when I told them, of how grand my job as Political Officer sounded, and how little I accomplished. These days I lived from Sunday to Sunday, and sex seemed to provide the only meaning to life – what else on earth was so important? There was nothing to compare with two warm bodies in a bed: this was wealth, freedom, and happiness; it was the object of all human endeavour. I was falling in love with Margaret Duboys.

I also feared losing her, and I hated all the other feelings that were caused by this fear – jealousy, panic, greed. This was love! It was a greater disruption in the body than an illness, but though at certain times I actually felt sick I wanted her so badly, at other times it seemed to me – and I noted this with satisfaction – as if I had displaced those goddamned cats.

It was now December, the days were short and clammy-cold; they started late and dark, they ended early in the same darkness, which in London was like faded ink. On one of these dark afternoons Erroll Jeeps came into my office and asked whether he could have a private word with me.

'Owlie Cooper – remember him?'

'I met him at your house,' I said.

'That's the cat,' Erroll said. 'He's in a bind. He's a jazzhead – plays trumpet around town in clubs. Thing is, his work permit hasn't been renewed.'

'Union trouble?'

'No, it's the Home Office, playing tough. He thought it would just be routine, but when he went to renew it they refused. Plus, they told him that he had already overstayed his visit. So he's here illegally.'

'What can I do?'

'Give me a string to pull,' Erroll said.

'I wish I had one – he seemed a nice guy.'

'He laughs a little too much, but he's a great musician.'

My inspiration came that evening as I walked across Chelsea Bridge to Overstrand Mansions and my apartment. I passed the public phone-box in Prince of Wales Drive and thought: Owlie Cooper was a man with a skill to sell – he made music, he was American, he was here to do business. He had a product and he was in demand, so why not treat it as a trade matter, Margaret?

I saw her the next day and said, 'There's an American here who's trying to do business with the Brits. He's got a terrific product, but his visa's run out. Do you think you can handle it?'

'Businessman,' she said. 'What kind of businessman?'

'Music.'

'What kind?' she said. 'Publishing, record company, or what?'

'He makes music,' I said. 'Owlie Cooper, the jazzman we met at Jeeps' house.'

Margaret sighed and turned back to face her desk. She spoke to her blotter. 'He can get his visa in the usual way.'

'We could help him sell his product here,' I said.

'Product! He plays the trumpet, for Pete's sake.'

'Margaret,' I said, 'this guy's in trouble. He can't get a job if he hasn't got a work permit. Look, he's a good advertisement for American export initiative.'

'I'd call it cultural initiative. Get Scaduto. He's the Cultural Affairs Officer. Music is his line.' Then, in a persecuted voice, she said, 'Please, I'm busy.'

'You could pull a string. Skiddoo doesn't have a string.'

'This bastard Cooper –'

'What do you mean, "bastard"? He's a lost soul,' I said. 'Why should you be constantly boosting multinational corporations, while a solitary man –'

'I remember him,' Margaret said. 'He hates cats.'

'No, it was dogs. And he doesn't hate them. He was mocking Al Sanger's dog.'

'I distinctly remember,' she said stiffly, 'it was cats.'

There was a cat-like hiss in her cross voice as she said so.

She said, 'People will say I don't want to help him because he's black. Actually – I mean, funnily enough – that's why I do want to help him – because he's black and probably grew up disadvantaged. But I can't.'

'You can!'

'It's not my department.'

I started to speak again, but again she hissed at me. It was not part of a word but a whole warning sound – an undifferentiated hiss of fury and rebuke, as if I was a hulking brutish stranger. It embarrassed me to think that her secretary was listening to Margaret behaving like one of her own selfish cats.

It was the only time we had ever talked business, and it was the last time. Owlie Cooper left quietly to live in Amsterdam. He claimed he was a political exile. He wasn't, of course – he was just one of the many casualties of Anglo-American bureaucracy. But I felt that in time he would become genuinely angry and see us all as enemies; he would get lonelier and duller and lazier in Holland.

Two weeks later I was calling Margaret from a telephone booth, the sort of squalid public phone-box which, when I entered it, excited me with a vivid recollection of her hair and her lips. She began telling me about someone she had found in the house quite by chance, how he had stayed the night, and eaten a huge breakfast, and how she was going to fatten him up.

I had by then already lost the thread of this conversation. I had taken a dislike to her for her treatment of Owlie Cooper. I hated the stink in this phone-box, the broken glass and graffiti. What was she talking about? Why was she telling me this?

I said, 'What's his name?'

'Who?'

'The person who spent the night with you.'

'The little Burmese?' she said. 'I haven't given him a name yet.'

My parting words were ineffectual and unmemorable. I just stopped seeing her, cancelled our usual date, and that Sunday I spent the whole day bleeding in my bedroom. She hardly seemed to notice, or else – and I think this was more likely – she was relieved that I had given up.

★ 11 ★

THE HONORARY SIBERIAN
★

One day I returned to my apartment at Overstrand Mansions and found a case of vodka outside the door – a dozen bottles of Stolichnaya Green Label. A week later it was a basket filled with small jars of caviare. Neither of these gifts contained notes or any indication of the name of the sender. But there was no question of my keeping them. I brought them to the embassy and put them in storage – in the same basement room in which we kept the originals of hate-letters and the left-behind umbrellas – and I had their existence entered in the Duty Officer's log. The next parcel was a box of chocolates, and the last one an imitation leather wallet. One thing was clear; whoever was leaving these things was running out of money.

'You have a secret admirer,' Everett Horton said. 'It's got to be a Russian. They're noted for their subtlety. Like German jokes, like Mexican food. A few years ago one of our guys on the third floor was approached by a Tass correspondent. They had lunch – our man was wired up. The Russian offered him money for information. Just like that – can you imagine. They still play the tape of the conversation upstairs for laughs.'

'What should I do, coach?'

Horton said, 'I'd put him on Hold.'

The next week there was no gift at my door. There was a phone call.

'My name is Yuri Kirilov,' the man said. 'You know me.'

I did know him, in the same way that millions of people in the West know Soviet defectors. But Kirilov's defection – in the middle of a television programme on the BBC – had been spectacular.

'Please to meet my wife,' Kirilov said, as I threw my lunch-bag into the litter-bin next to the bench. We were at the Piccadilly side of Green Park.

I was embarrassed for him, because this woman gave me a hot

adoring look, and took my hand. She said, 'You have beautiful eyes,' and kept staring.

Under the circumstances there was nothing I could say except 'Thank you' and 'Yuri didn't tell me he was married'.

'He is ashamed!'

I said, 'If I were married to you I'd never stop boasting about you.'

It was exaggerated and insincere, but what else could I say? She had made a little melodrama out of being introduced to me in Green Park and I was doing my best to turn it into a farce. Spouses who flirted in front of their partners seemed to me dangerous and stupid, and Helena – that was her name – had taken me by surprise. Kirilov had not mentioned his wife. He merely said that he urgently wanted to see me – somewhere quiet. I suggested my office at the embassy. He said, 'Not that quiet.' I suggested the Serpentine, which I often walked around at lunchtime. 'Green Park,' he said. 'Is better.' *Grin Park*: he had not been out of the Soviet Union very long.

'I must kiss him for these compliments,' Helena was saying. 'Take my photo, Yuri.'

Kirilov obediently snapped a picture as Helena sat me down beside her and threw her arms around my neck. We were, for a few seconds, the classic canoodling pair, kissing on a park bench.

'I like the taste!' Helena said. 'One more time, please.'

I tried to restrain her, but it did little good. I was sure that the photograph of this embrace probably looked much more passionate. The kiss made it seem a private moment.

'There is lipstick on your mouth,' she said. 'Your boss will be very shocked!'

I said, 'It would take more than this to shock my boss.'

'What if he knew it was Russian lipstick?' Helena said.

'He'd send me to Siberia,' I said.

'I would follow you,' Helena said.

I expected Kirilov to hit her, but all he said was, 'I was in Siberia. I write my novel in Siberia. With a little pencil. With tiny sheets of paper. More than eight hundred sheets, very tiny – very small writing, two hundred words to a sheet. I bring it here. It is *Bread and Water*. No one want to read it!'

'Siberia?' I said. 'Were you in a labour camp?'

'No,' he said impatiently. 'Writers' Union! They send me to Siberia to make books.'

Helena said, 'In Soviet Union, Yuri is famous. Have money. But here, not so famous!'

Kirilov looked rueful. 'I am honorary Siberian for my work,' he said. 'I can sell two hundred thousand copies of novel.' He made an ugly face. 'This is nothing. Others can even sell half a million. Even if I go to a shop I hear people say, "Kirilov, Kirilov," and pulling my sleeve. Moscow shop.'

Helena said, 'Pop star,' and smiled foolishly at him.

'In Soviet Union I have a car,' Kirilov said. 'Is better than that one.'

Now we were sitting on the bench, and Kirilov turned and pointed to a maroon Jaguar. He then let his tongue droop and with big square thumbs snapped his camera into its leather case.

Helena said, 'He have no car in London.'

'I don't have a car either,' I said.

'But you have a job,' Kirilov said. 'You have money. You can do what you like. I have nothing.'

'You have freedom,' I said.

'Hah! I have freedom,' Kirilov said. He twisted his mouth and made it liverish and ugly. 'All I have is freedom, freedom. Too much, I can say.'

Friddom: he made it sound like persecution.

'Is better more money,' Helena said. Each time she mentioned money her face became sensual. She spoke the word hungrily, with an open mouth and staring eyes. It occurred to me that you could know a great deal about a person by asking him to say, 'Money'.

Kirilov turned to her and said clearly in English, 'Now we make our discussion. So you go, Leni. Be careful – people can do tricks to you.'

Before she left, Helena said to me, 'You can come and visit me.'

'Perhaps I'll visit you both,' I said.

'Yes, that's nice,' she said, and made a soft sucking noise with her pursed lips.

When she was gone, Kirilov said, 'She likes you.'

'That's nice,' I said. But I wanted to say, How do you stand this damned woman?

'She never likes anyone before in London,' he said. 'But you – she like.'

'She's a very nice person,' I said.

Kirilov laughed. He said, 'No. She is very pretty. With big what-you-can-call. But she is not nice person. We say, she is like a doll – pretty face, grass inside.' He winked at me. 'Also like an animal.'

'I see.'

'She love to buy clothes. English clothes. American clothes. Blue-jeans. In Soviet Union, I buy clothes, clothes, clothes. I have money. I have respect. But here' – he made his ugly face again – 'nothing.'

'It takes time,' I said. 'You're luckier than some. There was a man here a few years ago who asked for political asylum like you, but before he was in the clear they drugged him – your embassy people – and sent him back.'

'He is not so unlucky,' Kirilov said.

'They might have killed him,' I said.

'You are like children – you believe anything,' he said. 'Maybe it was a trick. Just fooling the British. He is not unlucky. But I am very unlucky. These shoes – how much you think they cost?'

'Thirty-two pounds,' I said.

I must have guessed right, judging from his expression. He said, 'In Soviet Union, not more than ten pounds. And my rent! I have a tiny small flat here. Is better for a dog. I pay sixty-seven pounds a week. In Soviet Union I pay twenty for the same square metres. Is ridiculous in London.'

'Mr Kirilov,' I said, 'I thought you had something urgent to discuss with me.'

'Yes,' he said, then pettishly, 'But why you refuse me to have lunch?'

Dinner had been his first suggestion, lunch his second – 'I pay for you,' he had said. And I knew then that he wanted a favour. I wasn't interested in eating with him, and we had compromised on Green Park. If he had been any other Russian I would have refused to meet him, but he was enough of a celebrity to be harmless.

His defection, as I said, had been spectacular. He had been on a television programme with his interpreter, who was also his security man. And then, in the middle of the programme (something about writing and politics), Kirilov had simply stood up and walked off-camera, while the security man gaped. That was his defection. The clip of Kirilov hurrying away behind the wooden walls of the set, the security man squinting stupidly, was shown on the BBC many times, always with an hilarious effect, for it was known that, minutes after making a run for it, Kirilov had gone into hiding, in the depths of Kent. A week later he was granted political asylum.

Kirilov was not a political dissident. He was a defector, a well-known Soviet poet, a party man, a womanizer. He had always claimed that he was free to criticize Soviet life. He had made numerous trips to foreign countries. He was thought to be safe. He was well-connected. He went to writers' conferences, not only in eastern Europe, but also in the west – in Stockholm, Paris, and Milan. He had been to Cuba five times. His poems had been translated by the American poet, Walter Van Bellamy, and it was at Bellamy's house in Kent that he had hidden on the day of his defection. Anyone who read a newspaper knew these facts about Yuri Kirilov, and it was easy to tell from Kirilov's attitude on the telephone that he expected people to know him. He had the celebrity's easy presumption. He was on good terms with the world. I must have stammered or hesitated on the phone, because he had said, 'You know me.'

But he was annoyed that I had refused his invitation to lunch and I think he objected to our sitting on this park bench in the middle of a grey winter afternoon. He had imagined something grander, and he sat tetchily on the bench, making fastidious plucks at his trouser creases and fussing with his cuffs and his camera, and looking left and right.

I said, 'We can have lunch some other time.'

'You Americans,' he said. 'Always in a hurry. No time for relaxing. Even the British – so famous for their good manners. They behave like pigs, I can say.'

'That's nice, coming from you. I'm sure they'd love to hear you say it.'

'It is true. They are pigs.'

'When you ran away they gave you a place to hide. They let you stay. They could have sent you back. You'd be in Siberia, with your ass in a crack.'

'Siberia is lovely place! I am honorary citizen of Siberia!'

'You're an honorary citizen of Britain, too.'

He said, 'I am propaganda-value. I am worth millions. You saw the newspaper – "Famous Soviet Writer Chooses Britain." All of that. It is good for the British government. They would never have sent me back.'

'So you think you're valuable?'

'Millions,' he said, curling his lower lip and fattening it boastfully. 'I am not like some of these dissidents – troublemakers, cripples, Jews. Listen, I tell you they make trouble in any society – *any*. Solzhenitsyn! He is a trouble in Soviet Union. Yes, he is also a trouble in United States. You hear how he criticizes Americans – journalists, drugs, pop music. He is against!'

'Can you blame him?'

Kirilov laughed, snapping his jaws in the air. 'I can blame him! I like journalists, I like pop music, and some drugs I can say so what.'

'Then you must be very happy in London.'

'I am deeply unhappy, my friend. This is a terrible country, a corrupt country. So many people unemployed. No work. And how the people live! In small rooms, very cold rooms, eating bad food, taking the tube. Aargh! I hate.' He batted the air with his hands, pushing these images aside.

'Siberia must have been much better.'

He considered this, he nodded, he had not heard any sarcasm.

'I can say, yes, better. In Siberia I am a VIP. Here I am nothing. No one to publish Russian books, no one to read. I go to the library, I drink with Walter Bellamy, I look for money. Nothing, nothing, nothing. Better VIP in Siberia than nothing in London. There are flowers in Siberia!'

'It was your choice,' I said.

'Helena's choice,' he said. He winked at me. 'She likes you very much. You know?'

'She seems happy here.'

'Happy, yes. Because I let her do whatever she like' – he nudged me hard with a sharp elbow – 'whatever make her happy. Anything.'

'I see.'

'*Anything*,' he said. 'I am not a jealous man. She is very beautiful. Like an animal, I can say. Is cruel to make her unhappy. You think she is wild?'

'It's hard to tell,' I said, and now I was sure I wanted to walk away.

'In public park she is wild –'

'Yes, yes.'

'– but in bed, in bed she is a slave,' Kirilov said. 'A slave.' He watched my face closely, leering at me and waiting for me to react.

I was determined not to. I saw what he was offering me, but he stopped short of saying *Take her* –

Perhaps he noticed my impatience, because his face hardened.

I said, 'What do you want?'

'Brodsky,' he sneered. 'Brodsky has been declared a genius.'

'I haven't got the slightest idea what you're talking about.'

'Joseph Brodsky – Jew dissident – living in New York, good jobs teaching at three universities, nice place to live, plenty of money for bad poems. He writes his poems in a tiny room in Soviet Union. Fine. Good. Everyone say, "Good work – maybe a little decadent." Then he hate Soviet. He go to New York and "Please, mister, give me money for write poems in New York." This scumdrill have plenty of money, but he want more. To write bad poems! Then! American foundation say, "Brodsky is genius"' – he pronounced it *jayn-yoos* – ' "we will give him money! Forty thousand dollars, every year, for five years." Brodsky! Scumdrill!'

Kirilov was shouting. He had stood up, and his shrill voice penetrated through the roar of the traffic. The wind had risen, and it rattled the branches overhead, it pulled at Kirilov's coat, it yanked his trousers against his skinny legs and white ankles, making him look weak.

I said, 'I don't know anything about it.'

'Is in library, *New York Times*. Is your country. If you don't know about it I feel sorry for you. But I think it is an injustice.'

'This is the last time I ask you,' I said. 'What do you want?'

'You must give me a visa for New York City.'

'I'm not in the consular section.'

'You know the poet Bellamy. Famous American poet. He will vouch for me. He will sponsor me.'

'Bellamy's in the hospital,' I said. 'Anyway, you've already been turned down for a visa.'

'For what reason I want to know!'

'We're not obliged to give you a reason.'

He sat down beside me again – his shouting had tired him. He was a bit hoarse. He said, 'You can help me. They will believe you. Bellamy says you are the only honest man in the embassy – that's why I phoned you up. You have a reputation for being a fair man. That's why Helena is so attracted to you. She can't help it – she admires your honesty.'

I said, 'Do you know the word "bullshit"?'

'You are trying to insult me,' he said.

'You're wasting your time. If you had told me half an hour ago that you wanted a visa I could have saved you a lot of trouble. It's impossible.'

He said, 'It is not I who am insulted – it is my wife. You simply toss her away like a worthless thing.'

'Be careful,' I said.

His face darkened. 'Then you will be sorry.'

'Don't threaten me,' I said. I was smiling.

He said, 'You think you can mock me!'

'No, I was just thinking that you offered me lunch. All this might have been taking place in a restaurant. I would have had indigestion! Excuse me,' I said, and stood up. 'I have to go back to my office.'

'I have pictures of you with my wife!' he said. He shook the camera at me. 'I will send them to the newspapers. Hah!'

'It will be very embarrassing for you,' I said. 'In this country, pimping is a criminal offence. I would imagine that if the authorities heard that you'd been pimping for your wife they'd ship you both back to the Soviet Union.'

'That is a disgraceful lie,' he said. 'And you have no proof.'

'I've been recording our conversation,' I said.

He laughed. 'No, you haven't. When Leni kissed you she examined your clothes for a recorder. She found no wires, or she would have told me!'

I moved to the end of the bench and dipped my hand into the litter-bin. I retrieved the soiled lunch-bag I had thrown in, and took a small tape-recorder out of it. It was still whirring softly. I stopped it, rewound it, then pressed the *Play* button.

'*. . . ship you both back . . .*'

'You are disgusting,' Kirilov said.

I said, 'Get a job.'

I knew then that this honorary Siberian would spend the rest of his life as a refugee – unemployed, uttering threats, and pitying himself. He had actually believed that I would help him – perhaps sleep with his wife, or be tempted to collaborate with him in his flight to America. How old-fashioned the Soviets were in their quaint belief in blackmail! But Kirilov believed in nothing, really, which is why he was so ignorant. A more passionate man, a believer, would have been far more resourceful.

But he was right about this man Brodsky. The dissident who had written wonderful poems in prison (jailed for 'social parasitism') he had found that he could not produce a thing in New York for less than forty thousand dollars a year. And he *had* been declared a genius by the MacArthur Foundation, which would pay all his bills for five years. It was a bit like being an honorary Siberian, really, but the pay was better.

★12★
GONE WEST
★

They appeared to be husband and wife – man standing, woman seated: the classic married pose of Authority flanked by Loyalty – but when I got closer I saw they were both men. It was just after eight in the morning, a smudgy winter dawn in London, on the embassy stairs. The doors would not be open to the public for another hour. I mounted the stairs but couldn't get to the door without asking the man who was standing to move aside. He made a respectful noise, then spoke.

'We're going to America!'

Americans call it the States.

I said, 'You'll need visas.'

'That's why we're here,' the seated one said.

'You should be at the other door – the consulate, visa section. It's right around the corner, on Upper Grosvenor Street.'

The news that they were waiting at the wrong door didn't upset them. They laughed, as the English often do in such situations. They said, 'Silly old us!' and 'What a wheeze!'

It seemed to be a national characteristic. The English had been getting bad news for so long they had learned to cope. They disliked complainers, even when the complaint was justified, and regarded such people as spineless. Most of the English seemed rather proud of their capacity for suffering. It made them the world's best airline passengers, but had given them one of the world's worst airlines. Surely this 'mustn't grumble' attitude accounted for a great deal of Britain's decline? But of course it made the place nice and quiet. Our vices are so often our virtues as well.

'You must be cold,' I said.

'Absolutely freezing.' This was said, with one eyebrow raised, in the most matter-of-fact tone.

'Never mind. We'll soon be in California.'

'Fat lot of good that's doing me now,' the matter-of-fact one said.

'Oh, we're going to have a little moan, are we?'

'Listen to him – after his blameless weekend!'

'You said you were impervious to cold.'

'On your bike! I never said impervious – don't know what the flipping word means!'

This was all spoken with sharpness and speed, and the effect was comic – friendly, too – even in the misty brown dawn of a January morning. From that moment I began to wonder what would happen to them in California.

The dark-haired one, who was standing, faced the fairer one, who was still seated, and said, 'Lambie here got me up at the crack of dawn. Said we had to hurry – frightened me with stories about long queues and red tape. So off we go to stand at the wrong door! Feel me cheeks. They're solid ice! I haven't even had tea!'

'Forgot our thermal underwear, didn't we, chicken?'

'I'm wearing me serviceable string vest.'

I said, 'How about a coffee inside?'

This made them go very silent. They seemed a bit suspicious. But I had noticed that a kindness to an English person often arouses unease or suspicion. It is a very nervous nation. In a wary voice, the dark-haired one said, 'Do you think it'd be all right?'

'What about security? Laser beams and that,' the other said. 'You must get ever so many bomb scares.'

I said, 'You don't look very dangerous to me.'

'Him – he's the dangerous one,' the dark-haired man said. 'Oh, he's a hard lad!'

They followed me in – our Security Man squinting at them and giving their colourful shoulder-bags a close inspection for weapons – and I heard one of them say, 'Laser beams, you daft prat!'

The coffee urn was outside Al Sanger's office. This morning there was a plate of Danish pastries next to the urn. Sanger often bought them at a place off Curzon Street – deliberately there, so that he could say, 'I just picked up some tarts in Shepherd Market. Want one?'

I poured three cups of coffee and urged them to take some pastry.

'Don't mind if I do!'

'Our first American breakfast.'

So they had overcome their suspicion. I said, 'It's part of our job to encourage tourism.'

150

'It's lovely and warm in here.'

'Think I'll put me feet up!'

Their names, they said, were Cary and Lamb. Cary had the dark hair, and broad shoulders, and he had a tiny Irish chin and a high sweet voice. Lamb at first glance was a young man with reddish hair, but looking closer I saw he was quite old – over sixty – with rather nasty blue eyes and his hair harshly coloured and coarse-textured and spread across his crown to cover his baldness. He wore an earring, and Cary had a heavy chain around his neck.

Lamb said, 'You actually work here, do you?'

'Course he works here, you pillock!'

I said, 'But I can't give you much help with your visas.'

'We won't have any trouble,' Cary said. 'We've never been communists or prostitutes, and we haven't been in the nick. That's the kind of thing they want to know, don't they? We've been good lads, haven't we, Lambie?'

'Apart from your occasional lapses of taste,' Lamb said.

'Listen to the incurable cottager!' Cary shrieked. He pulled a pack of cigarettes out of his back pocket. But his trousers were so tight the cigarettes were squashed and unsmokeable. He said, 'There's another packet of fags gone west.'

'About time you gave up smoking. It'll stunt your growth.'

'Aren't you happy with me growth, Lambie?'

They both laughed at this. I couldn't see the joke, but the sight of them laughing so easily amused me.

'What are you planning to do in the States?'

'We're going to California,' Lamb said.

'I mean, after you get there.'

'We don't have any plans for after that. We're going to California a special way – an ingenious way. It's Cary's big plan, see. He does have the occasional brilliant scheme.'

'I'd like to hear it,' I said.

Cary had thrown his squashed cigarettes into the waste-paper basket. Now he was bent over the basket and reaching in, trying to retrieve them.

'Look at him,' Lamb said. 'Fossicking in the waste-paper basket!'

'I see one,' Cary said.

'He sees one,' Lamb said, rolling his eyes. 'Picking up fag-ends – can't take him anywhere.'

It was a double-act. They were spirited and mocking, and they kept it up until my secretary arrived. They found her presence intimidating, and they asked whether they should go. I said they shouldn't hurry away, and I kicked the door shut.

Lamb heard her tuning the radio for the news. There was a moment of music.

'Music,' he said. 'Oh, be still my dancing feet!'

'Give over,' Cary said.

'Tell him your brilliant scheme.'

'Yes, mum,' Cary said, and grinned and gave himself dimples, as he looked at me. 'We're second-hand furniture dealers, the kind of rubbish that innocent people call antiques. We find the stuff all over the place. You've seen the signs. "House Clearances Our Speciality."'

Lamb said, ' "Top Prices Paid for your Unwanted Furniture." '

Cary frowned. He said, ' "That Old Chest in your Attic Could Be Worth a Fortune." '

'Cary specializes in old chests. You have to watch him.'

'You flaming wally!' Cary said and, turning back to me, he said, 'It's absolute balls about the top prices, but we buy what we can afford, mainly tables, benches, mirrors, picture frames and that. Windsor chairs. Welsh dressers if we're lucky.'

'There's an awful lot of lifting,' Lamb said, 'I've done me back in I don't know how many times.'

'He's the original Welsh dresser, is Lambie,' Cary said. 'Aren't you, sunshine?'

'You're just saying that because you like me drawers.'

'That's what we should have called the shop, you know – "Chests and Drawers".'

'Do me a favour!' Lamb said in an actressy voice.

But I noticed that everything they said, no matter how mocking, was tinged with what sounded like real affection.

I said, 'What is your shop called?'

' "Pining for You" – isn't it horrid? We hate it,' Lamb said. 'We used to do stripping in our tank, to order. Anything you wanted stripped – within limits – we'd chuck in.'

Cary said, 'There's a boom in stripped pine in London at the moment. You get knackered scrubbing the paint off, but you can sell anything if it's stripped. We got top whack for a coffin once.

152

Can you imagine someone buying an old coffin? I suppose some clapped-out Dracula –'

'We've got a lot of American customers. They adore our refectory tables,' Lamb said. 'Or any sort of shelving. They're mad on shelving over there.'

'"Mad on shelving" – you make them sound a pack of flaming morons, Lambie.'

'Well, they are,' Lamb said, timing his pause after that word, 'mad on shelving.'

'Americans buy quality,' Cary said.

'Crawler!' Lamb said. 'You're shameless!'

Cary said, 'And that's what gave me the idea of the lorry. Did you know you can ship a lorry across the Atlantic and it costs the same whether it's full or empty?'

'That's Cary's brilliant scheme. We're going to take a lorry-load of country pine furniture to California.'

'And flog it,' Cary said, 'To pay our way.'

'We reckon on making a tidy fortune on it.'

'Don't tell me too much,' I said. 'If you do, I'll have to advise you about the regulations governing the import of dutiable goods.'

'Muggins put his foot in it,' Lamb said.

'Oh, belt up,' Cary said. But he was laughing.

'I won't report you,' I said. 'But you'd better go get your visas. The consulate opens pretty soon.'

'Crikey, I feel better. I needed that coffee. You're awfully kind,' Cary said.

'You're welcome,' I said.

'That's nice, isn't it? "You're welcome." English people never say that.' He looked at Lamb and said, 'You're welcome, sunshine.'

'Send me a postcard,' I said.

'We'll do better than that,' Lamb said. 'We'll report back.'

'When English people go to California,' I said, 'they either come back the next day or stay there for the rest of their lives.'

Lamb said, 'I wonder what we'll do.'

'You could do both,' I said. 'After all, there are two of you. Each one could –'

'There's only one,' Cary said. 'I mean to say, we're sticking together.'

Lamb gave Cary an affectionate push and Cary lowered his eyes.

I noticed again the great difference between their ages. Cary's neck was loose and the roots of his hair were grey and his hands were mottled with liver spots. But his voice and his gestures, the promptness of his wit, made him seem youthful.

'That's the idea,' I said. 'Stick together.'

'He's my wife,' Cary said. 'Aren't you, petal?'

I never thought I would see them again. I imagined them crossing the United States in an old English truck loaded with pine furniture – Cary at the wheel, Lamb riding shotgun, going west.

Of all the get-rich-quick schemes I had ever heard – and I had heard many – this was the best. It was a truckload of furniture, but they paid only for the truck. This would transport them to California, and the sale of the furniture paid for the trip. It had everything – sunshine, freedom, a good product, a free ride and a guaranteed profit. It had taken a little capital, but even more enterprise; and it gave me hope. Whenever London went dead on me, whenever I thought of ditching my job and clearing out, I thought of Cary and Lamb in their truck, with their pine furniture, bumping down the highway underneath a big blue sky. It made me want to get married and go.

I was sure they would wind up in San Francisco, overstay their visas, and go to ground. Many Europeans did these days – it was only Arabs who had the confidence to head home when their visas expired. I had met the two men in early January. In late February, the security man at the main entrance phoned me and said, 'A Mr Cary and friend down here, sir. Doesn't have an appointment – name's not in the book – but he says he wants to talk to you. What shall I tell him, sir?'

A Mr Cary and friend: they were back!

'Send them up,' I said.

But Lamb was not the friend, and I barely recognized Cary. He was thinner, he had grown a beard, and he was dressed like a man in the English Department bucking for a promotion – tweed sports jacket, leather tie, corduroy trousers, argyll socks and shiny shoes. He was a far cry from the junk-dealer in the ragged scarf and flat cap and greasy raincoat of six weeks ago. Some people look worse, much stranger, even crooked, when they dress stylishly. That was how Cary seemed to me – as if he was trying to pull a fast one on me. He was frowning, pushing out his lips, jerking his beard with his cheeks.

And the friend was a girl with a big soft face, who chewed gum with her mouth open. She wore a man's pea-jacket and a woolly hat. Cary introduced her to me as 'Honey'.

There are some nicknames that are obstacles to friendship. 'Honey' is one of them. At first it seems over-affectionate, and then it seems like mockery, and finally it sounds like a word of abuse.

Cary was holding her hand. He did not let go of it, even to smoke. He shook out a cigarette, put it to his lips and lit it, all with one busy hand. In itself his hand-holding was not strange, but he had never once touched Lamb.

I said, 'I'm glad you kept your word about giving me a report.'

Cary didn't smile. He sat stiffly in his chair with a look of vague incomprehension on his face.

'Just stopped in to say hello,' he said. 'And to introduce you to Honey.'

The girl snapped her gum at me and said, 'Cary told me how you helped him' – she was American – 'and he really appreciated it. Usually embassy people are such assholes. I remember once when I was in Mexico.'

Cary coughed and said, 'You must be busy.' He looked as if, already, he wanted to go.

'Tell me about the trip,' I said.

'There's so much to tell.'

'The crossing,' I said. 'What was the ship like?'

'I was seasick most of the time. It was a Polish freighter, full of butch sailors. The food was dreadful – turnips, swedes, cabbage, boiled cabbage, stews of rancid mince. It was a week of misery. I stayed in my bunk the whole time.'

'What about your friend?'

'Pardon?'

'Lamb,' I said.

'Oh, him. He started acting strange. He'd disappear for hours and then when I asked where he'd been he'd say, "In the bowels of the ship." He thought he was being incredibly funny.'

I smiled, remembering Lamb, imagining how he would have said that. Where was the little old comedian? – Where was the old Cary, for that matter? This one was entirely new – disapproving and full of seriousness. He was grave, but what was the point?

'It wasn't funny,' Cary said. 'He was always cracking jokes. When people who aren't funny start to make jokes it sounds stupid.'

His accent was gone, too.

I said, 'New York must have been quite a surprise.'

Cary shrugged. 'Lamb met a chap in a bar, and got very excited. "He's giving us a place to kip – he's got bags of room!"' It was a flash of the old Cary – he did Lamb's effeminate voice very well, and it reminded me of how his own voice had deepened. He glanced at the girl whose hand he was holding and said, 'The chap was into S and M. Well, "S" really. Very keen on spanking. "How do you know you don't like it if you've never tried it?"'

'How did you get out of that one?' I asked.

'A cobbler's bench and a lot of pleading. I reckon he's cobbling someone on it right this minute.' He weighed the girl's hand in his own, lifting it and considering it. 'Hungry?'

Honey squeezed her face into an expression that said, 'Sorta,' and Cary said to me, 'We have to go. I promised to show Honey around the neighbourhood where I grew up – Stepney Green.'

'But what about your scheme?' I asked. 'What about the trip?'

'Don't ask. The lorry broke down on the New Jersey Turnpike. Turnpike! Why is it that the most horrid places in the States have the prettiest names?'

'Like Stepney Green – the jewel of East London?'

Cary did not respond to that. He said, 'We were towed to a garage. It seemed we needed a water-pump. Two hundred for the tow, another two hundred for the pump. Nice round figures. We hadn't a penny.'

'How did you pay?'

'A refectory table, lovely it was, from a boys' school in East-bourne. It was covered with carved initials, some of them going back to the eighteenth century. Just the thing for a garage mechanic in New Jersey.'

I had the strong sense that I did not know this man at all; that we were talking about nothing; that he did not know me.

'The radiator packed up in Virginia, on something called "The Skyline Drive" – Lamb loved the name. The radiator cost us a beautiful Victorian chest – two drawers, and brass fittings, lots of carvings.' He looked at Honey again and waggled her hand and said, 'Hi.'

'Hi,' she said.

'Bored?'

She snorted a little air.

He kissed her. I felt I was watching someone taking a bite of candy. He licked his mouth when he finished kissing her.

'Let's go,' she said.

'So you didn't make it to California?' I said.

'We did, after a fashion. By the time we got to Missouri we'd traded most of the big pieces. And, over the next three weeks, the rest of it went, to buy petrol and food. We slept in the lorry. It was getting emptier and emptier. Pretty soon, all the best pieces were gone. We'd turned them into cheeseburgers.'

'Not all of them,' Honey said. She surprised me. Her voice was brighter than Cary's, and a little malicious and lively.

'Where are you from?' I asked.

'Pomona?' She made it a polite question, as some uncertain Americans do, when they give information. 'I go outside one morning and who do I see in the front yard but these two English guys.'

'So you met Mr Lamb,' I said.

'And his friend,' she said.

'Not me,' Cary said in a disgusted way. 'It was a chicken he found in Arizona. A hitch-hiker. "Oh, let's pick him up – he looks lost!" ' Cary squinted at me, giving me a powerful look of indignation, and he said, 'Lamb was really beastly to that kid. It was a revelation to me.'

Honey said, 'They were fags.'

Cary swallowed and said, 'I think he's sick. I think he's strange. I think he lost his bottle.'

Now Honey was smirking. 'My first husband is into English antiques. They really hit it off.' She uttered a coarse laugh and dragged Cary's hand off her lap and said, 'Let's go, sailor, we're wasting this man's valuable time.'

'We're looking for a flat,' Cary said. 'I'm not going to live over the shop any more – especially after I've seen the way they live in America.'

'We've got this grubby little room,' Honey said, 'in a dump called Kilburn!'

'We'll find something,' Cary said in a solicitous voice.

'What about Lamb?' I said.

Cary pretended not to recognize the name for a moment, and then he said, 'We were really shocked. It opened my eyes. Lamb's a corrupter. That's where he belongs – Pomona.'

'Shut up about Pomona,' Honey said. 'It's a hundred times better than this dump. Hey, are we going or aren't we?'

So they left. What had gone wrong on the ideal trip, I could not say. But what worried me was that, in half an hour of talking, in the presence of a woman he obviously loved, this very funny man had not smiled once.

★13★
A LITTLE FLAME
★

'I'm downstairs.' It was a dead man's voice, like my father talking from his grave. 'They say they can't let me see you without an appointment.' It had a slight stammer of fear or anger in it. 'I want to talk to you about my wife.'

'I didn't catch your name,' I said.

'Whiting.'

'Anthony?'

'James Whiting, from Hong Kong,' he said. 'Anthony's my cousin. He said he's met you. But Mei-lan –'

'Yes! You're married to Mei-lan! Now I remember.'

He said, 'It's in that connection that I want to talk to you. It's very important.'

'I see. I wonder if we could make it tomorrow. Lunch say – somewhere pleasant.'

'I'll be on my way back to Hong Kong tomorrow.' He spoke with a finality in which there was no emotion.

I said, 'I'm terribly tied up at the moment.'

'I can wait.' He sounded as if, already, he had been waiting a long time for me.

'Perhaps we could meet the next time you're here?'

'I'll never be in London again.' His voice was stone.

'I might be in Hong Kong one of these days,' I said.

'You won't find me. I'm leaving the bank for good. What time do you finish work?'

'I'll be here for ever, I'm afraid.' His silence demanded that I explain. 'The Vice-President's flying in next week from Washington. We're all working overtime. It might be eleven before I can get away.'

'Midnight, then,' he said, and I saw blackness.

'Impossible,' I said.

'I must see you.' The words rapped against my ear.

'Is Mei-lan with you?' I asked.

'Mei-lan is dead.'

'Oh, God, I'm sorry,' I said. 'I'll be right down.'

He was older than I had guessed he would be, but his frailty was partly grief. The strain was on his face, in his sideways glance, and his odd bereaved smile. He was a tough man who had been stricken with sorrow. His hair, raked into grey and white strands, was as dull as metal. His face was shadowy, there was no light behind the skin. It is that light that can make a person seem old or young.

Now that I was with him I was less anxious. He was just over sixty – I knew him to be sixty-one – not elderly, but rather old to be the husband of a Chinese girl in her mid-twenties. He had the shaky gaze of a widower. I could not match him to Mei-lan. He looked a little wild.

I had greeted him. I was still talking, commiserating, and walking much too fast. He replied in a breathless way. He followed me outside and down the embassy steps. He seemed to be chasing me. I stayed just ahead of the flap of his footsoles, one stride away from him.

He said, 'I'm at the Connaught. Shall we go there?'

That was a bad moment. I said, 'The Connaught,' and made it an idiot's echo.

'I'm sorry to have interrupted your work.'

Was this irony? Mei-lan was dead! We were heading across the square for Carlos Place.

'It's perfectly all right. I hadn't understood. I should have asked.'

'I didn't want to tell you on the phone. I find it hard to talk about. It's only been a month. The odour of her scent is still in the house. *Flammette*. It's very upsetting.'

He said no more until we reached the Connaught Hotel. The doorman saluted us. James Whiting raised his head and showed the man his bereaved smile, and we went inside. In the little lobby of armchairs and engravings, he said, 'Wouldn't we be more comfortable upstairs?'

He scratched the air with his hands, pointing the way.

'Right here is perfect,' I said. I sat down to show him I was satisfied and would not go farther. I hoped he would sit down.

I felt very young then, and sad and swindled, not just visited but haunted. This man had seemed to materialize in London with terrible news, and he looked terrible – the menace was a shadow on his face. I did not want to go upstairs. I did not want a white door to close behind me, in a room smelling of burning lavender, with a blue ceiling and the purifying light from tall windows.

He frowned at the chair across from mine. He blew out his cheeks in anger – but it might have been only impatience. He sat down in that chair, he sighed, he blinked at me, he tried to start.

'She stayed here, you know,' he said.

'They say it's a lovely hotel.'

'This is where she said she was happiest in London, when she came in October for her tests. That's why I'm staying here.'

'Those tests. I thought she was taking exams. She mentioned she was studying law.'

'To take her mind off it. She was trying to overcome it by means of will-power. She had so many tests! She didn't believe them. The best hospitals. The findings were always the same, even the same words – "The Black Spot," she said, when she got the reports. When she was too weak to travel – bedridden – she seemed to accept it. They gave her heroin injections. "Heroin for the heroine" – that was her joke. It was wonderful stuff. It made her death almost peaceful.'

I said, 'Please don't feel you have to talk about it.'

'I think it does me good.' He wore a look of wonderment for a few seconds. It lighted his face briefly, it made him look selfish and a little wild once more. Then it was gone and, with a kind of grumpy deference, he said, 'Unless you'd rather I didn't.'

'It's painful,' I said. 'I find it painful.'

'You young people.' He raised his head at me. 'When you get cancer it goes right through you. You burn up very fast. It's usually a matter of weeks, not months. Days sometimes. You just burn.'

'Please.'

He said, 'She was very fond of you.'

'I knew her father. I was the US Consul in Ayer Hitam. What a home-town for someone like Mei-lan!'

'You don't have to tell me anything. I know about you. She spoke about you a great deal. What are you looking at?'

The waiter had slipped behind Whiting to inquire whether there was anything we wanted.

'Nothing for me,' I said.

Whiting exercised his right as a guest of the hotel and ordered a whisky – it was after three-thirty. He did not speak again until it arrived, and then he merely held the glass, sometimes lifting and inhaling its fumes, but not drinking. It seemed to allow him to hide his glance in an innocent gesture. His eyes seldom left me and they scorched me with aching heat wherever they rested. They were deceptively dangerous, like dull metal that looks the same hot or cold.

'She greatly enjoyed her time in London.'

'The old man's customers were British – always talking about London. It was home for those colonials. Sentiment can be catching. People had so little to be sentimental about in Malaysia. I mean the Chinese. He wanted Mei-lan to come to London.'

'It wasn't London – it was you.'

Whiting, a banker, did not have the heavy-faced and chairbound look of a banker. No paunch, no watch-chain, no money-moralizing, nor any apologies that were in reality sneers. He had a lawyer's alertness showing through his boney face of grief. He had watchful eyes, the pretence of repose, the pounce ('It wasn't London –'). Bankers are bullfrogs, lawyers are lizards. And his tongue was quick for a grieving man.

He said, 'We were in London together when we first got married. It seems like yesterday. It *was* yesterday. Two years ago. Funny' – he didn't smile – 'she didn't mention you then.'

'The old man liked me to keep an eye on her. He was my first friend out there. He worried about her.'

'You call him the old man,' Whiting said, and raised his glass and looked at me from over its rim. 'He and I are the same age.'

I said, 'We did some business with him. We were winding up the consulate. I needed office equipment. It would have been expensive for me to buy things outright and sell it two years later. He leased all of it to me at a fair rate. He was one of the first in that part of Malaysia to go in for leasing in a big way. He was progressive. So were his children. Very modern-thinking. They were stifled there.'

Whiting pushed at his face with his fingertips as he listened to me.

'I left my wife for Mei-lan.' He looked at me through spread fingers. 'I have grown-up children.'

'Her father was a bit upset about that. Strife in a Chinese family can be violent. Threats, fights, suicides. It's all or nothing. The old man was worried.'

'My eldest son was Mei-lan's age,' he said.

'How did he take it? Some kids never come to terms with their parents' divorce.'

'Didn't bother him.'

'He's unusual.'

'He's divorced,' Whiting said. 'Three years ago. But he loved Mei-lan. Everyone did.'

I said, 'She was the sort of woman who inspired men to make sacrifices for her. They'd do anything.'

He merely looked at his whisky and at me. He drew his lips up in a mock smile like a man with a bad pain hiding his distress and after I said *They'd do anything* one of his eyes widened on me.

I said, 'Her father gave her everything. It made him a little uneasy – he knew he was in danger of spoiling her. I'm proud to say he trusted me. I liked him.'

Whiting gave me his sideways look. I noticed that his grey-white hair was yellowing in places, as it does in certain ageing men. It gave his head a strange heated appearance.

He said, 'Frankly, I found the old man a bit slippery.'

'He was a businessman.'

'I don't mean that. I'm a businessman myself. He seemed sly.'

'A lot of people respected him for being careful.'

'A double-entry man. Hong Kong's full of them. Twisters.'

'I found him truthful. I knew the whole family.' As I said this, Whiting raised his head, lifting his chin at me, seeming to reject what I said. I paused, then said, 'The family must have been very sad about Mei-lan.'

'Shattered. You see, Mei-lan wasn't very truthful. All along she had denied that she was seriously ill. She claimed it was hepatitis.'

'That takes courage.'

'No.' His bright eyes challenged me to deny this. 'She found it easy to lie.'

'I said, 'Perhaps in unimportant matters.'

'Unimportant? I am talking about her death. But not only that.' He now sat like a man on a waggon travelling over a bumpy road. He worked his shoulders as he spoke. 'She told lies because truth bored her. She didn't know that a good liar needs a good memory. She was always contradicting herself. It could be rather touching sometimes, like my daughter who used to swear she hadn't touched

163

the sweets and then would show me her purple tongue. God, I loved her.'

'You're saying she was deceitful.'

'No. She was virtuous. She didn't really know what the truth was. Lying was just a bad habit with her.'

'So she was innocent,' I said. 'She looked innocent.'

'She looked like a child,' he said. 'She was tiny. She had such a simple clean face. Some Chinese women never grow old. They have skin like silk. It grows finer, more beautiful with the years. Mei-lan was like that. A person ages and dies – the ageing is a kind of preparation. But if there is no decline, no ageing process – if the person looks ageless and beautiful, they seem immortal.' He glanced behind me as if a new thought had come into his head. 'Then they die and it is like the end of the world.'

'Didn't you know she was ill?'

'Having cancer isn't being ill,' he said. His head was turned towards me, but his eyes were glazed with memory. 'This is going to sound horribly naïve to you, but I thought she was pregnant. It took my first wife that way. In bed all the time, that sort of ravishing pallor, the tears. I thought she was below-par. It made her more beautiful.'

'She seemed fine when she was here,' I said. 'It must have been London.'

'Perhaps it was your company.'

'I saw very little of her, I'm sorry to say.'

'Somehow, she was satisfied.' He drank half his whisky in a sudden gulp and breathed hard. He said, 'She wanted to be well.'

'Mei-lan wasn't desperate,' I said.

'It's not desperation I'm talking about – it's urgency. Do you known anything about death?'

'A certain amount. My parents were killed in an aircrash when I was five. I was old enough to miss them.'

He said, 'With all respect, I'm talking about a different kind of intimacy with death. I mean, a dying woman will do anything to save herself.'

'So will a dying man.'

'For a man, death is a door. Everyone dies ugly, but that ugliness makes it terrible for a woman. You can't imagine. And there are worse things. A woman will do anything to get well, but she'll also do anything if she knows she's not going to get well. What are your restraints if you know you're doomed?'

'Mei-lan was a rational person. She was studying law,' I said. 'She had sense.'

'Law was only one distraction. She became obsessed about her appearance. She had beauty treatments. Injections. She did all the hospitals, she was tested again and again. She travelled, she needed old friends, she saw you.'

Whiting still sat solidly across from me with a patient intensity. He was large, his gaze was steady, and yet it was not a stare. He glanced from my eyes to my lips when I spoke, and at my hands when I moved them. We were not alone in that little Connaught parlour. It seemed to bother him. Whenever someone entered, Whiting flicked his eyes at them and dropped his voice.

I said, 'I hadn't really expected to hear from her.'

'She liked to startle people, show up without warning, catch them off-guard.'

'That can be charming,' I said.

'It gave her the upper hand. She could get anyone to do anything. I had never met anyone like her. Do you know, I lost most of my friends when I married her. I was glad. I didn't want them. She was everything. And such greed! I wanted someone who was greedy, who wanted me in a fiery way. That is passion. To me she was a friend, an enemy, a mother, a child.'

I must have looked puzzled.

'Wife, too,' he said slowly. 'I felt like an old man before I met her. After we married, I felt young – she gave me youth. I had never had a real childhood. Some of us don't, you know. An English childhood can seem as serious and grey as middle-age – all that silence, all those exams, we're always indoors. Mei-lan set my spirit free. My only regret was that she would outlive me – she would be on her own. I knew she had to be provided for. She gambled, you know.'

'I wasn't aware of that.'

'No?' He sat straighter. He seemed glad that I didn't know. I wondered how he got such a close shave – his skin was pink, not a hint of whiskers. It made me think of razors.

'She'd bet on anything,' he was saying. 'On an ant crossing a carpet. Very Chinese, that. I didn't mind the expense. It gave me something to spend my money on. It made her happy. Past a certain figure it's impossible to know what to do with your money. I had everything when I had her. I don't mean it was all good – it was diluted, that was the best of it. She kept my feet on the ground. You look blank.'

'I'm not sure what you're talking about.'

He shrugged. He didn't smile, yet he looked pleased – confident. In the past half-hour he had grown larger but less menacing. He said, 'When she died, nothing mattered. I came close to death myself then. What was the point of carrying on? I wanted to turn to wood. I spent a week in a chair with my mouth open. I suppose that sounds a bit crazy to you.'

I denied that it did. His eyes never left me and there was watchfulness even in his two hands, poised like crabs on his knees.

'When I finally got out of the chair, I wrote my letter of resignation. Now I want to find a smaller flat. I don't want anything more if I can't have Mei-lan.'

He turned away but glanced back at me quickly as if he expected to catch my expression changed.

He said, 'Sometimes I can't bear to think of her.'

'That's only natural.'

'You don't understand.' He flung that sudden gaze on me again. Was he sinking, was he drowning? He said, 'But I had to trust her. I came here yesterday and realized that I was looking for her. That's not good. Don't you agree?'

'You'll never find her,' I said.

I had hesitated, and now he gave me his lizard look of scrutiny.

He said, 'No, no. That's not the point. I could find her – I could know her better. But it might be very upsetting.'

He wanted me to agree with him. But I said, 'People should be allowed to have secrets.'

'People's secrets are the most interesting thing about them,' he said. 'How could you love anyone who didn't have a secret?'

I said, 'How is it possible to go on loving someone after you know the secret?'

He was watching me very closely now. He seemed to want to trap me, lowering his judge's face on me and exerting pressure with his eyes.

He said, 'I want to think of her as I knew her – like a little flame, burning, burning, slightly malicious, tempting, loving, doing harmless damage. The coquette is a tormentor in a good cause. I want to think that she would always have been mine.' His face moved closer to mine. 'What colour was her dress?'

I made a memory-prodding gesture, showing my effort by masking my eyes with my hand. I experienced a slow moment of grief, and it seemed to pinch a bruise on to my soul.

In this darkness, Whiting spoke to me, 'You don't remember,' he said. 'She wouldn't have liked that. She went to a lot of trouble to buy her London clothes.'

I said, 'She was only here a few days.'

'A week,' he said.

'I only saw her one day.'

'A day has twenty-four hours in it,' he said.

'We had tea,' I said. 'One hour. I didn't see her dress. She never took her coat off.'

Whiting frowned at me in pleasure, and lapsed into a comfortable silence. He said, 'In a hurry, that was Mei-lan. Hello, goodbye. What a life. It's perfect when you think about it. She was a little flame. She –'

At first I thought he was about to cry, but then I saw the flicker of a smile on his mouth. He had not smiled so far.

He said, 'The chaps at the bank think I'm stupid. "You're wrecking your career – throwing it all away, everything you worked for." But they didn't know Mei-lan. A woman's secret is the essence of her character, isn't it? She is what she tries to hide. They didn't know her.'

His eyes changed in focus, leaving me and peering into a greater distance.

He said, 'If I thought for a minute that she had betrayed me, I wouldn't have left the bank. I'd carry on as normal. And I don't think I'd ever trust a living soul again.'

He invited my attention with a beckoning of his head, lifting it at me and saying. 'What would you do if you were in my shoes?'

'Just what you did,' I said. He was surprised into a little silence by my prompt reply.

'She was rather special,' he said. 'What?'

'Yes,' I said.

And then he smiled. He said, 'And you hardly knew her!'

14

FURY

One of the first Americans Mary Snowfire met in London was a girl named Gretchen, who told her she was doing graduate work on the European Economic Community, and then smiled and smoothed her chic velvet knickerbockers and said she also worked for an escort agency. 'You have to, here. It's the only way you can manage financially.' Gretchen had a Saab Turbo and a big apartment in Fulham. She talked about 'Saudis'. 'I've met some really interesting people. It's not what you think. I'm not a hooker.'

But escort agency meant hookers for hire, didn't it?

'You have dinner usually. Or you go to a play. After that it's up to you.'

Gretchen was also a tennis player. She spoke French. She had a tan. She owned a sun-bed. Some weekends she went to Paris.

'Do they pay you?'

'You wouldn't believe how much! Some of those girls could retire. They make a fantastic amount.'

'Sure,' Mary said, 'but what do they have to do for it?'

She said 'they' but she meant Gretchen.

Gretchen said, 'They do everything.'

Everything seemed frantic, pleasureless, repetitive, exhausting.

Gretchen said, 'They're really well paid.'

'Doesn't that mean it's prostitution?' Mary asked.

'Oh, no. It's much more than they're worth,' Gretchen said. 'That's why it's not prostitution.'

Gretchen offered to introduce her to the manager of the agency, but Mary laughed and said no thanks, and she did her best to hide her disgust. She was also shocked by the easy way that Gretchen confided this matter. If you had to do these things to live here, why live here?

Gretchen changed the subject. She began talking about the EEC in a dull and knowledgeable way, and wasn't it a scandal that the French farmers were paid a subsidy to produce butter that was sold cheap to the Soviet Union in order to keep the prices high in the European butter market?

Mary listened to the pretty girl and later got a nanny job, looking after three small children. She lived at the top of the house, which was just off the Fulham Road. She could hear the buses. For this job she was paid ten pounds a week – less than twenty dollars. Her room was part of her salary. Some girls were not paid at all, the woman said: they were jolly glad to have a place to live in return for helping with the kids! And Mary thought: No wonder girls like Gretchen met Arabs in the Hilton and went to bed with them. ('At midnight you say, "I've really got to go. I've got a heavy day tomorrow at the Institute," and you walk out with three hundred pounds.')

Mary had wanted to live in London more than she wanted a husband or a lover. She was from Gainesville, Florida, an English major from the university there. She had very little spare money, but the standby fare to London was a hundred and fifty dollars. After a month at the Fulham Road house she saw that a bookstore near the cinema had a card in the window saying *Sales Staff Wanted*. She was interviewed by the manager, Mr Shortridge, and hired. When she resigned from her nanny job she did not tell the woman that her husband had made an improper suggestion (kept pinching her hard and saying 'How about it?') and this was the main reason she was leaving.

In her new job, Mary discovered what many people like Gretchen already knew – that there was a great deal of good-will towards Americans in London. We had style, we worked hard, we were full of life, we understood money, we succeeded where others failed. We were associated with luck.

By planning her life and measuring what she earned against what she could afford, Mary established herself. She had moved to a bedsitter which was directly over an Italian grocery store. She painted her room, she sewed new curtains, Mr Shortridge gave her Penguin posters – portraits of Virginia Woolf, Doris Lessing, and William Faulkner. Each one said, *A Penguin Author*. Their orange matched her orange room. She had a bike (five pounds from a junk shop – she fixed it up), a gas-fire and a plug-in radio (batteries made radios expensive). Her geraniums, her small avocado tree, her pots of ivy she had all grown herself. The bright ferny tub of marijuana which thrived in a sunny corner of the room had been left by the last tenant.

She became friendly with the owner of the grocery store and his wife. They knew how little money she had and gave her a discount, and sometimes they gave her packaged food when the date stamp had just expired. This Italian couple, who had an English accent, had relatives in Newark, New Jersey! Mary knew that they looked upon her as another exile, trying to make her way in this city of cold rooms, and hallways smelling of dust and bacon fat, and wet streets and brown skies.

London was not the London of her Gainesville dreams. It was sadder, darker, stranger, narrower, newer, dirtier, more oppressive. Now she understood why Gretchen had become a prostitute in an escort agency. But Mary felt that London was teaching her how to live against the odds.

She knew she could not have a boyfriend or a lover. They required too much time, they demanded favours, they crowded her and made her careless. In her first weeks in London she had gone out half a dozen times with men she had met. She went to pubs, to the movies, and once to a disco. She insisted on paying her share – it was expensive! One drink in a pub was around two dollars! The British seemed easier about money – no one had any. But Mary could only manage by living narrowly. It was hard and comfortless and sometimes very lonely. It was a delicate balance, but friends could be unpredictable, and everything depended on close planning, because she had so little.

She had never smoked, she stopped drinking, she became a vegetarian. She began to dislike cats for being meat-eaters. She had never felt healthier or tougher. It was a satisfaction, this kind of survival. She didn't care that it made her seem a little selfish. She had started with nothing. She had discovered how to be independent, and she was glad, because she was a woman, and they weren't expected to be loners. When she thought of Gretchen or saw a woman with a rich man who was obviously keeping her, Mary Snowfire smiled and thought, 'She lays eggs for gentlemen.'

Mary was twenty-four, and slim, and had long legs. She could run five miles. She told the truth. She became so angry when someone lied to her that she couldn't sleep. Occasionally, customers in the bookstore lied to her: 'That's what I said the first time' or 'I gave you a ten pound note and you gave me change for a fiver'. She wanted to hit them.

After six months she considered that she had won her freedom. It was then that she became friendly with the fellow Brenhouse. He worked as a deliveryman for Howletts, the book publisher, but Brenhouse also supplied books from the Blackadder Press, a publisher of Trotskyite literature. This bookstore reflected Mr Shortridge's political views. Mr Shortridge had been to Cuba.

Brenhouse was extremely thin, in his early twenties, and from Whitby, in Yorkshire, where the Blackadder Press was. He had hair to his shoulders and a drooping moustache and a long nose. He looked like Robert Louis Stevenson. His hands were skinny and usually dirty and he bit his fingernails until they bled. But Mary regarded him as sort of romantic, because he lived outdoors, in a lean-to on Mitcham Common. It was perfectly legal there – it was common land: men lived there like savages, squatting near smokey fires, and boiling soup in black kettles. In cold weather they wore socks on their hands and lined their coats with old newspapers and stuffed them up their pants. They carried their belongings in baby-carriages twenty miles or more. Brenhouse told her these things. Mary thought: The poor kid sleeps in a Surrey ditch with hobos and homeless men and he still works every day! He had build his own shelter and had a sleeping bag. He said he was better off than many people in this country. Mary admired him for saying that.

She had once thought she was living the life most men led, until she met Brenhouse, who slept on the ground. There was sometimes a cloudy droplet at the tip of his nose. He offered the information that he kept clean by using public baths. London was full of bath-houses for people who didn't have tubs at home. This was 1981! His talk made her grateful for what she had.

Some nights, in her warm room – the warmth brought the scorched smell of new paint off the wood – she thought of Brenhouse and shuddered, feeling faintly ashamed. Though she knew there was no virtue in living outdoors like that, she felt it was beyond her capabilities. Shouldn't women be able to endure such hardships? If you had to do it, you could, Brenhouse said. But Mary thought: If I had to do it I would die.

The cold winter forecast for London was colder even than the predictions. Snow fell in big white crumbs and made the streets simple and small. It was not ploughed, no one shovelled it, it did not melt. After a week it was still on the ground, but dirtier, and the temperature dropped. Walking down the Fulham Road was treacherous. Mary saw dead sparrows in snow holes where they had fallen and frozen. Cats walked in the soft snow in a high-stepping tentative way, making spider's legs. Strangers spoke to each other in worried reminiscing voices. This London weather was remarkable, almost unbelievable, and everyone had something different to say about it. The first week of storms was exciting, but the city was changed and the next week similar storms were cruel.

And one night, the coldest night so far, there was a rapping on Mary's door.

It was Brenhouse. Five minutes ago she had been thinking of him! He did not ask to come in. He did not speak. His skin was red and grey, his cheeks looked bruised, but after an hour in the room he became pale. His breathing was harsh. He stayed the night, sleeping on the floor. He did not take off his clothes, and though he was wrapped in two blankets he smelled of dirt and oil-smoke.

'I thought I was going to die,' he said the next morning, his first words, and he was still pale.

Mary knew that he planned to stay. He was afraid of the cold for the first time. The snow lay everywhere in London like black slop.

She said, 'Don't you have a friend somewhere?'

'No,' he said. 'Only you.'

How could this be true of a man who lived in his own country when it was not true even of Mary who had lived in London less than a year?

Suddenly he said, 'It's only seven-thirty!'

'I have to open the bookshop,' Mary said.

'In Mitcham I never get up before nine.'

He made it sound like luxury, and he was talking about a scrap-wood lean-to on a scrubby common in the dead of winter. The rigid tip of his long nose that had been very red last night was pale as gristle today.

Mary said, 'What about your job?'

'I'm not going in today. I'll call in sick. Want to go to the pictures?'

This was why she hated men and boyfriends. They recklessly decided to tell lies or turn their back on things. Maybe it was their strength, but it was crooked strength.

She said, 'You'll get fired.'

Brenhouse swore. Obscenity was always an ugly foreign language to her and she translated what Brenhouse said as 'To hell with them.'

'I can find work back home.' He snorted, pushing at one nostril with a knuckle. 'Whitby.'

When Mary returned to her room that night, he was wrapped in a blanket and sitting cross-legged on her bed, reading a Blackadder pamphlet, something about wealth and property. He looked contented. His hair was still damp from his bath, his nose was shiny. Where had he found the towel?

The gas-fire was hissing and the room was so warm it raised his soap smell and the paint and the geraniums and some lunch odours – he had made himself a fried egg, the greasy skillet still on the hotplate. Mary began to tidy the room and, seeing her, Brenhouse tried to help.

'I'm not used to bourgeois living,' he said.

What about the bath, the meal, his leisurely reading? And he had scrubbed the dirt out of his fingernails.

Brenhouse was at the sink doing his dishes. Mary would have done them: she liked cleaning the room alone, but with Brenhouse doing it too the housework seemed like drudgery. He was talking.

'We can go up the pub.'

'I hate pubs,' she said.

'Then I'll go out and get a bottle of plonk,' he said. 'It's the least I can do.'

That was true: it *was* the least he could do. It was a characteristic of too many Englishmen, Mary thought, this doing as little as possible, and presuming; and some of them lived like pigs. He brought back a two-litre bottle of Spanish wine and she remembered that she had given up drinking.

She bought cheese from the Italian downstairs and made cannelloni and salad. They ate, sitting on cushions in front of the gas-fire.

Brenhouse said, 'There's no meat in this, love.'

'I'm a vegetarian,' she said.

'I eat anything,' Brenhouse said. He had a weevil's nose. He stared at her and smiled, and when she shrugged he filled her glass to the brim with the cheap wine.

She drank it because this bottle was his gift to her. He filled the glass again and she drank that. He began wickedly again with the big bottle. Mary tried to stand up, but couldn't; nor could she sit. She lay on the floor until the side of her face grew hot. Before she sank completely she felt his hands on her. He was lifting her clothes in a rough and hurrying way. And then for an hour or more she had little glimpses of herself being pushed and pulled by him. At the end, he shouted at her in a doomed and adoring way.

In the morning Mary woke up in her bed and saw he was gone. The room had been turned upside-down. The truth was easy to see in a room so small. He had stolen her money, he had taken her keys, her watch, her earrings, her one bracelet, her Florida paperweight, her radio. His smell was on the bed. It was that, his dreadful smell, that made her cry. Then, remembering the way he had shouted in his passion, she became angry. She ran to the book-shop. It was eight-thirty.

Mr Shortridge was already inside.

'We've had a break-in,' he said. 'It must have happened in the night. The till's empty.'

He was trying not to be cross. He always said that the Tory government deserved crime and that property owners and land-lords were thieves. Now his hands were in the empty cash drawer. He said no more. He chewed his tongue.

Mary said, 'It wasn't a break-in,' and explained, and began to cry again, and only her anger stopped her tears.

Then she had no time for grief, none for tears; she was falling. She had no job – Mr Shortridge sorrowfully fired her and when she mentioned the week's pay that he owed her his lips trembled and he said, 'You should be paying me.' Her rent was due. Bren-house had taken her chequebook – but there was no money in the account. He had taken her Parker pen! Everything shiny, every-thing of value, the savage had taken. He had stuck his horrible nose everywhere.

Mary had nothing in this dark brown winter-wet city.

Gretchen was glad to hear from her, though Gretchen's first

mood on the phone was a mixture of sex and suspicion – her escort voice. Then her tone was girlish. 'Have you changed your mind about the agency?'

'I need some money,' Mary said. 'A loan. Would ten pounds be all right?'

'You could earn two hundred by dinner-time,' Gretchen said.

Mary said, 'I'd kill the first man that touched me.'

They met for tea that day. Gretchen handed some money over. It was fifty pounds.

Mary counted it and cried because it was so much. She was aware that she wore a starved and crazy expression but she couldn't help it.

'I'll pay you back.'

'Nothing to pay back,' Gretchen said. 'Fifty quid isn't money.'

But to Mary's mind it was money, but a man had given it to Gretchen, but what had she done in return? But she was really generous. But it was no way to live.

Gretchen talked about her work at the Institute, and the European oil-fields and the future of Arab oil. Mary thought only of the thief Brenhouse. There was a glut, Gretchen said, and everyone thought there was a shortage. Gretchen said, 'I could show you the figures – I've made an amazing flow-chart. Oh, God, I've got to run.' She made a friendly face. 'A date.'

Mary was still holding the money rolled into a tube. She said, 'I have to get my bike fixed and buy a few things.'

'You're funny,' Gretchen said. 'But I think you're right. You'd hate being an escort.'

Mary felt there was a yellow flame of anger in her that kept her alive. She wanted to find this man who had treated her like an ignorant animal. He was the animal – he had the snout for it! She walked to Fulham Broadway and bought a light for her bike. She set off for Mitcham Common, pedalling fast. She knew she was behaving like the animal he had made her. But he had created this rage in her.

Two old men sat on their heels in front of the fire, watching it with pink watery eyes. They didn't know Brenhouse. Had she been over to the spinney? They sent her to this wooded part of the common, not far, but she noticed they were following her like stupid hungry hounds. There was no sign of anyone else here. They were trying to confuse her or trap her! She hissed at them, and they stood aside, and her bike took her quickly away.

There were fires and camps all over this common. Scraps of snow still lay on the ground like filthy bandages.

She surprised a pair of schoolboys smoking cigarettes. They guiltily agreed to help her. Perhaps she looked like their teacher? Their search turned up Brenhouse's ditch and the lean-to and the dead smelly fire. Brenhouse had cleared out. She did not pity him at all when she saw this rat's nest – she hated him much more.

A man with a grey face and a coat of long rags was watching her. This place was full of tramps! This one was young, about Brenhouse's age, but heavier, and this weight made him look shabbier and nastier.

'I've got news for you,' he said.

'I hate that expression,' she said. It was a man's belittling expression, *I've got news for you.* She wanted to hit him.

The young man laughed. He knew she was wasting her time.

'He's gone home!' His grey mocking face seemed to say, and there's nothing you can do about it!

Mary said, 'Where does he live?'

'He's a Yorkshireman, isn't he?' But it was not a question. He added, 'I've got no time for Yorkshiremen' – to insult her, because she was involved with Brenhouse, the fat young man could see that.

She remembered Whitby.

'Don't go away,' she said to the schoolboys, who had helped her find this camp-site. The fat young man would not touch her while they were around. The boys escorted her to the road, but said nothing, and even refused the tangerine she offered them as a present.

Howletts, the publishers, confirmed that Brenhouse was in Whitby. They were very angry with him, and when she said he owed her money they understood and in an encouraging way – she felt – they gave Mary his address.

She did not sleep that night. The room was no longer hers. Brenhouse had robbed and ruined her. Her life had depended on a delicate balance. Brenhouse had stumbled into her little room and betrayed her, all the while looking down his nose at her. She had never once asked anything of him. He was a pig, he deserved worse than death. She cried, feeling trapped in a ditch where he had thrown her and tried to smother her. Why are men thieves?

Each night after that she cried again. But she was crying because it was dark and she could not travel in the dark. Her tears were fury.

She had sold everything that she could sell and bought an army sleeping bag – arctic model. She had then dressed herself in her warmest clothes (bleak-brown February had turned the snowfields to dampness and mud) and set off on her bike for Whitby. In this small country of four directions she had taken the longest one.

She was fighting the wind as soon as she left London. Her head was down and her body bent double and braced over her bike frame. She had rejected the train, the bus, or hitch-hiking. She needed this effort so that she could use her fury. Each day on her bike her anger gave her strength. It was food, it refreshed her, it kept her warm. She did not sleep easily beside the stone walls of villages and farms, but her fury enlivened her when she was awake. And sleep that was too deep was dangerous on cold nights: you could freeze and not know it.

The roads were clear, the thaw was general and filthy. And, even with the rain pelting against her, she flew. Some days in high winds she screamed curses at him. She hated the thought of his beaky face.

She had become possessed. Fury made her a demon, but it also made her efficient. She saw nothing unusual in this speeding along back-roads on her bike, but her throat burned with shrieks as she beat uphill towards Yorkshire. Men stood in muddy fields or against high brambly hedges and watched her. They were curious, but after they had had a good look at her they were afraid. She went fast, the effort strengthened her; she felt she was being flung towards Whitby by black winds.

From Ely and the Fens, she skirted the Wash and made for the Lincolnshire Wolds, then across the Humber to York and the long hills of that dark county to Scarborough. She was in Whitby the next day, she knew it by the ruined abbey – her gaze continually travelled up to it.

She did not stop. She had by now memorized Brenhouse's address and the roads to it. Hunger had increased her fury: she had not eaten since morning – it was now a cold windy mid-afternoon muffled by cloud.

She had imagined him alone in an empty room and defenceless. Her mind had simplified the imagining and made it helpful, and had tricked her. The truth was a tiny brick house in a bottled-up lane, with no view either of the moor or the sea. There was no answer to her knock. She drank a cup of tea at a café. She had four pounds and sixty-seven pence left, but once this was done nothing mattered.

Her dirty face and red hands frightened the woman at the tea urn.

Leaving the café, she saw him – she was sure it was Brenhouse – walking down the road. And he saw her. But he smiled and looked away, probably guessing that he had imagined her in this distant place, and smirking at his mistake. How could she have got here so fast in the winter with no money?

Furiously, she followed him. She was impatient. Now, hearing her rapid steps, he looked again. This made her eager. She held her weapon up her sleeve. No: he had not recognized her.

He had pushed through the door of a pub, but when Mary entered she could not see him. There was smoke and chatter, nearly all were men, some staring at her. She saw her own scarf around someone's neck! It was one she had bought in London. The person's head was turned, but she knew whose it was. Two strides took her to the chair and then she had his long hair in her hand and was yanking his head back, so that he faced the ceiling.

Brenhouse tried to stand up. He shouted. His look of horror filled her unexpectedly with pity, and it frightened her, too. No one made a move to help him, or to restrain her in her swift movement. The cloudy light came through the painted pub window with gulls' nagging squawks. Brenhouse was clutching his face, blood streamed from his hands. Then Mary was seized from behind.

'His throat's cut,' she heard.

And, 'She never cut his throat.'

She hadn't touched his throat but she had cut him with the scissors she surrendered to the men.

All this she told me on the train south from York, after her two weeks in the hospital. She was treated for exhaustion and dehydration, and Brenhouse was there, too, in another ward – severe laceration of the face, as the newspapers said. She had scissored a little more than half an inch from the end of his nose.

But there were no charges laid against Mary Snowfire. The London embassy was involved because she had no money – and I was sent to escort her back to London and arrange her repatriation. We flew her to Florida. She said she would repay every cent. I felt sure she would keep her word.

15

NEIGHBOURS

★

I had two neighbours at Overstrand Mansions – we shared the same landing. In America 'neighbour' has a friendly connotation; in England it is a chilly word, nearly always a stranger, a map reference more than anything else. One of my neighbours was called R. Wigley; the other had no nameplate.

It did not surprise me at all that Corner Door had no nameplate. He owned a motorcycle and kept late nights. He wore leather – I heard it squeak; and boots – they hit the stairs like hammers on an anvil. His motorcycle was a Kawasaki – Japanese of course, the British are only patriotic in the abstract, and they can be traitorously frugal – tax-havens are full of Brits. They want value for money, even when they are grease-monkeys, bikers with skinny faces and sideburns and teeth missing, wearing jack-boots and swastikas. That was how I imagined Corner Door, the man in 4C.

I had never seen his face, though I had heard him often enough. His hours were odd, he was always rushing off at night and re-turning in the early morning – waking me when he left and waking me again when he came back. He was selfish and unfriendly, scatterbrained, thoughtless – no conversation but plenty of bike noise. I pictured him wearing one of those German helmets that looks like a kettle, and I took him to be a coward at heart, who sneaked around whining until he had his leather suit and his boots on, until he mounted his too-big Japanese motorcycle, which he kept in the entryway of Overstrand Mansions, practically blocking it. When he was suited up and mounted on his bike he was a Storm Trooper with blood in his eye.

It also struck me that this awful man might be a woman, an awful woman. But even after several months there I never saw the person from 4C face to face. I saw him – or her – riding away, his back, the chrome studs patterned on his jacket. But women didn't behave like this. It was a man.

R. Wigley was quite different – he was a civil servant, Post Office,

Welsh I think, very methodical. He wrote leaflets. The Post Office issued all sorts of leaflets – explaining pensions, television licences, road-tax, driving permits, their savings bank and everything else, including of course stamps. The leaflets were full of directions and advice. In this complicated literate country you were expected to read your way out of difficulty.

When I told Wigley I wouldn't be in London much longer than a couple of years he became hospitable. No risk, you see. If I had been staying for a long time he wouldn't have been friendly – wouldn't have dared. Neighbours are a worry, they stare, they presume, they borrow things, they ask you to forgive them their trespasses. In the most privacy-conscious country in the world neighbours are a problem. But I was leaving in a year or so, and I was an American diplomat – maybe I was a spy! He suggested I call him Reg.

We met at the Prince Albert for a drink. A month later, I had him over with the Scadutos, Vic and Marietta, and it was then that talk turned to our neighbours. Wigley said there was an actor on the ground floor and that several country Members of Parliament lived in Overstrand Mansions when the Commons was sitting. Scaduto asked him blunt questions I would not have dared to ask, but I was glad to hear his answers. Rent? Thirty-seven pounds a week. Married? Had been – no longer. University? Bristol. And, when he asked Wigley about his job, Scaduto listened with fascination and then said, 'It's funny, but I never actually imagined anyone writing those things. It doesn't seem like real writing.'

Good old Skiddoo.

Wigley said, 'I assure you, it's quite real.'

Scaduto went on interrogating him – Americans were tremendous questioners – but noticing Wigley's discomfort made me reticent. The British confined conversation to neutral impersonal subjects, resisting any effort to be trapped into friendship. They got to know each other by allowing details to slip out, little mentions which, gathered together, became revelations. The British liked having secrets – they had lost so much else – and that was one of their secrets.

Scaduto asked, 'What are your other neighbours like?'

I looked at Wigley. I wondered what he would say. I would not have dared to put the question to him.

He said, 'Some of them are incredibly noisy and others down-right frightening.'

This encouraged me. I said, 'Our Nazi friend with the motor-cycle, for one.'

Had I gone too far?

'I was thinking of that prig, Hurst,' Wigley said, 'who has the senile Labrador that drools and squitters all over the stairs.'

'I've never seen our motorcyclist,' I said. 'But I've heard him. The bike. The squeaky leather shoulders. The boots.' I caught Wigley's eye. 'It's just the three of us on this floor, I guess.'

I had lived there just over two months without seeing anyone else.

Wigley looked uncertain, but said, 'I suppose so.'

'My kids would love to have a motorcycle,' Marietta Scaduto said. 'I've got three hulking boys, Mr Wigley.'

I said, 'Don't let them bully you into buying one.'

'Don't you worry,' Marietta said. 'I think those things are a menace.'

'Some of them aren't so bad,' Wigley said. 'Very economical.' He glanced at me. 'So I've heard.'

'It's kind of an image-thing, really. Your psychologists will tell you all about it.' Skiddoo was pleased with himself: he liked analysing human behaviour – 'deviants' were his favourites, he said. 'It's classic textbook-case stuff. The simp plays big tough guy on his motorcycle. Walter Mitty turns into Marlon Brando. It's an aggression thing. Castration complex. What do you do for laughs, Reg?'

Wigley said, 'I'm not certain what you mean by laughs.'

'Fun,' Scaduto said. 'For example, we've got one of these home computers. About six thousand bucks, including some accessories – hardware, software. Christ, we've had hours of fun with it. The kids love it.'

'I used to be pretty keen on aircraft,' Wigley said, and looked very embarrassed saying so, as if he were revealing an aberration in his boyhood.

Scaduto said, 'Keen in what way?'

'Taking snaps of them,' Wigley said.

'Snaps?' Marietta Scaduto said. She was smiling.

'Yes,' Wigley said. 'I had one of those huge Japanese cameras that can do anything. They're absolutely idiot-proof and fiendishly expensive.'

'I never thought anyone taking dinky little pictures of planes could be described as "keen".' Scaduto said the word like a brand-name for ladies' underwear.

'Some of them were big pictures,' Wigley said coldly.

'Even big pictures,' Scaduto said. 'I could understand flying in the planes, though. Getting inside, and air-borne, and doing the loop-the-loop.'

Wigley said, 'They were bombers.'

'Now you're talking, Reg!' Scaduto's sudden enthusiasm warmed the atmosphere a bit, and they continued to talk about aeroplanes.

'My father had an encyclopaedia,' Wigley said. 'You looked up "aeroplane". It said, "Aeroplane: See Flying-Machine."'

Later, Marietta said, 'These guys on their motorcycles, I was just thinking. They really have a problem. Women never do stupid things like that.'

Vic Scaduto said, 'Women put on long gowns, high heels, padded bras. They pile their hair up, they pretend they're princesses. That's worse, fantasy-wise. Or they get into really tight provocative clothes, all tits and ass, swinging and bouncing, lipstick, the whole bit, cleavage hanging down. And then – I'm not exaggerating – and then they say, "Don't touch me or I'll scream."'

Good old Skiddoo.

'You've got a big problem if you think that,' Marietta said. She spoke then to Wigley. 'Sometimes the things he says are sick.'

Wigley smiled and said nothing.

'And he works for the government,' Marietta said. 'You wouldn't think so, would you?'

That was it. The Scadutos went out arguing, and Wigley left: a highly successful evening, I thought.

Thanks to Scaduto's pesterings I knew much more about Wigley. He was decent, he was reticent, and I respected him for the way he handled Good Old Skiddoo. And we were no more friendly than before – that was all right with me: I didn't want to be burdened with his friendship any more than he wanted to be lumbered with mine. I only wished that the third tenant on our floor was as gracious a neighbour as Wigley.

Would Wigley join me in making a complaint? He said he'd rather not. That was the British way – don't make a fuss, Reg.

He said, 'To be perfectly frank, he doesn't actually bother me.'

This was the first indication I'd had that it was definitely a man, not a woman.

'He drives me up the wall sometimes. He keeps the craziest hours. I've never laid eyes on him, but I know he's weird.'

Wigley smiled at me and I immediately regretted saying, 'He's weird,' because, saying so, I had revealed something of myself.

I said, 'I can't make a complaint unless you back me up.'

'I know.'

I could tell he thought I was being unfair. It created a little distance, this annoyance of mine that looked to him like intolerance. I knew this because Wigley had a girlfriend and didn't introduce me. A dozen times I heard them on the stairs. People who live alone are authorities on noises. I knew their laughs. I got to recognize the music, the bedsprings, the bathwater. He did not invite me over.

And of course there was my other subject, the Storm Trooper from 4C with his thumping jackboots at the oddest hours. I decided at last that wimpy little Wigley (as I now thought of him) had become friendly with him, perhaps ratted on me and told him that I disliked him.

Wigley worked at Post Office Headquarters, at St Martin's-le-Grand, taking the train to Victoria and then the tube to St Paul's. I sometimes saw him entering or leaving Battersea Park Station while I was at the bus stop. Occasionally, we walked together to or from Overstrand Mansions, speaking of the weather.

One day, he said, 'I might be moving soon.'

I felt certain he was getting married. I did not ask.

'Are you sick of Overstrand Mansions?'

'I need a bigger place.'

He was definitely getting married.

I had the large balcony apartment in front. Wigley had a two-room apartment just behind me. The motorcyclist's place I had never seen.

'I wish it were the Storm Trooper who was leaving, and not you.'

He was familiar with my name for the motorcyclist.

'Oh, well,' he said, and walked away.

Might be moving, he had said. It sounded pretty vague. But the following Friday he was gone. I heard noise and saw the moving van in front on Prince of Wales Drive. Bumps and curses echoed on the stairs. I didn't stir – too embarrassing to put him on the spot, especially as I had knocked on his door that morning hoping for the last time to get him to join me in a protest against the Storm Trooper. I'm sure he saw me through his spy-hole in the door – Wigley, I mean. But he didn't open. So he didn't care about the awful racket the previous night – boots, bangs, several screams. Wigley was bailing out and leaving me to deal with it.

He went without a word. Then I realized he had sneaked away. He had not said good-bye, I had never met his girlfriend, he was getting married – maybe already married. British neighbours!

I wasn't angry with him, but I was furious with the Storm Trooper who had created a misunderstanding between Wigley and me. Wigley had tolerated the noise and I had hated it and said so. The Storm Trooper had made me seem like a brute!

But I no longer needed Wigley's signature on a complaint. Now there were only two of us here. I could go in and tell him exactly what I thought of him. I could play the obnoxious American. Wigley's going gave me unexpected courage. I banged on his door and shook it, hoping that I was waking him up. There was no answer that day or any day. And there was no more noise, no Storm Trooper, no motorcycle, from the day Wigley left.

16

FIGHTING TALK

★

Some repeated noises seem to erupt with numbers, making the chatter of counting, a kind of syncopation that turns *bop-bop* into *one-two*. But, staring out the window of Vic Scaduto's office at the rear of the embassy, I was only dimly aware that I was hearing a noise at all. I seemed to be hearing the words *three-four-five*. It was only after I saw the policeman hurry out of the glass booth near our staff garage that I realized that what I had heard were gunshots.

'What is it?' Scaduto said.

He had just been telling me about meeting the father of Hussein Something-or-other, one of his kids' schoolfriends – at least he had thought the man was a parent, an unusually friendly guy among all those snobs at the school rugby match – and he turned out to be Hussein's bodyguard and chauffeur! 'Hey, listen, Arabs are Jews on horseback –'

'It sounded like gunfire,' I said.

Blackburnes Mews was very still for several minutes, and then it was awash with scrambling policemen setting up barriers at the mews entrance and blocking Culross Street. I heard the ear-splitting donkey hee-haw of a British police siren.

Scaduto had joined me at the window. His ears twitched, the hairline of his scalp gave a little jerk. He shaped his mouth as if preparing to take a bite.

'Libyans,' he said.

We had had an urgent memo about Libyans earlier that week. Teams of gunmen had been dispatched by the wild-eyed President Gaddahfi. We had been sent blurred pictures of the moustached assassins.

Scaduto's phone rang. Panic invests commonplace objects with menace. He picked the receiver up with fearful fingers – would the thing explode? He listened for perhaps twenty seconds. He said, 'We've been expecting something like this,' and then he replaced the receiver gently, again behaving as if it were explosive.

'There's been a shooting,' he told me solemnly. 'Stay inside and keep away from the windows. Those are orders. It might be Arabs. That was Horton on the phone.'

'It was right down there,' I said, pointing into the mews.

'You're a witness.'

'I didn't see anything,' I said.

Scaduto said, 'I'm glad they didn't give me Rome. It's worse there.'

While he phoned his wife I tried to determine what the police were doing with their chalkmarks on the surface of the mews. It looked like the beginning of a children's game.

'I'm not kidding, honey. I heard the shots,' he was saying. 'Hey, I'm glad they didn't give me that Rome job. It's an everyday thing there. Sure, it's terrorists! No, don't worry. I can take care of myself.'

He looked pleased, even smug, when he hung up. 'How about a drink?' he said. 'Someone's bound to have the poop on this downstairs.'

The bar-restaurant in the embassy basement had no windows, and it was perhaps this and the semi-darkness that suggested a hide-out or bomb-shelter to me. It was full of huddled whispering embassy employees rather enjoying their fear.

'Reminds me of when I was in Rawalpindi,' Scaduto said, still looking pleased. He went for two beers and returned with the name of the man who had been fired upon – Dwight Yorty, a relatively new man in Regional Projects, whom I had never met.

'I shouldn't laugh,' Scaduto said.

But near disasters, especially when an intended victim seems to have been miraculously reprieved, are often the occasions for lively gossip.

'Yorty!' Scaduto said. 'A month or so ago, he told me the most amazing story. He hit his wife over the head. She fell down, *wham*, flat on the floor. Go ahead, ask me what he hit her with.'

'What was the weapon, Vic?'

'A cucumber,' he said, pressing his teeth against his smile. 'Isn't that incredible? You'd think he'd use something sensible, like a sledgehammer. But they were having an argument about cucumbers at the time. He had it in his hand, then he hauled off and belted her with it.'

187

'You can't do much damage with a cucumber,' I said.

'It paralysed her!' Scaduto was tipping forward in his chair, trying not to laugh. 'That's what she said – she couldn't move. An ambulance came to take her away on a stretcher. The stretcher wouldn't fit through the kitchen door. She had to get up and walk into the hallway and lay down on it. That's the funny part.'

I said, 'That's not the only funny part.'

'Exactly,' he said. 'Ask me what happened to the cucumber.'

'You'll tell me anyway.'

'He ate it!' Scaduto said. 'That's what they were arguing about. She didn't want him to eat the cucumber, so he whacked her over the head with it and then ate it. He didn't count on her faking brain damage. You don't believe this, do you?'

'It sounds a little far-fetched.'

'If you were married you'd believe it,' he said. 'You'd think it was an understatement. This kind of thing happens all the time to married people.'

'But shootings don't,' I said. 'Someone just tried to kill Yorty. Maybe it was his wife.'

'No. His wife left him – she's in the States. Poor guy.' Now Scaduto looked contrite. 'I shouldn't have told you that cucumber story. But that's all I know about him.'

The next morning, Ambassador Noyes gave the senior officers a briefing.

The crueller ones among us called him 'No-Yes'. He was a tall whitefaced man with thin pale hair and the stiffness and exaggerated sense of decorum that you often associate with people of low intelligence. He often said he liked golf an awful lot. He had the shoulders and the plodding gait of a golfer. He had no interest in politics and had never before held a diplomatic post. But he was a personal friend of the President, and this post of US Ambassador to Britain was regarded by many people as membership in the ultimate country club. It was expensive but it offered real status. It also proved that money could buy practically anything.

Ambassador Noyes had another trait I had noticed in many slow-witted people: he was tremendously interested in philosophy.

'I guess you've all heard about the shooting,' he was saying. 'As far as I'm concerned, this is just about the most serious thing that's happened since I took up this post.'

Although he was nervous and rather new, he did not find his a difficult job. His number two man, Everett Horton, was a career diplomat who had been in London ten years and had wonderful sources. And of course the eight hundred of us at the London embassy were each working towards the same end: to prop up the ambassador and put him in the know. I could think of twenty people who were directly responsible to the ambassador. There was Horton, Brickhouse, Kneedler and Roscoe, besides Scaduto, Sanger and Jeeps. There was Pomeroy, MacWeeney, Geach, Baskies, Pryczinski and Frezza, Schoonmaker, Kelly, Kountz and Toomajian, Shinebald and Oberlander. There was me. There were the boys on the third floor. And that was just the inner circle. We were at his service; we were his eyes and ears; we were the best, most of us overqualified for the jobs we were doing. How could he fail?

'I'm determined to get to the bottom of it,' he went on. 'I want to show these people – whoever they are – that we are not afraid of anyone, and that we are, if provoked, quite able to hit back.'

He was a reasonable man. He was also a multi-millionaire. How he had made his fortune was a mystery to me, but it was no mystery to me how he had kept it. He was unprejudiced and fair; he gave everyone a hearing; he was also unsentimental. I suspected he was strong. He was certainly practical, and I knew from the way he lived that he was a simple soul. He knew how to delegate power and how to take decisions. I was sure he knew his weaknesses – if he hadn't he would not have been so successful.

All this is necessary background – I mean, the reasonableness of his character – because his next words were very fierce indeed.

'When I find out who did this, I can promise you that it'll be the last time they try it. We're going to jump on them hard. Our flag will not be insulted.'

The mention of 'flag' put me in mind of Dwight Yorty and the cucumber, and I lowered my eyes as I listened to Ambassador Noyes's tremulous voice.

'I spoke to the President last night and he assured me that he will support us to the hilt. I don't have to tell you gentlemen that we are more than a match for anyone who takes up arms against us.'

This was fighting talk. We muttered our approval, and there was

189

a little burst of appreciative handclapping. But I could tell that the response was mixed. The older men seemed very pleased at the prospect of kicking someone's teeth in. The younger men and all the women were clearly irked by the threats. Most of us judged the ambassador to be uncharacteristically credulous. Perhaps he was trying to make an impression by swearing revenge. I wondered how it would sound after it was leaked to the press.

Everett Horton spoke next. At times like this he was captain of the team rather than coach. He was correct, modest, loyal and deferential. He gave a good imitation of controlled anger – I doubted that he had been angry at all. His voice expressed intense indignation.

'The Ambassador has been forthright – and with reason. This is the sixth terrorist incident involving American Embassy personnel in the past two months. It is the first one we've had in London. Obviously, there's a movement afoot in Europe to frighten us.' He paused and said, 'I'm not frightened, but I'm kind of mad.'

Ambassador Noyes smiled in agreement at this, and some of us shuffled our feet in embarrassment.

'One American has been killed, and another wounded – both in Paris,' Horton said. 'Three incidents have been kept out of the papers, as you know. But the Ambassador has decided, and I agree, that this attempt on the life of one of our serving officers should be given maximum publicity.'

He then read us the press release, with the details of the shooting: At approximately fifteen-thirty hours ... Dwight A. Yorty fired upon ... unknown assailant ... believed to be political. He showed us a street map of the embassy neighbourhood, and as he took us through it step by step he looked more and more like a quarterback explaining a game-plan that had gone wrong.

'Any questions?'

No hands went up, perhaps because the Ambassador was in the room standing behind Horton with his arms folded, ready for battle.

I decided to risk a question. I stood up and said, 'Everett, you called it a terrorist incident. Have we any proof of that?'

Before Horton could speak, the Ambassador stepped forward. 'A man was terrorized – shot at,' he said. 'There's only one sort of person who does that. Everett?'

'I think we're in total agreement, Mr Ambassador,' Horton said.

I was still standing. I said, 'What I meant was, has any group like the IRA or the PLO or Black September – or anyone – claimed credit for it?'

My question exasperated the Ambassador. He sighed and stepped away, seeing me as an obstruction. He said, 'I'll let you field that one, Everett.'

'No terrorist group has come forward,' Horton said. 'In one of the Paris shootings the same pattern was followed – an unknown assailant. But it wasn't robbery in either of the incidents. It's got to be political.'

Now Oberlander was on his feet. 'Excuse me,' he said, 'but isn't it somewhat premature to call this shooting political?'

'No,' Horton said, 'because we've got a good description of the man. Dark hair, dark eyes, swarthy features, a slight build, about five-foot-six. Arab. He may be the same man who was responsible for those Paris incidents. We're sure they're linked. And frankly' – Horton made a half-turn towards the Ambassador – 'I'd love to nail him.'

Al Sanger said, 'What about the guy who was picked up right after the shooting?'

This was news to me.

'He was released,' Horton said. 'He didn't fit Yorty's description.'

'I hope you won't find this question malicious,' Errol Jeeps said, 'but how is it the guy took six or seven shots at point-blank range and missed?'

'Five shots,' I said.

Horton said, 'We haven't found any of the cartridges, so we don't know how many shots. Maybe it was one. Apparently he missed because Yorty was parking his car at the time – in the staff garage.'

'Instead of looking for cartridges,' Sanger said, 'why not look for the slugs?'

'That is up to the British police who, so far, have done a superb job,' Horton said.

Horton repeated that we would not give in to intimidation, and the Ambassador refolded his arms in defiant emphasis. And he fixed his jaw and nodded stiffly as Horton advised us to take all necessary precautions. If any of us had reason to think we were under threat, he said, we could apply for police protection.

Erroll Jeeps said, 'These British cops don't have guns but they got some real loud whistles.'

'We'll ignore that remark, Mr Jeeps,' Horton said. 'In the meantime, remember, the best defence is a good offence. Thank you, gentlemen.'

And then, unexpectedly, I was asked to leak it to the British press. I had been very doubtful about the whole affair, but what made my nagging questions the more urgent was the Ambassador's request, relayed by Horton, for me to see a reliable journalist on the *Telegraph* or *The Times* and spell it out.

I said I would need time to think about it.

'Thinking is not necessary in this case,' Horton said. 'I just want you to give an accurate summary of our attitude. You were at the briefing.'

'The whole team was there.'

'You were taking notes,' he said. 'I saw you.'

'I was writing down questions, and wishing I had answers to them.'

'You asked questions. I gave you answers.'

'I didn't ask you the most important one, because I thought Yorty might be in the room. I didn't want him to feel he was on trial.'

'Ask me now, if it'll make you feel better.'

'Okay,' I said. 'Yorty didn't see the gunman. I re-enacted the shooting with Scaduto standing in Culross Street. If Yorty was in the garage – and he must have been, because I was right above him – there is no way that he could have seen the man who was shooting at him.'

Horton said, 'That's a statement, not a question.'

'This is my question,' I said. 'He didn't see the gunman, so how was Yorty able to supply you with a description of him?'

'Your premise is false,' Horton said. 'Therefore, the question doesn't arise. He saw the man. That's how he gave us a description.'

'Couldn't have – impossible. And that's the problem, because it leaves us with two answers to the question. And both of them put Yorty in a bad light.'

'Yorty's a married man with a spotless record,' Horton said crossly.

'His wife's in London?'

'She's on sick-leave,' Horton said. 'I don't know why I'm answering these questions.'

I said, 'Listen. He gave you a description because he knew the gunman beforehand, and he didn't have to see him to describe him accurately. That's the first possibility.'

'If Dwight Yorty was the sort of man who ran around with those sort of people I think the boys on the third floor would know about it.'

I ignored this. 'The second possibility is that because Yorty knew the gunman he deliberately didn't describe him accurately. In which case, he doesn't want us to catch the guy.'

'You just sit there assuming that Yorty knows this killer!' Horton said. 'That's incredible!'

'He definitely knew him,' I said.

'Prove it.'

'Because he definitely didn't see him, and he definitely gave us a description of the man.'

Horton said, 'This is interesting. Thinking always is. It's fun, let's face it. But you're not paid to contradict the Ambassador. I can tell you he's really mad. He knows that I'm asking you to pass this along to the press.' Horton put his fingertips together and flexed them. 'And when he opens his paper in a few days he will expect to see an accurate version of his point of view, not a garbled mess that impugns the honesty of a serving officer –'

I wanted to say: Yorty hit his wife over the head with a cucumber, and then he ate it, and now she's trying to sue him for brain damage.

I said, 'I'd like to know a little more about the man who was picked up after the shooting.'

'He didn't fit Yorty's description,' Horton said. 'He was released.'

'Yorty's description doesn't really count, because he didn't see the gunman. The suspect was seen running down Park Street.'

'Jogging,' Horton said. 'He was a jogger.'

'That's useful. He's athletic. It could explain the gun. A runner might have access to a starter's pistol – one that shoots blanks.'

'Just because no cartridges were found doesn't mean that no shots were fired.'

'True,' I said, 'but no bullet-holes were found either. No slugs. No marks on the garage walls.'

Horton said, 'You've been working overtime.'

'I was looking out of the window when it happened. I didn't see anything. Yorty couldn't have seen anything.'

And he hit his wife with a cucumber and she called it attempted murder.

'I'm glad you've told me all of this speculation,' Horton said, 'because if any of it gets into the paper I'll know who to blame. Maybe someone else should be found to leak the story.'

'No, no,' I said. 'I want to do it – please let me. Just give me a little time. I've got to find the right paper, one that the wire services will pick up on.'

Horton smiled. 'Remember, you're doing this for the Ambassador. He didn't like your performance at the briefing – you asked too many questions. He'll be watching you.'

'Do you trust me, coach?' I hated saying the word, but with Horton it always worked.

'Of course I do.'

'I'll do exactly what I'm told,' I said. 'But I'd appreciate it if you'd ask Yorty one question on my behalf. There's no harm in asking. It might even be a good idea. After all, since we're accusing Libya of sponsoring an assassination attempt, we really ought to have most of the facts. And it's a simple question.'

'Go ahead,' Horton said.

'Just this – and it would help if you reminded him that it doesn't matter whether he swears on a stack of Bibles that he's telling the truth, because this fact is checkable. It concerns the man who was picked up right after the shooting, the one you said was innocent. Has Yorty ever seen him before?'

'What if he says yes?'

'Then that's your man, because Yorty didn't see him at the time of the shooting. He knew him – perhaps very well, perhaps so well that he wanted to hide the fact.'

Horton said, 'Then why did the guy try to kill him?'

'He didn't,' I said. 'Only ex-lovers shoot to kill.'

Two days passed, and on the morning of the third I entered my office to find Everett Horton seated at my desk.

He said, 'Have you leaked the story yet?'

'Not yet,' I said, but in fact I'd had no intention of doing so until we had all the information, which was why I was so eager to take sole responsibility for it.

'That's a relief,' Horton said.

'He answered the question,' I said.

Horton nodded. 'Yorty is leaving us,' he said. 'He's leaving the Foreign Service, too. And his wife is leaving him – already left him, so I understand.'

'I feel sorry for him,' I said.

'Forget it,' Horton said. 'The Ambassador wants to see you. Don't bring up the incident in our backyard to him. He was impressed, I think, by your tenacity, but it's rather a sore point.'

Ambassador Noyes said, 'I was wondering whether you're free to join us for dinner on the twenty-first. We'd like to see you at Winfield House.'

'I accept with pleasure.'

He said, 'The Prime Minister will be there.'

So that was my reward.

17

THE WINFIELD WALLPAPER
★

Dinner at Winfield House, the American Ambassador's residence in Regent's Park, was usually regarded as a treat, not a duty. But the guests of honour tonight were the Prime Minister and her husband. I had guessed that my invitation was a reward, and then I began to suspect that I was being put to work. I did not really mind – I had nothing else to do. After more than a year in London I still had no lover, no close friends, no recreations. I had plenty of society but not much pleasure: it was not an easy city. And perhaps I over-reacted to Ambassador Noyes's invitation. I bought a new tuxedo and a formal shirt. The shirt cost me forty-seven dollars.

I was heading home to change, and reflecting on the safest topics to discuss with the Prime Minister, when I saw the car. Every Friday evening since early in January I had seen this car parked on the corner of Alexandra Avenue and Prince of Wales Drive, and always two people inside. As the weeks passed I began to be on the watch for the car. The man and woman in the front seat were either talking quietly or embracing. On some evenings they sat slightly apart, sipping from paper cups. Three months later, but always on Fridays, they were still at it.

There was something touching about this weekly romance in the front seat of an old Rover. It was ritual, not routine. Sometimes the two people seemed to me as passionate and tenacious as a pair of spies – lovers clinging together and hiding for a cause; and sometimes they made me feel like a spy.

I supposed they worked in the same office, that he drove her home, and that on Fridays – using the heavy traffic as an excuse – they made this detour in Battersea to spend an hour together. It was their secret life, this love affair. The parked car seemed to say that it was kept secret from everyone. It was probably the only hour in the week that mattered to them.

Tonight they were kissing. The spring air was mild, and the trees in the park were blossomy, pink and white, palely lit by the lingering sunset and the refracted riverlight that reached past the embankments and cast no shadows. We had had high clouds, mountains of them, all day, and every new leaf was a different shade of green. Spring was magic in London, the city seemed to rise from the dead. There was no winter freeze, as in some northern cities, but rather a brown season of decay and bad smells. April brought grass and flowers out of the mud, and healed the city with leaves, and made it new. This was my second spring, and it was, again, a surprise.

The couple in the car helped my mood. I set off for Winfield House, whistling a pop song I had been hearing, called 'Dancing on the Radio'. I was wearing new clothes. I had done my exercises, and had had a shower and a drink. It had been a good day. In my cable I had summarized in a thousand words yesterday's by-election; a month ago I had correctly predicted the outcome. I had borrowed Al Sanger's Jaguar, and as I drove up Park Lane I turned on the radio and heard a Mozart concerto, the one for flute and harp. It gave me optimism and a sense of victory. I had solitude and warmth, and all my bills were paid, and I had a general feeling of reassurance. Everything was going to be all right. It began to rain lightly and I thought: Perfect.

When I came to the iron gates of Winfield House, four armed men appeared. I opened my side-window and heard noises from the zoo, grunts and bird squawks. The men examined my invitation and found my name on their clipboard, and I was waved in. The security precautions reminded me once again that the Prime Minister was coming. I was by now excited at the prospect of meeting her.

I was announced by the doorman. Ambassador Noyes sprang forward when he heard my name. He seemed nervous and rather serious. Everett Horton and Margaret Duboys were there and, soon after, more guests arrived. Most of them were nice American millionaires who lived part-time in London. There was also a journalist, and an American academic and his wife, and a novelist – he was fortyish and talkative, delighted to be there, and his smug square face was gleaming with gratitude. One group of guests had already been more or less herded into the green room to admire the wallpaper.

'I think it's best if we sort of gather in there,' Ambassador Noyes said. This was an order, but he said it uncertainly, which was one of the reasons he was called 'No-yes'.

He was the shepherd, and Horton and I were the sheepdogs, and the non-diplomatic people were the sheep. The idea was to keep them from straying without making them panic or feel penned in.

Horton whispered, 'Not a word about interest rates tonight, please.'

Then he hurried to the far end of the room and began helpfully pointing at the wall.

The wallpaper in this room was famous. It was Chinese, four centuries old – or was it five? – and had been found in Hong Kong by a recent ambassador, who had had it restored and hung. It was the colour of pale jade and there were pictures of birds and flowers on it, hummingbirds and poppies and lotuses. It was a classic item, it had the look of a Chinese cliché, even to the predictable pagodas. It had been so carefully repainted it looked like a copy – it was too perfect, too bright, not a crack or a peel-mark anywhere, and every figure on it was primly arranged in a pattern of curves. The pattern was old and slightly irregular, but the surface design had been scoured of its subtlety with the fresh paint, and there was not an interesting shadow on it anywhere. You scrutinized it because it was famous, and then you were dis-appointed because you had scrutinized it. Such interesting wall-paper, people said; but if it had been less famous it might have looked more interesting. And I felt that the prettier wallpaper was, the worse the wall it hid.

It had another feature, this wallpaper – it inspired the dullest conversation: how old was it, and was it really paper, and how much had it cost?

It made me want to change the subject. I was talking with Debbie Horton, telling her the correct version of a story about me that had been going the rounds. A few months before I had attended a fund-raising dinner and at my table I had spoken to a man whom everyone present had been referring to as 'Sonny'. Sonny was a tall rosy-cheeked man with the subdued manner of a botanist or a handyman. 'What do you do?' I had asked. He became awfully flustered. 'Nothing much,' he then said, and was silent for the rest of the meal. Afterwards, a smirking, sharp-faced woman said, 'That was Sonny Marlborough – the Duke of Marlborough, to you.' It was a good story and, as President Nixon used to tell his aides with a sweaty little grin, it had the additional merit of being true.

Debbie had heard the gossip version, that he had said, 'What do I do? I'm a duke –'

Then I forgot everything. I couldn't think. I was looking at a young woman's back, and at her yellow hair, the way it came out in little wings over her ears, and the curve of her hip, a line from where her small hand rested on her waist, to her knee, and the way her green dress was smooth against her thigh. I went weak as if suddenly standing up drunk, and I felt lost in admiration and anticipated failure and the kind of hopeless fear in a flash of blindness that is known only to those who feel desire. I wanted to touch her and talk to her.

Debbie Horton was saying, 'You're not even listening to me!'

'I heard every word you said.' Insincerity made my voice over-serious and emphatic.

'What are you looking at?' Debbie said.

A stir in the room saved me. There was a shifting of feet, the guests looking at each other and then at the door, which the Prime Minister and her husband were just passing through with the Ambassador and his wife. We fell silent, and the Prime Minister began talking in a loud friendly way about how much she liked the wallpaper.

'It's silk, of course,' the Prime Minister said.

This silent smiling mob at my end of the room was already tremendously impressed. This was how you talked about wall-paper!

The young woman had also turned to see the Prime Minister. She was about thirty, her face was bright with intelligence and a kind of shyness. She had a little smile of fear on her lips, giving her mouth a pretty pair of parentheses, and there was something lovely and unglamorous about her that gave her real beauty. Her dress was a simple one, but the neck of it was edged in lace. Her eyes were green, she had small feet, her skin looked warm.

No one spoke. The Prime Minister was being introduced, and most of us were beaming horribly at her in case she should look up.

'I have a law degree myself!' she was saying to one guest. She spoke in a hearty headmistressy shout.

Two steps took me nearer the young woman with green eyes, and I whispered, 'We haven't met.'

She smiled and looked towards the Prime Minister, who was approaching us.

I said in a low voice, 'What do you think of the wallpaper?'

She laughed a little and said, 'I like its lame uncertain curves.'

'Flora Domingo-Duncan,' Ambassador Noyes said, appearing next to her. 'Doctor Duncan is currently doing research in London.'

'On Mary Shelley,' she said, with hesitant bow to the Prime Minister.

'Frankenstein!' the Prime Minister shouted, and moved on. She had already put herself in charge of us.

I again wanted to touch Flora Domingo-Duncan. I could not think of anything to say to her. I needed time, and I knew I looked stupid and slow.

At this point, the Prime Minister's husband came forward, and was introduced. This man had been made into a celebrity by an English comedian, who had portrayed him in a popular farce as a sour-faced paranoiac in a cardigan, interested in nothing but drinking and playing golf. In this unlikely way he had become as famous as his wife, but something of a joke-figure. I could see at once that the comedian had got him wrong. He was kindly, he was funny, and he had an easy laugh – a way of throwing his head back and braying his approval. He scowled and smiled; he was skinny and nimble; he had a very funny upper-middle-class drawl.

'Is this your first time in London?' he asked Dr Duncan.

'No,' she said. 'I did graduate work at Oxford three years ago.'

'I know who you are,' he said to me. 'You're with the firm, aren't you? Yes' – and threw his head back and laughed – 'you see I've done my homework! I read that sheet of names they gave me – all your little biographies.'

This was surprising candour – dinner-party homework was never mentioned – but it made me like him. He saw it properly as both a joke and a duty.

I said to Doctor Duncan, 'You have a lovely name. Flora Domingo-Duncan.'

'My mother is Mexican.' She was polite and patient, and I wondered whether she was bored by me.

The Prime Minister's husband said, 'Yes, some of these Mexicans actually do have blonde hair.'

'My mother's hair is brown,' Doctor Duncan said.

We were getting nowhere. I wanted to be alone with her. I wanted to meet her later in the week for dinner. Maybe she had a boy-friend?

Horton joined our little group; he introduced a lady by the name of Bloomsack, then whispered to me, 'That was a wonderful cable you wrote today on the by-election.'

'Thanks, coach,' I said, and for some reason thought of the old Rover car parked on the corner of Alexandra Avenue and Prince of Wales Drive, and the two people in it, kissing, and I stepped nearer Flora Domingo-Duncan.

Horton was whispering behind me, 'If the subject of interest rates come up with the PM, I'll give you a signal. I'll need some back-up.' And he went away.

I was watching Doctor Duncan's pulse at her neck, an almost imperceptible flutter between a branch of bones.

Mrs Bloomsack said, 'I was at Carrington's last night,' to the Prime Minister's husband.

'Yaaas,' he drawled warily, tipping his head back.

The woman had equivocated – 'Carrington,' she had said, not 'Lord' or 'Peter'. Lord Carrington was the Foreign Secretary.

'Wasn't he the man,' Doctor Duncan said, 'who settled the Rhodesian issue?'

'Yes,' said Mrs Bloomsack.

'No, no, no,' the Prime Minister's husband said. 'I'll tell you who did that. I'll tell you who brought both sides together and did most of the preliminary work.' And he turned and with an owlish face and immense pride he said, 'It was that lady over there. That's who it was. Yaaas.'

He was smiling fondly at the Prime Minister. She saw him and smiled back. She had a hard pleasureless smile and slightly dis-coloured teeth, and her skin was like flawed dusty marble. Her face was vain, unimpressed, and attractive, and her body square and powerful. Her eyes were heavy-lidded, and there was a sack-like heaviness in her, a wilfulness and impatience that gave her an aura of strength. Even her hair looked hard. In every way she was the opposite of her husband.

Ambassador Noyes stared at me. He was with the Prime Minister and I think he wanted help. I pretended not to see him.

'I'm interested in your research on Mary Shelley,' I said to Doctor Duncan. 'I re-read *Frankenstein* recently. "Misery made me a fiend. Make me happy, and I shall again be virtuous." That poor monster.'

'Frankenstein's the doctor, not the monster,' Mrs Bloomsack said, seeming pleased with herself.

'Yaaas,' the Prime Minister's husband said, lifting his sharp nose at the woman.

'Most people get it wrong,' she said.

'Do they?' the Prime Minister's husband said. 'I had no idea.' He shook his head at her and in a gentle way watched her stumble. Did he know how funny he was?

I said, 'I have a theory that this novel represents a fear of childbirth. Mary Shelley's mother died giving birth to her, there had been several miscarriages in her family – or Shelley's family – and she wrote it when she was pregnant. Can't *Frankenstein* be seen as an expression of the fear of giving birth to a monster, or a corpse?'

'But a lot of people have that theory,' Doctor Duncan said. She tossed her loose gold hair and smiled at me. 'But she wasn't pregnant, and anyway is Dr Frankenstein the father or the mother of the monster?'

'Does it make a difference?'

'We are being summoned to dinner,' the Prime Minister's husband said, and stood aside to let the ladies pass.

'As a feminist, I think it makes a big difference,' Doctor Duncan said. 'You don't believe me.'

'No, no, it's not that,' I said. 'Feminists are usually such scolds. But you're so nice.'

'I'm not nice,' she said lightly. 'I'm selfish, I'm bossy, I'm opinionated, and I'm a scold, too. My students are afraid of me.' She was grinning, giving her mouth the pretty parentheses. 'And I'm impossible to live with.'

'You're full of surprises,' I said. 'When I asked you about the Chinese wallpaper you said, "I like its lame uncertain curves." That's pretty funny.'

'It's a quotation,' she said, 'from Charlotte Perkins Gilman. You don't know her story, *The Yellow Wallpaper*?' She smiled at my ignorance. 'She was another impossible woman. It was very nice to meet you.'

And I felt, furiously, that she was saying good-bye to me.

The table was set for sixteen people. Flora Domingo-Duncan was sitting at a distant corner, between Everett Horton and Mr Sidney Bloomsack. The Prime Minister was halfway down the table, next to Ambassador Noyes, and her husband was just across from her. I saw Doctor Duncan speaking to Mr Bloomsack, who had the tanned white-and-brown head of a yachtsman in his sixties – he radiated money and virility – and I became uneasy and thought how funny and spirited Doctor Duncan was, how self-possessed and surprising. She was pretty, she was bright-eyed, she was frank. I had nothing to offer her, but again I felt the sad urgency of desire for her.

It is customary at such a dinner to speak to the person on your immediate right. This was Mrs Fentiman, wife of the New York publisher, who was in London in a take-over bid for the English firm of Howletts.

Mrs Fentiman said, 'I can't think of anything to say to the Prime Minister's husband.'

'Ask him about Zimbabwe or North Sea Oil,' I said. 'Don't mention interest rates or unemployment.'

But I was watching Flora Domingo-Duncan, and my heart ached when I saw how far away she was. I was in an undertow – I was very far from shore.

The meal was served. It began with pheasant consommé and sherry, and then *Navarin de homard*. The main course was *Escalopine de veau Normande*, with broccoli and dauphine potatoes and a *Gateau de carottes aux fines herbes*, and the wine with it was Pinot Noir 1977. There was red salad and deep-fried camembert, and dessert was *Bombe glacée* with fresh strawberries and cream, and I had three glasses of champagne.

I ate, I listened to Mrs Fentiman, and, instead of watching the Prime Minister to see how she was getting on with the ambassador, I stared hopelessly at Doctor Duncan, trying to catch her eye. She never once glanced in my direction. Several times, while watching her, I saw her laugh – she had a loud energetic laugh. I loved her laughter, and yet it made me feel rueful. Why was I sitting so far from her?

There were toasts – to the Queen, to our President – and then speeches. The Ambassador's, made with notes, was a simple affirmation of Anglo-US friendship; the Prime Minister's speech was an eloquent and graceful rejoinder which had the effect of making Ambassador Noyes seem as if he had asked an intelligent question – he looked surprised and pleased. At their best, the British could be very courtly, and the Prime Minister made us seem that night as if we were her dearest friends.

It was one of the best meals I had ever eaten; this was one of the most distinguished guest lists imaginable; Winfield House was one of the loveliest private homes in Regent's Park; the speeches were uplifting; and all that beautiful wallpaper! But I would have swapped it all for an hour of privacy with Flora Domingo-Duncan.

'And you're a pretty fussy eater,' Mrs Fentiman said. She was still talking! 'You hardly touched your meal. Are you one of these food cranks?'

'No. I just got very strange when I was in the Far East,' I said.

She did not smile. She twitched a little. I hated women who looked like men.

'The State Department has a lot to answer for,' I said.

Having successfully bewildered Mrs Fentiman, I scrambled to get near Doctor Duncan, nearly knocking down Mrs Bloomsack. Doctor Duncan was smiling at me, seeming to invite me over to join her! Just behind me, I heard Horton clearing his throat, and then he threw his arm around me.

'The word is that she wants to hear about interest rates. We'll have an informal session over coffee. You're going to like her. She is really an amazing human being.'

I said, 'I don't know anything about interest rates.'

'Improvise,' Horton said.

'It seems to me that's what all the economists are doing,' I said. 'Improvising.'

'That's kind of a cute opening – why don't you use it on her? She'll appreciate it.'

Flora Domingo-Duncan had joined Margaret Duboys and Debbie Horton and the distinguished Sidney Bloomsack, who I could tell had taken a shine to her. He was a rich, idle man – he would make everything easy for her. He looked like the sort of man who had had every dollar and every woman he had ever wanted. It was awful to think that she and I might never have a chance to talk, and she might go off with S. Bloomsack thinking he wasn't a bad guy – generous at least. Some women in the company of vain and ridiculous men look vain and ridiculous themselves, and some look like hookers. Doctor Duncan looked serene. She had the prettiest shoulders. She was listening, giving nothing away.

'Hurry up,' Horton said, squeezing my arm. 'She hates to be kept waiting.'

I heard a loud sudden burst of laughter and recognized it as Doctor Duncan's. What a wonderful laugh! What had Bloomsack said that was so funny? They were all laughing now, over there, the millionaires, the academics, the journalist, the novelist. They were having a swell time.

My whole life had been like this. Working in second-floor offices in Africa, in Malaysia, in London, I had looked out of the window and seen lovers strolling on the ground, or people smiling at nothing; I had seen the casual way that people met, the way they chatted, how they held hands. And I was always doing something else. My work was my life. I had never been idle. I was always a little late for an appointment, a little overdue with bills, a little behind in my work, and there was always someone in the next room with a problem for me. I was seen by everyone as a master; but no one was a more put-upon servant, keeping regular hours and at the mercy of anyone at all who demanded to see me.

It seemed wrong to like solitude so much, but I had always lived in empty rooms, and craved privacy, because I was overworked. And now, like any servant, I saw how completely I had surrendered and how much I had wasted. I had been praised, but praise was not enough; I was well-paid, but what did money matter? I had never had the time to spend it. It seemed that I had always been a bystander, watching life through a second-storey window and expected to talk about the wallpaper. Love was for after work, but I was always at work.

This woman had woken in me desire, and a realization of my own envy, cowardice, loneliness, and disappointment – I couldn't say despair. But I began to think that I did not deserve her, which is one of the gravest sins of all, self-doubt. What a lovely name, what a ringing laugh, what a pretty mouth.

Watching Flora Domingo-Duncan, and thinking about myself, I was taking a chair in front of the Prime Minister.

'The Prime Minister was wondering about interest rates,' Horton said to me.

'I was told,' she said in a hectoring, too-loud voice, 'that you could quite easily put me in the picture. Just how long are your rates going to go on rising?'

She was known for her directness. I sat down and began explaining, and again I heard the sudden laughter of Doctor Duncan. She was with that other group – the ones drinking port and cognac, who would go away thinking what a wonderful time they had had at Winfield House with the Prime Minister and those powerful London embassy people. We were drinking water. We were talking in abstractions. From my point of view the evening was a failure, because I wanted for once to be on the far side of the room. The only thing that mattered was human happiness; however distinguished or powerful we looked here in this corner beside the expensive fake-looking wallpaper – the Prime Minister, Horton, Ambassador Noyes and myself – we were merely temporary people, actors with small speaking roles, reciting lines that were required of us: we knew what an uncertain thing power was. We were talking about the world, and pretending that we had a measure of control over it, but it was mostly bluff. Or did we really believe that this concern was more important than that laughter?

We had done with interest rates and grain sales and the Polish debt, and then a silence fell.

To fill it, I said, 'Prime Minister, the unemployment rate in Britain strikes some of us as a serious matter. Have you any –'

'No one is more concerned about it than I am,' she said, with the force of someone who believed she might soon lose her job. 'I take it very seriously indeed. But the long-term projections are encouraging, and we believe it will be substantially reduced in the next quarter.'

'I don't see how,' I said, and I looked for Flora Domingo-Duncan across the room.

I had, through inattention, been too sceptical. This aroused the Prime Minister, and she began to speak in a venomous way. 'There are a few vicious, self-serving, greedy, desperate, power-seeking –'

Flora Domingo-Duncan was leaving.

I said, 'It seems hopeless.'

'Don't you believe that for a moment,' the Prime Minister said; she had never looked plumper, and her plumpness was like armour.

What had I started? They were all staring at me! Was it unemployment. Oh, God, I thought, and I saw that the hardest thing in the world for me to do would be to leave that little group. I had to stay, to give the Prime Minister a chance to say her piece, and to satisfy the Ambassador and Horton. But there was no time, and in the swing of that silence I stood.

'Excuse me.'

And turned my back on them.

She was in the large, wood-panelled foyer, speaking to the Bloomsacks. Mrs Noyes was saying good-night to the Fentimans. Chauffeurs were being summoned from the rain and darkness.

'Do you need a ride home?' I said. 'I have a car.'

'The Bloomsacks are taking me,' Doctor Duncan said. 'But thanks anyway.'

I said, 'We didn't have much of a chance to talk.'

'I saw you talking to the Prime Minister,' she said. 'I mean, you were actually *talking* to her. That was –'

'No, no!' Mrs Bloomsack exploded. 'Mine is the dark blue one!' Pumping her arms, this short stout woman crossed to the cloakroom where a blank-faced servant held the wrong coat in both of his hands.

'May I get your coat, Flora?' Mr Bloomsack said.

'It's a green cape,' she said.

And then we were alone, Flora Domingo-Duncan and I.

'I want to see you again, very much, for a meal – or anything.' I was talking fast.

'That would be nice.' She looked at me with curiosity, and her gaze lingered in a tipsy way. She had the slightly out-of-focus look in her eyes of someone who wears contact lenses.

'What's your telephone number?'

She told me. I scribbled it on my wrist in ballpoint.

'Call me,' she said.

Mr Bloomsack was returning with her coat. His teeth were gleaming. He was pushing towards me.

'When?' I said, with such insistence that she smiled again.

'Tonight,' she whispered, and then turned so that Mr Bloomsack could help her put on her cape.

★ 18 ★

DANCING ON THE RADIO
★

Flora Domingo-Duncan said, 'I used to be a mess,' and laughed and said, 'It was my mother. So I went to graduate school in California and put three thousand miles between us. God, am I boring!'

'You're not boring,' I said.

'I don't want you to get sick of me.'

'I'll never get sick of you.'

We were naked in bed on our backs and speaking to the ceiling.

'Anyway, I was a wreck,' she said, and clawed her blonde hair away from her forehead. 'I had a shrink. I wasn't embarrassed, I just didn't want to talk about it, so I told people I was seeing my dentist. Twice a week! "You must have terrible teeth," they'd say. But it was my mind that was a mess. Hey, why are we talking about my mind?'

Because during our love-making we had become very private and fallen silent. I thought then that no one was more solitary than during orgasm. We were resuming an interrupted conversation.

'I like your mind,' I said. 'I like your green eyes. I like your sweet et cetera.'

'Good old E. E. Cummings.' She was expert at spotting quotations. We agreed on most things, on *Wuthering Heights*, *To the Lighthouse*, *Dubliners* and *Pale Fire*; on Joyce Cary, Henry James, Chekhov and Emily Dickinson. We shared a loathing for Ernest Hemingway. That night we had gone to the National Theatre to see *La Ronde*, by Arthur Schnitzler; and then I made omelettes; and we went to bed, and talked about *La Ronde*, and made love. But literature was as crucial as sex – we were getting serious. Liking a particular book opened a bright new dimension of pleasure and experience. Taste mattered: who wanted to live with a philistine, or to listen to half-baked opinions? Everything mattered. And there was her Mexican side, a whole other world. It was not exactly revealed to me, but I was aware of its existence. In all ways, with Flora, I seemed to be kneeling at her keyhole. She loved that expression.

It was spring, and the windows were open. The night-sweet fragrance of flowering trees was in the air.

'This is luxury,' she said. She pronounced it *lugzhery*, because she knew I found it funny, like her comic pronunciation of groceries, *grosheries*.

'But I have to go,' she said.

'Stay a while longer.'

'Just a little while.'

She lived off Goldhawk Road, at Stamford Brook, in two rooms. It was there that she worked on Mary Shelley, with occasional visits to the British Library. Her time was limited. She had only until July to finish her research; then back to the States and summer school teaching. She worked every morning, and so it was important to her that she left me at night.

'I have to wake up in my own bed,' she said. 'Otherwise I won't get anything done.'

I admired her enterprise and her independence, but I was also a bit threatened by them – or perhaps made uneasy, because her life seemed complete. She had a Ph.D., an Oxford D.Phil., and was an assistant professor at Bryn Mawr. She was presently on a travelling fellowship, working on a biography of Mary Shelley. She was beautiful, and I never wanted her to go. She had never spent a whole night in my bed.

I said, 'I wish you needed me more.'

'That's silly. You should be glad I'm independent,' she said. 'I can see you more clearly. Don't you know how much I like you?'

I liked her. I craved her company. I liked myself better when I was with her. The word 'like' was useless.

'But I need you.'

'There's no reason why you have to say it like that,' she said, smiling gently and kissing me. 'Anyway, you have everything.'

'I used to think that,' I said.

She said, 'It's scary, meeting someone you like. Friendship is scarier than sex. I keep thinking, "What if he goes away? What if he stops liking me? What if . . . what if . . . ?" '

'I'm not going anywhere.'

'But I am,' she said. She could be decisive. She kissed me and got out of bed and dressed quickly. And minutes later I was

209

watching her car pull away from Overstrand Mansions and already missing her.

I had thought that once we were sexually exhausted we would be bored with each other, and yet boredom never came, only the further excitement at the prospect of my seeing her again. Every succeeding time I was with her I liked her better, and discovered more in her – new areas of kindness, intelligence, and passion. I lusted for her.

She was not romantic. She was gentle, she was practical, and a little cautious. She had warned me against herself – she told me she was selfish, bossy, opinionated and possessive. She said, 'I'm impossible to live with.' But later she stopped talking this way. She said I made her happy. I had known her a month, but I saw her regularly – almost every evening.

We had made love the first night we met, after the Ambassador's party, at two in the morning, in distant Stamford Brook. We made love most evenings, always as if we were running out of time. It became like a ceremony, a ritual that was altering us. Each occasion was slightly different and separable, and fixed in my memory. So this continued, both of us burning, both of us expecting it to end. But we did not become bored – we were now close friends.

I had had lovers, but I had never had such a good friend, and for this friendship I loved her. I didn't tell her – I was afraid to use that word. The sex was part of it, but there was something more powerful – perhaps the recognition of how similar we were in some ways, how different in others, how necessary to each other's happiness.

Love is both panic and relief that you are not alone any more. All at once, someone else matters to your happiness. I hated to be parted from her. But she was busier than I was! She had just until July to finish her work, and then it was back to the States and her teaching. We lived with a feeling that this would all end soon, but this sense of limited time did not discourage me. I found myself making plans and, in an innocent way, falling in love with her.

It reassured me. I had never thought that I would fall in love with anyone. Then it seemed to me that living with another person was the only thing that mattered on earth, that this solitary life I had been leading was selfish and barren – and turning me into a crank – and that Flora was my rescuer. Part of love was bluff and fumbling and drunkenness, I knew that – but it was the pleasant afterglow of moonshine. The other part of love was real emotion; it was stony and desperate, it made all lovers shameless, and it did not spare me. I was alive, I was myself, only when I was with Flora, and that was always too seldom.

I could not see her on Friday nights. She did not say why, but Friday was out. I had a colleague – Brickhouse in the Press Section – who told me that after he got married he and his wife decided to give themselves a night off every week – it was Wednesday. Neither could count on the other's company on Wednesday, and neither was expected to reveal his plans. They weren't married on Wednesday night. Of course, most Wednesdays were the same – a meal, television, and to bed – in different rooms that night, that was the agreement. But some Wednesdays found Jack Brickhouse on his own and Marilyn inexplicably elsewhere; on other Wednesdays it was the other way around. This marriage, which was childless, lasted seven years. Brickhouse said, 'It was a good marriage – better than any I know. It was a good divorce, too. Listen, my ex-wife is my best friend!'

I used to wonder if for Flora it was that kind of Friday, keeping part of her life separate from me. It certainly disturbed me, because I was free most Fridays. I spent Fridays missing her, thinking of her, and wishing I was with her. Perhaps she knew this – counted on it? On the weekends when I was Duty Officer I did not see her at all.

I had asked her about her Fridays once. I said, 'I get it. It's the night you go on your meeting of Alcoholics Anonymous.'

I could not have been clumsier. But worry, self-pity, and probably anger, had made me very stupid.

She said, 'Do you have to know everything?' and then, 'If it is Alcoholics Anonymous I'm hardly likely to tell you, am I? The A A is very secret, very spiritual, and no one makes idiotic jokes about it. That's why it works.'

Maybe she was an alcoholic? But a few weeks later she told me that her father had had a drinking problem, and I knew somehow that she didn't.

Still, every Friday night I seemed to hang from my thumbs. On two successive Fridays I called her at her apartment, but there was no answer. Was she in bed with someone else and saying, 'This is our day off'? I wondered whether I could live with her and allow her her free Fridays. But of course I could – I would have allowed her anything!

And from this Friday business I came to know her as someone who could keep a secret. She did what she wanted, she stuck to a routine, she would not be bullied. So, not seeing her on Fridays, I learned to respect her, and to need her more; and it made our Saturdays passionate.

She never stayed the whole night with me, not even on the weekends. On the nights when I went back to her apartment she woke me up and always said, 'You're being kicked out of bed.' It was so that she could work, she said. She was determined to finish her Mary Shelley research on time.

On one of those late nights, when I was yawning, getting dressed sleepily, like a doctor or a fireman being summoned at an unearthly hour – but I was only going home to go back to bed – she said, 'By the way, I'm busy next weekend.'

'That's okay,' I said. But the news depressed me. 'What are you doing?'

Her beautiful silent smile silenced me.

That weekend passed. I missed her badly. I saw her on the Monday, and we went to the movie *Raging Bull*. She hated its violence, and I rather liked its Italian aromas – boxing and meatballs. I took her home in a taxi, but before we reached Stamford Brook she kissed me lightly, and I knew she had something on her mind.

'Please don't come in,' she said. 'I'm terribly tired.'

Well, she looked tired, so I didn't insist. I had the taxi drop me at Victoria and I walked the rest of the way home. It was not unpleasant, walking home late, thinking about her. And it did not seriously worry me that there was a part of her life that she kept separate from me, because when we were together we could not have been closer. I had never met anyone I liked better. It became a point of honour with me that I did not discuss her absent Fridays or that weekend. It was the only weekend she asked for – there were no others.

Enough time had passed, and we were both committed enough, for us to think of this as a love affair. Flora must love me, I thought, because she is inspiring my love. But so far, the embassy knew nothing about it.

This was just as well. Not long after Flora's mysterious weekend, we were given a talk on the anti-nuclear lobby in Britain. The feeling was fiercely against our installing nuclear missiles in various British sites. Every party hated us for it – the Labour Party because it was anti-Soviet, the Liberals because it was dangerous, the Conservatives because it was an iniquitous form of national trespass. We knew it was unpopular. We had five men gathering information on it. They had the names of the leaders of the pressure groups, they had infiltrated some of these groups, they had membership lists. They filmed the marches and demonstrations and all the speeches, whether they were at Hyde Park or at distant American bases in the English countryside, where the more passionate protesters chained themselves to the gates.

One of the films concerned a group calling itself Women Opposed to Nuclear Technology. It was not an anti-war movement, they weren't pacifists, they did not advocate unilateral disarmament. Their aims struck me as admirable. They wanted Britain to be a 'nuclear-free zone', no missiles, no neutron bombs, no reactors. And they were positive in their approach, giving seminars – so the boys on the third floor said – on alternative technology.

This film showed them marching with signs, massing in Hyde Park, and demonstrating at an American base. The highlight of this weekend of protest was an all-night vigil, which won them a great deal of publicity. They didn't shout, they didn't make speeches. They simply stood with lighted candles and informative posters. It was a remarkable show of determination, and one of the women in the film was Flora Domingo-Duncan.

I sat in the darkness of the embassy theatre and listened to the dead-pan narration of one of our intelligence men, and I watched him take his little baton and point in the general direction of the woman I loved.

'This sort of thing is doing us an awful lot of harm,' he said.

I smiled, and loved her more.

Did she know she was on film?

'No,' she said, 'but I'm damned glad you told me. The others will be mad as anything. Why did you tell me?'

'It's every citizen's right to know,' I said. 'Freedom of information.'

She laughed. She said, 'Now you know about my Friday nights.

213

But I thought that if I told you about it you'd have to keep it a secret.'

'It wouldn't have mattered,' I said.

'Something else to think about. You're busy enough as it is.'

It never occurred to her that I might disapprove of her agit-prop because I worked for the US Embassy. It was nothing personal. She had acted out of a sense of duty.

I said, 'If I say I admire you for this – acting on your beliefs – will you think I'm being patronizing?'

'You're very sweet,' she said. She wrinkled her nose and kissed me. 'Let's not talk about atom bombs.'

The matter was at an end. Everything she did made me love her more.

We went on loving, and then something happened to London. In the late spring heat, the city streets were unusually full of people – not tourists, but hot idle youths who stared at passers-by and at cars. Battersea seemed ominously crowded. They kept near the fringes of the park and they lurked – it seemed the right word – near shops and on street-corners. They carried radios. There was a tune I kept hearing – I could hum it long before I learned the words. 'Dancing on the Radio', it was called.

> We start the fire
> We break the wall
> We sniff the smoke
> Which covers all the monsters
> Look as us go
> Dancing on the radio,
> Hey, turn up the volume and watch!
> Turn up the volume and watch!

And there was a chanting chorus that went *'Make it, shake it, break it!'* It was a violent love-song.

The youths on the streets reminded me of the sort of aimless mobs I had seen in Africa and Malaysia. These south London boys looked just as sour and destructive. They lingered, they grew in numbers, and their song played loudly around them.

Flora called them lost souls. She said you had to pity people who were unprotected.

214

'Then pity the poor slobs whose windows are going to be broken,' I said.

'I know. It's a mess.'

I said, 'All big cities have these little under-developed areas in them. They're not neighbourhoods, they're nations.'

Flora said, 'They scare me – all these people waiting. They're not all waiting for the same thing, but they're all angry.'

Many were across the road from Overstrand Mansions. They sat at the edge of the park; sometimes they yelled at cars passing down Prince of Wales Drive, or they walked towards the shops behind the mansion blocks, and paced back and forth. There was always that harsh music with them.

'If this was the States and I saw these people I'd be really worried,' Flora said. 'I'd say there was going to be terrible trouble. But this is England.'

'There's going to be trouble,' I said.

She looked at me.

'We're getting signals,' I said.

The boys on the third floor, the ones who had filmed Flora, were now showing us films of idle mobs.

Then the trouble came. It did not begin in London. It started from small skirmishes in Liverpool and Bristol, and it grew. It was fierce fighting, sometimes between mobs – blacks and whites fighting – sometimes against the police. The sedate BBC news showed English streets on fire. It did not have one cause, that was the disturbing part; but that also made it like the African riots I had seen. There was trouble in a town and all scores were settled – racial, financial, social, even family quarrels; and some of the violence was not anger, but high spirits, like dancing on the radio.

When it hit London there were two nights of rioting in Brixton, and then spreading to Clapham it touched my corner of Battersea. One Sunday morning I saw every window broken for a hundred yards of shop fronts in Queenstown Road. There had been looting. Then the shop windows were boarded up and it all looked uglier and worse.

I had been at Flora's that night. We heard the news on her bedside transistor, and on the way home I had seen the police standing helplessly, and seen the running boys, and the odd surge of night-time crowds.

I was then deeply in love with Flora. Sex was part of it. I had been looking for her, I knew. She said the same and this well-educated woman quoted a Donne poem that began, 'Twice or thrice had I loved thee, Before I knew thy face or name ...' But in finding her I had discovered an aspect of my personality that was new to me – a kinder, dependent, appreciative side of me that Flora inspired. If I lost her it would vanish within me and be irretrievable, and I would be the worse for it.

She was different, but that did not surprise me. All women are different, not only in personality but in a physical sense. Each woman's body is different in contour, in weight, in odour, in the way she moves and responds. It is possible, I thought, that every sexual encounter in life is different and unique, because every woman is a different shape and size, and different in every other way. But what about men?

Flora said, 'I've stopped wondering about that. "Men" is just an abstraction. I don't think about men and women. I just think about you and me.'

We were at my apartment, one Saturday, sitting on my Chinese settee from Malacca. I wanted to tell her I loved her, that sex was part of it, but that there was something more powerful, something to do with a diminishing of the fear of death. It was an elemental desire to establish a society of two.

'Let's talk about love,' I said.

'*Folie à deux*,' she said. 'It's an extreme paranoid condition.'

There was an almighty crash. I ran to the balcony and saw that a gang of boys had stoned a police car and that it had hit a telegraph pole. The police scrambled out of the smashed car, and ran; the boys threw stones at the car and went up to it and kicked it. Then I saw other boys, busy ones, like workers in an air-raid scurrying around in the darkness, bringing bottles splashing the car. They set the car on fire.

I shouted. No one heard.

Flora said, 'It's terrible.'

'This is the way the world ends,' I said.

She hugged me, clutched me, but tenderly, like a daughter. She was afraid. The firelight on the windows of my apartment came from the burning car, but it looked more general, like the sprawling flames from a burning city. And later there were the sounds of police sirens, and shouts, and the fizz of breaking glass, and the pathetic sound of running feet slapping the pavement.

We sat in the darkness, Flora and I, and listened. It was war out there. It seemed to me then as if we had been transported into the distant past or future, where a convulsion was taking place. How could this nightmare be the here and now with us so unprepared? But we were lucky. We were safe, and had each other. And, in each other's arms, we heard the deranged sounds of riot, and much worse the laughter.

Past midnight, Flora said, 'I'm afraid.'

'Please stay the night,' I said.

'Yes, I'm so glad we're together. Maybe we have no right to be so safe. But nothing bad can happen to us if we're together.'

Her head lay against my chest. We had not made love, but we would sleep holding each other and we would keep death away.

She relaxed and laughed softly and said, 'You didn't really think that I'd leave you tonight. I'm not brave –'

'You're brave, you're beautiful,' I said, and I told her how every night that we spent together was special and how, when it came time to part, it hurt and made me feel lopsided. I told her how happy I was, and how many places in the world I had looked for her – in Africa and Asia – and had practically given up hope of ever finding her, though I had never doubted that she existed. All this time the windows were painted in fire, and I heard Flora's heart and felt her breath in a little listening rhythm. Tonight was different, I said, because we could spend the whole night together – it was what I had wanted from the moment of meeting her. And what was so strange about liking her first of all for her hair and her green eyes? That's how I had recognized her! She had been funny and bright and had made me better, and this nightmare world did not seem so bad now that we were together, and –

'To make a long story short,' I said.

And then she laughed.

'Isn't it a bit late for that?' she said.

MEMO

★

When I took up my post at the London embassy I entered into a tacit agreement to share all the information to which I became privy that directly or indirectly had a bearing on the security of the United States of America, or my own status, irregardless of my personal feelings.

I feel it is my duty therefore to report on an American national now resident in Britain.

The Subject is a 32-year-old female caucasian; slight build, blonde hair, green eyes; no visible marks or scars. She is single. She has no criminal record, although our files show that she was arrested once on a charge of Obstruction; the charge was later dropped. She was born in Windsor, New Jersey, of mixed Scottish-Mexican ancestry. Education: Wellesley College, and Oxford University, England. She is presently on a one-year sabbatical from Bryn Mawr College, where she is a member of the Department of English, specializing in Women in Literature.

As an undergraduate at Wellesley, the Subject was a founder-member of several feminist groups; and at Bryn Mawr she has continued to support feminist organizations by acting as Faculty Advisor. She was arrested in 1980 at a sit-in protesting against the non-adoption of the Equal Rights Amendment; as stated above, the charge against her was dropped. More recently, she led a demonstration at a nuclear power station in central Pennsylvania.

The Subject entered the United Kingdom on a student visa in January, 1981, and became caretaker/tenant of an apartment in Stamford Brook, West London. Her stated reason for being in London was to complete her research for a biography of Mary Shelley, author of *Frankenstein* (1818), and *Lodore* (1835), as well as *Valperga, or the Life and Adventures of Castruccio, Prince of Lucca* (1823). This research did not fully occupy the Subject, and soon after her arrival, together with some British nationals, the Subject founded a group calling itself Women Opposed to Nuclear Technology.

The US Embassy Fact-Finding Task Force on Security here in London has a substantial file on this (legally-registered) organization, as well as tapes and films of its activities, and a membership list on which the Subject's name appears as Chairperson of the Agitprop Committee. The Subject attends the weekly Friday meeting of this committee.

What the Fact-Finding Task Force on Security is evidently not aware of is that the Subject has twice been entertained as a guest of Ambassador L. Burrell Noyes at Winfield House. Ambassador Noyes and the Subject's father are graduates of Amherst College, class of '47.

It was at Winfield House earlier this year that I became acquainted with the Subject, though it was some weeks before I learned of her activities in the areas of feminism and anti-nuclear protest. She struck me as tough-minded, independent and a somewhat combative intellectual. She is extremely personable. She is also lovely. In a short time in England she has managed to make friends with British people – most of them women, most of them opinion-formers – representing a wide spectrum of political thought.

The Home Office has refused to extend the Subject's visa, claiming that her student status is no longer applicable, as she has completed her work on Mary Shelley. Personally I think the Home Office is somewhat antagonized by the Subject's political activities, but there has been no direct comment on this by the Home Office.

The foregoing is necessary to you because of the sensitive nature of my job, and my involvement with the Subject. But none of it is of much importance, and the only fact really worth recording is that roughly two months ago I fell in love with the Subject. Yesterday, having consulted no one – why should we? – we met at the Chelsea Registry Office, where my part of the dialogue went as follows:

Registrar: 'Do you, Spencer Monroe Savage, promise to take Flora Christine Domingo-Duncan as your lawfully-wedded wife' etc.

And I said, 'I do.'

MORE ABOUT PENGUINS, PELICANS
AND PUFFINS

For further information about books available from Penguins please write to Dept EP, Penguin Books Ltd, Harmondsworth, Middlesex UB7 0DA.

In the U.S.A.: For a complete list of books available from Penguins in the United States write to Dept DG, Penguin Books, 299 Murray Hill Parkway, East Rutherford, New Jersey 07073.

In Canada: For a complete list of books available from Penguins in Canada write to Penguin Books Canada Ltd, 2801 John Street, Markham, Ontario L3R 1B4.

In Australia: For a complete list of books available from Penguins in Australia write to the Marketing Department, Penguin Books Australia Ltd, P.O. Box 257, Ringwood, Victoria 3134.

In New Zealand: For a complete list of books available from Penguins in New Zealand write to the Marketing Department, Penguin Books (N.Z.) Ltd, P.O. Box 4019, Auckland 10.

In India: For a complete list of books available from Penguins in India write to Penguin Overseas Ltd, 706 Eros Apartments, 56 Nehru Place, New Delhi 110019.

Paul Theroux in Penguins

THE CONSUL'S FILE

Paul Theroux's diplomat in *The London Embassy* began his career as resident American Consul in Malaysia ... Here is a sequence of twenty episodes in the life of Ayer Hitam in Malaysia – sharp *aperçus* of celebrated scandals, eccentricities and passions in the tiny community. The whole spectrum of life in Malaysia is evoked, from adultery to murder, from ghost stories to the vagaries of diplomatic politics, until the small town atmosphere takes on the significance of an entire world.

THE MOSQUITO COAST

Allie Fox was going to recreate the world. Abominating the cops, crooks, scavengers and funny bunnies of the twentieth century, he abandons civilization and takes the family to live in the Honduran jungle. There his tortured, quixotic genius keeps them alive, his hoarse tirades harrying them through a diseased and dirty Eden towards unimaginable darkness and terror.

'Stunning ... an adventure story of classic quality' – *Sunday Times*

'An epic of paranoid obsession that swirls the reader headlong to deposit him on a black mudbank of horror' – *Guardian*

'As oppressive and powerful as its central character. It bursts with inventiveness' – *The Times*

Paul Theroux in Penguins

WORLD'S END

London, the wilds of Corsica, a tropical island, provincial Holland ... All are ends of the world in one way or another for the characters in this superb collection of short stories. Stranded in alien landscapes, searching for the vitality and happiness they consider their due, they are comically tragic refugees from life.

'Altogether brilliant' – *Guardian*

'Cruelly amusing ... tinged with sadness ... and composed with a stylish, sometimes savage confidence' – *Sunday Times*

'Read a story a night and you've got a fortnight's gritty dreams – and one or two nightmares' – *Time Out*

THE FAMILY ARSENAL

A novel of violence in the tradition of *Brighton Rock*, set in the grimy decay of South-East London.

'One of the most brilliantly evocative novels of London that has appeared for years ... very disturbing indeed' – Michael Ratcliffe in *The Times*

'Mr Theroux has the ability to turn the familiar into the fabulous' – Francis King in the *Sunday Telegraph*

and

GIRLS AT PLAY
THE GREAT RAILWAY BAZAAR
JUNGLE LOVERS
THE OLD PATAGONIAN EXPRESS
PICTURE PALACE
SAINT JACK